Finding True North

Finding True North

A Texas Sisters Novel

Audrey Wick

TULE
PUBLISHING

Dedication

This book is dedicated to Brian, my true north.

Acknowledgements

Writing is not something I just teach. It's something I do. And I've been fortunate to have many people help me do it.

Beth Wiseman, you have taught me the industry and been a constant cheerleader and friend. Connecting me with Jamie Foley expanded my writing circle and helped me learn the technical side.

Janet and Ed Murphy as well as Suzanne and Eric Batchelder, providing homes in Port Aransas and Angel Fire gave me the physical space in which to work on this project. And Barbara Collins Rosenberg, the idea would have never happened had you not encouraged it as my agent.

Jeff and Rayna, years ago when we made our trip to Seguin, little did I know the seed was planted for the setting in this book. What a journey!

Daryl, your friendship and shared understanding of the writing process have been invaluable.

Working toward novel writing became possible because of all the past writing opportunities I was given through Blinn College, Sam Houston State University, and Cengage Learning. Thank you to my colleagues there.

The Tule team in San Clemente was willing to take a chance on me, and I appreciate the expertise from so many: Meghan, Michelle, Sarah, Sinclair, Lee, Monti, and Jane. Seeing the way Tule works is empowering.

Luke, you share my love of books and bring me so much happiness.

Finally, Brian, this materialized because of you. As a critique partner, you help me tell great stories, and as a life partner, you keep us both on track for a happily-ever-after. Thank you for supporting all I do.

Chapter One

THE BAG OF Cheetos rode prominently in the upper basket of the grocery cart, in the small space usually reserved for a toddler.

But Paige's two-year-old wasn't with her. Not today.

On a pass through the chip aisle, she added a box of whole wheat crackers for good measure. They would balance the lack of nutrients in the Cheetos.

This was what Paige's life had become—one of extremes and trying to find balance.

Alone.

She sighed as she navigated her cart around an endcap to see what else she absolutely couldn't do without. She glanced at her watch, calculating there was a little over an hour remaining before she had to pick up Nathan from day care. She fought the urge to run to him immediately after the court hearing, scoop him up, and hold him tight because she knew better than to interrupt his nap. It was best to let him sleep, have his snack, and then pick him up at his regularly scheduled time. Even though nothing in her own life felt normal, she wanted Nathan's schedule to remain as uninterrupted as possible.

So here she was killing time at the grocery store since the

hearing at the courthouse didn't take as long as she had planned. It didn't even last close to the time her divorce attorney warned her it might, if her husband had actually shown.

But he hadn't.

His lawyer was his voice for the uncontested divorce. So she didn't even see him.

"It's better that way," her attorney whispered in her ear as she saw Paige scanning the seats at two p.m. Paige just nodded, letting the lawyer take the lead because she had guided clients through the process more times than Paige cared to count. Was it better? Was any of it really better?

She returned her hand to the cart, resolving not to dwell on the afternoon. As of today at 2:27 p.m., she was a divorced woman.

And a single mom.

Her naked left ring finger was the physical reminder. That outward change was the easy part. The inward changes—the constant feeling of absence in the pit of her stomach and the looming fear of being less than enough as a single parent to Nathan—weren't something she could simply remove with the same ease as slipping off a diamond band.

But in the short term, a few comfort foods were going to help her get through her first weekend of this new normal.

She tugged the edge of the bag staring back at her. *Cheetos are normal, right?* They'd have to do.

She clicked her kitten heels against each perfectly square tile on the grocery store floor, looking down as she walked. If she timed it right, she could place a shoe completely inside the boundaries of one, taking them in single file through each aisle. It was a simple movement, one foot in front of the other. That was her divorce attorney's advice when Paige had asked her "Now what?" as she shuffled her feet in the courthouse hallway after the anticlimactic end to her divorce proceedings.

"Now you're single," her attorney answered. "So move forward from this. One foot in front of the other, Paige." That was all she said before she waved, turned, and called back, "Final bill next month." As if Paige needed a reminder of the attorney's two hundred and fifty dollar an hour fee that was sucking her own modest paycheck dry each week.

After becoming accustomed to those hefty fees, the cost of today's grocery store run was going to pale in comparison. And because of that, Paige felt completely entitled to Cheetos.

And that bag of powdered donuts.

And ready-to-eat chocolate swirl pudding.

As much as she planned on drowning her miseries this weekend with empty calories and the bottle of ibuprofen she tossed in, Nathan's needs were always on her mind. She steered the cart toward the far end of the store, heading to an aisle to get his foods. She picked up the pace as she strode, no longer paying attention to her foot placement.

As her focus shifted from the floor to eye level, she noticed how many shoppers were walking in raincoats or pushing wet umbrellas in their carts. Gray skies had held for most of the afternoon, the symbolism of ominous weather not lost on Paige. It represented the type of day she was having—soggy and bitter, with just enough annoyance to ruin.

But from the looks of the crowd forming in the store now, the skies were emptying. Clothes were wet. Carts were damp. Floors were splotchy. And Paige's *Dry Clean Only* dress and tan kitten heels were going to be no match for Mother Nature when she stepped outside.

"Great," she muttered, already mentally debating whether she'd need to buy a disposable poncho just to make it to her car without completely ruining her outfit. She didn't know why she had even dressed up for the proceedings. Maybe just to show Barry Van Soyt what he was letting go after their four-year marriage . . .

Suck it up, buttercup. She willed herself to remember this piece of advice using her daddy's nickname for her. Paige couldn't let herself go to that dark place in her life during the divorce.

Fruit snacks and the cinnamon oatmeal Nathan loved so much.

That was where her head needed to be now.

Paige pushed the cart with the same force she used on Nathan's jogging stroller, ignoring more displays of tempting cookies, candy, and junk food as she went. She'd get what she needed, then would make her way through the checkout. She'd still have plenty of time for a trip to the bank and maybe some drive-through coffee before picking up Nathan.

A crash of thunder reverberated the industrial roof, echoing through the aisles and alarming customers as they brought their carts to screeching halts. Drastic weather changes in the south—sun to clouds, wind to stillness, clear to threatening—were just part of the package living in Texas. The big sky she loved so much could morph faster than a burning candle.

Another loud thunderclap shook the ceiling above, momentarily outing the streaming music from overhead speakers that entertained shoppers. Maybe she had been wandering the store aisles longer than she realized. Perhaps the weather was getting dangerous out there.

Paige stopped her cart, adding what she needed even as another aisle nearby called her name. "That's right. Mommy might need a little wine," she mumbled.

Paige wasn't much of a drinker, not even before Nathan was born. But her life was different now. A cheap bottle of something in a blush variety might pair well with the powdered donuts . . .

Paige turned her cart around in the aisle and told herself it wouldn't hurt to browse the alcohol selections when a third thunderclap did more than interrupt the store's music. In a single, terrifying instant, the store went dark. No overhead bulbs, no attractive display lighting, no single source of electricity glowed to illuminate the space in front of her. Paige gasped, then froze.

And, from the sounds of it, every other patron in the store reacted the same way. A wave of auditory surprise rippled across the darkened interior. Usually, when her lights flicked off at home during a storm, they didn't stay that way for long. Surely, the electricity would cut back on any second.

But moments passed, and Paige realized this was more than a flicker. A store employee yelled something about a generator. She took a few gingered steps in the same direction she had been heading across the tile, her eyes adjusting to the absence of light just enough to see shadows and outlines.

She fished her cell phone from her purse and swiped with her thumb to the flashlight icon. But before she could tap it, secondary lighting flicked to life overhead with minimal intensity. The renewed illumination was just enough glow for her to see in front of her while a firm hum replaced the echo from the thunder.

When she was a kid, she imagined what it would be like to be stuck in a grocery store during a storm. It wouldn't be such a bad place to get stranded. She'd head to the checkout aisle and read all the forbidden magazines on display. After she finished there, she'd treat herself to a melted popsicle or ice cream that surely the employees wouldn't want to go to waste. Maybe she'd be able to use some scented lotion or try out a nail polish. So much was waiting to be explored in the expanse of a store. Or so she thought as a kid. But now, as an adult, being stuck in a grocery store during a blackout was the last place Paige wanted to be.

"Patience, please!" An employee yelled over the din of muttered "What happened?" and "Check your phone" instructions shifting from shopper to shopper.

She looked down at her phone. A National Weather Service announcement was issued from nearby San Antonio. She slid her thumb over the teaser to read the full message.

Guadalupe County was included, and her town of Seguin as the county seat was in the path of rapidly moving
showers. The message warned of possible flash flooding in
low-lying areas due to the amount of rain possible in such a
short time, but it didn't warn of hail, high winds, or anything else more severe.

Lightening probably just knocked out a city transformer,
or maybe a dead limb from one of the town's mighty oaks
had downed a line. Either way, disruption in electricity was
probably the worst of it.

Paige clicked her phone off and dropped it back into the
side pocket of her purse. With the generator powering part
of the store, surely she'd be able to pay for her groceries and
put the whole afternoon behind her. She rounded the corner
to head into the checkout area when she nearly steamrolled
another shopper.

"Woah, there!" A man arched his back like a shocked cat
and sidestepped her cart, narrowly missing being plowed in
the stomach.

"Oh!" Paige brought one hand to her mouth in reaction.
"I'm so sorry about that." She snapped her mouth shut,
stunned by the stranger's words and their surprise eye
contact.

He squinted. "Paige?"

She recognized his squared jaw and granite-like face, a
classically handsome profile. This was no stranger. But she
asked anyway. "Everett?"

In a flash, he maneuvered to the front of her cart and
wrapped her in an embrace before she could make a move

one way or another. "It's so good to see you."

Paige melted into his arms. Her attorney had been so distant in the courtroom and aside from Nathan this morning, she hadn't had anyone come close to her. To feel the arms of another human being around her was the mark of humanity she had longed for all day. It felt good to be held.

And by Everett. With those arms.

And his broad chest.

Even through his clothes, she could tell he had maintained just as fit a physique as she remembered from high school.

She could barely manage a decent reply. "Wow, it's been something like—"

"Over a decade!" he answered for her, releasing his grip and dropping into a rhythm of conversation that made it seem like they had never lost touch. "We should be having a reunion or something. Was there one at ten years?" He leaned back on one foot, balancing a red hand basket in his grip to take her in. "You look fantastic."

Heat rose to her cheeks at the compliment. "Thanks." She wanted to add "*If you only knew.*" Could Everett see the tension of the day and the stress with which she had been living on her face? She certainly hoped not.

In spite of her embarrassingly short replies and her attempt to masque her insecurities, he continued the conversation. "Some blackout, isn't it?"

"I'll say." Paige wished she could say more, but two words were now all her mouth would articulate.

"I just rushed in for some cough syrup." He pointed to

two bottles in his hand basket. "My mom's chemo has really dried out her throat. I told her she should ask the doctor about taking this stuff, but she insists it makes her feel better and she's already asked the good doctor enough questions." Everett rattled off the words with an ease that nearly camouflaged the seriousness of the content.

"Chemo?" Paige managed to squeak.

"Four weeks in." He nodded. "Breast cancer." Paige's heart broke any time she heard someone else was diagnosed with a disease as serious as cancer. She knew of Everett's parents, though she didn't keep up with them. Still, she was surprised she hadn't heard about the diagnosis through the grapevine. At the land and title office where she worked, gossip was as plentiful as the paperwork.

Everett shifted his weight. "I've been driving her to San Antonio for some appointments. That's actually why I'm back here." He balanced his basket with one hand so he could gesture around the store. "Well, not here, exactly. Grocery stores are not my idea of a fun place to spend free time."

Though he probably didn't mean it as such, Paige took his comment as a bit of a cut to her own use of the grocery store today. Killing time and buying junk food was how she was spending her free time. She wished she could hide the contents of the garbage filling her cart. How could she explain away those Cheetos . . .

Everett continued before she could try. "But even I'll admit a grocery store during a blackout has a certain charm about it."

If this were a pickup line and Paige were a teenager, she might have bitten. But she wasn't in high school anymore. And this wasn't a pickup line.

Was it?

More heat flushed her cheeks. How would she even know flirting if it bit her on the ankle? Her mind was a mess, and thoughts raced in confusing circles.

Paige cleared her throat, finding her voice. "A grocery store blackout is a first for me." So was today's courtroom hearing.

And signing the divorce paperwork.

And remembering to use her maiden name of "Fredrick" instead of married "Van Soyt" again.

But she didn't share any of that with Everett.

He just smiled, a dimple visible in his left cheek as he volleyed back to her, "And me." He grinned again, though Paige couldn't be sure for what reason he was really smiling. "So, um . . ." A conversation was proving more challenging than buying healthy foods today.

"Paige." Everett filled the absence, his rich contralto voice dominating the space. "What's been new with you? I mean since, I don't know, the last time we saw each other at Seguin High School? Are you married? Have kiddos?" It was an honest enough set of questions. Banter, really, more than anything substantial. Two people getting reacquainted with small talk.

Harmless.

Until Paige blurted a lie she couldn't take back. "I'm widowed."

Chapter Two

PAIGE WASN'T READY to share her truth of divorce just yet. Publicly branded with the weight of an unsuccessful marriage, she had worried that she was a failure, no matter how many friends and family told her she wasn't. Still, keeping that part of her past to herself made her feel guarded and safe.

Upon hearing Paige's words, Everett's face paled with shock. "Oh, Paige," he whispered, shifting the grocery hand basket to one side of his body, taking a step toward her. The corner of her cart still edged Everett at a distance, but that didn't stop him from reaching out. His hand extended gently to her arm.

Paige had already experienced judgement from people who knew of the divorce. Looks of compassion tinged with disapproval revealed the truth: people in town were not accepting of a broken family.

Her divorce attorney counseled that the tide of public reaction was normal but it would go away. Gossip today would be forgotten tomorrow. But a public court proceeding was not a way to sweep news under the rug of open attention. Divorce was something people asked about and that they talked about in the small-town pressure cooker of

Seguin.

But widowhood didn't carry shame.

So her words were a snap decision, a way to sidestep an otherwise embarrassing conversation with Everett. She didn't want to talk about her life, and she certainly didn't want to remember this day.

If Everett were trying to steady himself from the surprise of hearing the widowhood lie, the bit of skin-on-skin contact wasn't enough to do it. But Everett's touch was enough to send a charge through Paige's forearm. Her skin prickled underneath the pads of his fingers, though her heart was in no place to process anything but sorrow. It vaulted shut inside her chest and her voice wilted. "I'm—um, it's really . . ." Flashes of intensity too quick for Paige to catch flooded through her.

Defeat at the day.

Frustration at the grocery story blackout.

Alarm at seeing Everett.

Guilt at the lie.

Guilt, shame—once again, Paige was used to shouldering burdens like this. She was the one who filled that role in her marriage, for Barry was not a burden-bearer. His coping mechanism had always been to ignore. Just like he shopped, if he pretended he didn't see something, then it wouldn't exist to him.

Paige just never thought she and Nathan would be on the receiving end.

He never wanted children. But along came Nathan, and Paige was over the moon. With time, she expected Barry would be too. It simply never happened. He was an absentee parent, just like he was absent from the proceedings.

Paige willed herself to focus on ending the conversation with Everett. A weekend of coping with self-misery through junk food therapy was waiting. If she could just get out of this grocery store. "I really need to get going."

Everett blinked hard, withdrawing his hand. "Right." His voice stayed low. "I'm so sorry," he repeated. Then, with firm eye contact, Everett offered, "Widowhood isn't easy."

Neither is being divorced.

But instead of such a biting response, she closed the conversation with a simple statement. "I don't like to talk about it."

Everett took a step back, stiffening his posture. "Of course."

That was one way to shut down a conversation. The tiniest burst of pride swelled in Paige at success in avoiding the topic of divorce, though there was nagging guilt about the lie. Still, she was saving face through it all. It wasn't like she was going to see Everett again.

Everett glanced over his shoulder. Paige followed his gaze. "Looks like the checkout lines are moving a bit." The generator still hummed, keeping the store limping along to power a few registers. "I need to get this cough syrup back to my mom."

Now, it was Paige's chance to react with internal shock. She had no idea of the extent of the cancer Everett's mom was battling, but in her attempt to camouflage her own situation, had she been insensitive of his? Was widowhood something Everett's father could soon be facing?

Paige's heart was bigger than completely ignoring something so major. "I will be thinking about your mom, and I'm glad you can be there for her." She softened her voice and added, "I hope she gets to experience good days." The words only scratched the surface of sensitivity, but Paige couldn't let Everett escape without verbalizing something.

His kind eyes registered with reciprocal sincerity. "Thank you."

Determined to leave on a high note, Paige pushed her cart as Everett walked through the dimly lit aisle to the *Ten Items and Under* lane. Paige's binge of comfort foods and impulse purchases wouldn't qualify, so she chose the next lane over from Everett. But neither was progressing too quickly. Customers were eager to leave, though the blackout slowed everyone's movement in the store, especially the cashiers.

Everett's parallel presence feet away as Paige waited was a reminder of how often she was likely to run into people like this. She frequently had, though during her marriage, there had always been something pleasant to say. News about the house they were buying, an event they were attending, and then Nathan's birth.

That reminded Paige again of the need to pick up Nathan. She glanced at her watch. With the storm outside, she might have to drive more slowly than normal, but there wasn't a rush. Thankfully, day care was a short distance away. In Seguin, everything was like that—five minutes here, ten minutes there. Metropolitan San Antonio next door was a world of difference, but the urban sprawl hadn't yet hit Seguin, at least not the heart of it.

As cashiers completed transactions, shoppers advanced through the line. Paige reminded herself not to look right at the rows of eye-level candy. She turned her head in the opposite direction, focusing on the headlines of the gossip magazines on display.

Words like *lies, deceit,* and *divorce* peppered the covers while headlines like *Marriage Sham Revealed!* and *It's Over!* screamed for shoppers' attention.

Paige sighed. Maybe looking to the left wasn't better after all.

With only one customer now in line ahead of her, Paige started to unload her purchases onto the conveyor belt. She stacked them as closely together as she could, letting the shape of an object drive its placement and proximity each to each. She focused on the arrangement of items as if they were the most interesting things in the world, which gave her reason not to look over at Everett.

"Remember, shoppers." A manager was using his loudest octave to verbalize another directive to the small crowd. "The card reader machines are not working. Cash only."

"Cash only?" Paige repeated under her breath.

She ducked her head as she dug desperately through her purse for her wallet. She wasn't in the habit of carrying much cash. Her purchases today weren't her usual fare, so how much was this even going to cost?

She counted just short of nine dollars, and that was including the quarters she recognized in haste as she unzipped the change pocket of her wallet, hoping to see a surprise twenty by chance stashed in there.

Nope.

Paige sighed a second time, this time with exasperation at the decision she'd have to make. She could tell the cashier she decided against some of the items, but what? Nathan needed the toddler foods, and she needed the ibuprofen, so those items alone would surely amount to at least nine dollars. She could put everything back in the cart, then reverse and excuse herself to the end of the line until the machines started working again. But how long would that take? Either choice would—once again—be embarrassing.

She figured she could wait it out. Leaning forward, she scooped as many objects into her arms as she could, and deposited them back into the cart. "Go on ahead of me," she said to the middle-aged woman behind her. "I don't have cash."

"Cash?" She repeated the word as if it were foreign to her tongue.

Paige resumed her rewind. "That's right. Card readers aren't working. Cash only." She grabbed the Cheetos by their edge. "Did you hear that?"

The woman narrowed her eyebrows. "Don't scold me."

Paige immediately shrunk into herself, not intending to sound curt. "I didn't mean . . ." She tossed the Cheetos back into the basket. "I'm sorry. Excuse me. Just go ahead of me." She placed her hands on the back of the cart as she readied to push it out of the line, if this woman would move out of the way.

Like a reprimanded puppy, Paige sulked to the back of the line. Her cart wobbled as she maneuvered it in reverse. The woman had the last word. "You're not going to find any cash back there."

Paige didn't respond. Maybe she had overlooked something in her purse, a loose bill at the bottom or money hidden in a side pocket. She didn't bother to straighten the cart or reposition it in line. She bowed her head and dug through every inch of her bag.

She found another couple of quarters, a half dozen pennies, and a rewrapped Dum-Dum she never remembered even putting in there. But no bills. She plucked the lollipop and held it in her line of sight, as if she could transform it into cash by glaring at it.

No luck there either. The Dum-Dum just stared back at her.

The whole trip to the grocery store was turning into a bust. At least with the blackout, she had a half decent reason not to buy everything in her cart. Maybe she would just have to buy the couple of necessities and make a return trip tomorrow with Nathan.

"Need some cash?" She spun and held the Dum-Dum like a weapon against the sound of the voice. "I can spot you some." Everett called from where he had stepped out of his line.

She lowered the lollipop and dropped it back into her still opened purse. "I can't do that." Everett already thought she was a widow. Now he would think she was a poor one.

Taking charity wasn't Paige's style.

"Really, it's no problem." Everett was already reaching into his back pocket. "All I'm buying is cough syrup anyway." He glanced over her cart, as if mentally tallying the cost. Would he notice the fruit snacks? Or could he even tell they were designed for kids if he did?

Please, she willed. *Don't ask about a child.* She couldn't bear another lie.

He extended two twenty dollar bills. "Here. That should cover it."

She shook her head. "No. No way." Being offered a bailout, even if it was just for groceries, was almost as unsettling as her widowhood lie. And nothing good could come of her accepting cash from a man whose mother was battling cancer.

"Come on." He stepped to her and tried to fist the money into her palm, but Paige kept fingers clenched at her side. "No telling when those card readers will come back online."

True, Paige couldn't wait forever, but she could wait a bit longer. Or at least long enough for Everett to leave to avoid another humiliating encounter. "I don't mind waiting."

Everett maneuvered diagonally at Paige, trying again with a gesture toward her hand. "Just take it."

Maybe she should tell Everett the truth. "This is, um . . . " She cleared her throat for honesty. "When you . . . that is, when you asked earlier—"

But Everett had other plans.

"This is the way I see it." He squared his stance in front of Paige, his half foot of height taking charge of the space along with his voice, which he lowered. The richness of his tone exuded charm. "You've got two choices. Number one, you stay here, eat those Cheetos, and hope the card readers come back online by the time you finish." Paige cracked her first smile all day at the thought. As stressed as she was, grocery store snacking while shopping was not one of her coping mechanisms. Everett reacted with a smile of his own at seeing her relax enough to reveal human emotion.

And when he smiled, his countenance softened, revealing that single dimple she glimpsed earlier. "So what's the second option?"

"Option number two," Everett withdrew his hand and slipped the bills into the pocket of his jeans. "You can let me pay for what's in that cart when I check out."

That still sounded like charity.

"You better think fast," Everett urged. He threw back his head and tilted his chin. "Because I'm going to lose my place in line if you don't."

Paige admitted, "Such pressure." She was only half joking.

Everett stayed silent waiting for an answer.

"Well," she started, knowing Everett wasn't a complete stranger. And he was in town, at least for a while. Surely she could find a way to pay him back, which she wanted to clarify before they proceeded. "If you have extra cash anyway, then I can pay—"

"Option two it is!" Everett announced the words with the flourish of a bingo caller.

Paige didn't share the excitement, but it would guarantee

she could get her groceries, get out of the store, and get Nathan.

Everett excused himself from the *Ten Items and Under* lane and joined Paige in hers. He righted her cart with a gentle push before falling into step behind her. She couldn't remember the last time she had even been grocery shopping with another adult. Barry never liked to shop . . .

She snapped her face straight ahead and away from Everett as she squinted her eyes shut, trying to block another invasive thought of Barry. He was her ex, and *ex* meant *past*. She had to stop these intrusive little reminders of a man who didn't want to be in her life.

Everett's whispered words tickled her ear. "I prefer the puffs."

What?

Paige would have spun around, but awareness of his body in proximity prevented her.

"I see you're a fan of the crunchy Cheetos." His contralto voice trailed like a song. "Puffs are good too."

She had to give Everett credit for trying to keep this encounter light. Bantering about snack foods was, at least, a much safer option than the personal ones they had already broached. So she did her part in the conversation. "I love anything flavored with cheese."

Everett responded with something about Gouda and European cheeses. Paige was only half listening, pushing the cart closer to the conveyor belt where she'd finally be able to check out. His last words registered. "That's when I was in the Netherlands."

Maybe she should have been listening. That sounded like more than banter. "What was that?"

"The Netherlands," he repeated.

Paige truly had no idea what Everett did for a living. Searching her memory for his interests in high school would be a lost cause—that was so long ago—and if he had mentioned his career earlier, she clearly had forgotten already.

"I could tell you more about Europe. Say, over lunch?"

Paige's step forward slowed as she processed what she heard. She placed her foot heel first onto the tile, stiffening as she did. "What did you say?"

"Lunch." The word was as matter-of-fact as a hello. "I would like us to go to lunch."

Paige called it. This was another humiliating encounter.

If Everett was genuine in his offer or if this was a continuation of Paige as his surprise charity case, she wasn't yet sure. A lie could get her out of this, but already the one big lie to Everett was more than she intended. Plus, food had been on her mind lately.

That, along with so much more.

"You know . . ." Everett filled the void as she formed an answer. "I haven't been out for a restaurant meal at all since I've been back in town."

Residents didn't starve for lack of food choices. Besides Tex-Mex, there were some wonderful barbeque and comfort dish restaurants. Maybe it was because Seguin was one of the oldest towns in Texas. Its storied past made for rich and varied cuisine. But even though the options existed, going out to eat wasn't one of Paige's regular luxuries lately.

Dining out in the evenings at a nice restaurant was out of the question since it was just her and Nathan. And lunches were usually working ones at the land and title office. Her best friend Danica, who worked at the county appraisal district, would occasionally ask her, but more typically the time was spent at her desk with a sandwich in one hand and a pencil in the other.

A restaurant lunch was an underrated event for most people. Normal people had satisfying lunches all the time, not clock-ticking, crumb-dropping sessions alone. She breathed out the stress of her day and her thoughts, nearly shutting her eyes while admitting, "I really could use a nice lunch."

Paige should have looked Everett in the eye and clarified her rushed comment. Because she nearly teetered off balance of her kitten heels when he rephrased what he had heard. "So, it's a date?"

Paige dipped her head. *Not quite what I meant.*

Chapter Three

EVERETT DIDN'T WANT to push Paige. Seeing a blast from his past wasn't exactly on the radar when he decided to help his aging father with temporary care of his mother. He intended to see his mother through the worst of her chemotherapy sessions, complete a few handyman fixes around their tired homestead, and lift both his parents' spirits. He was able to take off a month from work in Amarillo for family leave. His mother's care qualified.

North Texas was where he made a life, in part due to an excellent job as a water well pump and sales supervisor. Oil was Texas' most precious natural resource of the past, but water was its most precious one for the future. And Everett had entered the industry at just the right time. Water titans were more powerful than oil barons.

So Everett worked hard, but that dedication resulted in a lot of flexibility too.

Seguin, then, became his home again, at least for these four weeks. Relocating the eight hours away was more like a second move. Though it was still in the same state, the distance in Texas made it seem like a world away.

He did enjoy the change in topography. Further north, flat plains, low shrubs, and tumbleweeds characterized the land. Here, grand shade trees, clear springs, and gently rolling hills were the charm. And in a town of approximately twenty-five thousand, the land was familiar and peaceful.

So were the people. And that included Paige.

Like the thunderstorm, old memories rushed in with no warning the moment he saw Paige. She was a high school crush—but she didn't know that. At least, if she did, she never let on. Or asked. Or reciprocated if she did suspect something. But that was over a decade ago.

Still, when Everett approached her, it was as if time hadn't passed. Paige was Paige. There was a naturalness in talking with her, as there always had been. She was the opposite of insipid, shallow female schoolmates, which was why he was drawn to her years ago. That same luster was present now, though perhaps shadowed by time. She was older, yes. With shorter hair and wispy bangs. Maybe a bit of a tired look, but certainly not a frumpy one. More like the look of someone emotionally set back, a sort of semipermanent unease he noticed even in the store that didn't seem to be a reaction to the blackout. It was deeper.

He didn't intend to pry. Truly, the small talk just turned. And then when Paige revealed she was a widow, her look made perfect sense. She was trying to appear presentable. She was trying to cope. But she was hurting.

Everett knew plenty himself about love. And loss. And coping.

That was why he didn't ask her any more about it. Private matters and those of the heart were better left alone.

But a lunch invitation seemed both practical and possible. After all, everyone had to eat, right?

Still, maybe he shouldn't have used the word "date" when Paige agreed. Her flummoxed reaction with a scrunched face made him want to take it back. Instead, he tried to cover with understatement.

"What I meant was," he started. Paige was still not facing him since the grocery line was slowly advancing, which only made their exchange more difficult. "I meant that we could, um, pick a date from the calendar. Maybe a certain *day*." He paused, emphasizing the word to distinguish it from *date*. "Decide on one that would work?"

Paige busied herself by removing items from her cart, stacking them on the conveyor belt, and then positioning herself opposite the cashier. Her tight waist and lean torso shone as she stretched in different directions. Her body was mature, but she carried herself with the reserved grace of someone not fully aware of her attractiveness. "Hi, again," she said to the female employee, a terse expression set on both their faces.

Looks like everyone's a bit tense.

Still, Everett didn't want to drop the offer. Surely, a widowed woman—no matter how long it had been since her husband's passing—should be entitled to a pleasant lunch.

The cashier scanned item after item, and Paige went around the corner of the line to bag. During a blackout, employees seemed to be stretched thin running in other directions. Everett took her place at the helm of the register, opposite the cashier.

"Hi," he offered as he did, mirroring Paige.

The cashier kept her face low to complete the transaction. "Is all of this together?" She pointed to the two bottles of cough syrup Everett had placed at the end.

"Yes," he confirmed. The cashier's question was a simple one, but the intensity of self-recognition sucker-punched him. He hadn't been shopping with a woman in so very long. He placed his hand on the side of his torso, pressuring the fake wound. *Hold it together.* A spasm lingered in his gut. He still needed to finish his conversation with Paige, but the distance and her preoccupation with the groceries wasn't making it easy.

"That will be forty-two fifty-seven. Cash only," the woman reminded, "until these card readers come back online."

Everett had the two twenties, though he needed to dig for a few more dollars. "I've got change." Paige raised her head, buried her hand into her purse, and emerged with a handful of loose coins, reaching over the bagged groceries to the cashier. Together, Everett and Paige pooled their money, as if they were a couple.

Everett pinched himself through the fabric of his shirt, needing a reminder that this scene was real. If Paige only knew how long it had been since . . . but how could he tell her anything after what she just revealed about being a widow? He needed to tread lightly.

He accepted the receipt from the cashier with an exchanged thank-you as she stacked his hand basket in a tower of others. He smiled as he wrapped his fingers around the handle of Paige's cart and gave it a gentle push forward.

"I can get that." Paige placed the last bag of her groceries in the cart, though she held a plastic bag with Everett's cough syrup out for him. "Here you go."

As he reached to accept the bag, she eased the cart forward and took charge. "I appreciate you helping me out, and I'll get the money back to you—"

"Don't worry about it," he dismissed, twisting the top of the plastic bag and following Paige to the store's exit. "It's nothing, really."

"It's forty dollars," she reminded, marching with clicked heels across the tile.

Her outfit didn't appear cheap, but maybe looks were deceiving. Women often were. Perhaps Paige was strapped financially. A major life change—like widowhood—could do that.

Everett needed to sort this before they left. But his practical side couldn't keep from asking, "Do you have an umbrella?" No telling, after all, what she carried in that purse the size of a throw pillow slung over her shoulder.

"No," she added quickly, "but I'm fine."

They reached the front of the store, and dark skies emptied quiet rain in a steady mist. The big alligator tear drops he imagined earlier falling from the sky simply weren't there. "See, it's not so bad," Paige observed.

He liked her dismissive strength. Then again, he remembered that from high school. Paige always had a strength of character and action that set her apart from the flighty cheerleaders, the dainty drama wallflowers, or the obnoxious sports standouts. She was kind to everyone, and she was resolute in making the best of any situation. A grocery store blackout, unavailable cash, and a little rainfall weren't going to stop her.

The automatic doors of the store were propped open, and an employee was managing the light flow of people in and out. Paige and Everett stepped through the doors, pausing under the covered storefront to assess the situation outdoors. Streetlamps were off, signaling a widespread power outage. Paige glanced at her watch. "I've got to get going."

But before she dashed to her vehicle, Everett needed to make sure. "So, about that lunch . . ."

"Everett," Paige began, a tinge of exhaustion in her voice. "I just don't know if I can—"

"Then let me." He didn't want to make her uncomfortable, but this chance meeting was his only shot at scheduling a lunch. He didn't even know her last name—*did she keep her married one after her husband passed?*—or where she was living or working. He just saw her as Paige from the past, and he wanted to see her again, Paige in the future. If for no other reason than to make himself feel a bit more normal with a lunch outside of his parents' house and conversation about something besides cancer.

A low roll of thunder spoke instead of Paige. He saw her eyes dart toward the gray clouds followed by a second look at her watch. Maybe he was keeping her from something after all. When the growl of Mother Nature settled into the turbid air, Everett made a final attempt. "How about we meet Tuesday? I drive my mom on Monday to San Antonio for her appointment, but I have no plans for Tuesday." He didn't delay the day for any other reason. "Straight up noon? Total lady's choice of where to meet." He wanted to give the appearance of offering her some say in the matter, even if it was only the location.

Paige kept her hands tight on the cart, her voice holding a soft shame. "I can pay you the money back then."

"I'm not even worried about the forty dollars." Everett treaded through the conversation like they were both standing on glass.

Paige rolled her shoulders, easing her stiffness as if contemplating an answer. She didn't make eye contact when she repeated, "Tuesday?"

Everett rushed his response. "Absolutely. Tell me where."

Paige paused before offering a name. "Chili's."

"The one off Interstate 10?" A chain restaurant on the interstate wasn't exactly Everett's idea of the best Seguin had to offer.

"Yes. There's only one in town." But Everett hadn't been home long enough to know that for sure.

"Sure," he confirmed, though he had wanted something more quaint. Private. Less ordinary. "Chili's it is." He hoped his feigned excitement at her choice wasn't evident.

Paige wasn't taking much notice of his expression anyway. She instead pushed the cart into a bay and looped the plastic grocery sacks around her wrists as she lifted them up. "Chili's. Noon," she confirmed. Everett recognized the technique of verbalizing to remember. He did that too.

"Well, be careful driving today." He didn't have a clue where Paige was headed, but thoughtful warnings were in order. "And stay safe out there."

"Don't worry about me." She flashed a thin-lipped expression devoid of much emotion. Then, she spun on her heel and turned toward the parking lot. She dashed off the curb and pranced on the balls of her feet through puddles, her prim silhouette enveloped by the falling rain until she disappeared.

PAIGE SLAMMED THE hatchback of her silver Mini Cooper closed after tossing everything in as swiftly as she could manage. She tiptoed through a veritable river across the pavement on now-soaked heels. The rest of her attire was as drenched. She swung the driver's side door open, shimmied in, and shut it with force. She instinctively wanted to look at her reflection in the rearview mirror to survey the damage, but she was afraid just the same.

A quick glance revealed usually wispy bangs matted in moisture to her forehead. Mascara and liner darkened, making her eyes look tired. What exactly had Everett seen? Hopefully not this. Even on Texas' most humid day, she didn't look this much like a wet cat.

"Urgh," she verbalized.

Pursing her bottom lip and blowing breath at her bangs didn't help. She grabbed a fast food napkin from the console and patted her locks instead. She used the corners to dab her eyes. "There." She settled back into her seat. "Almost normal," she muttered.

Time to pick up Nathan.

Paige turned the key in the ignition, set the wiper blades, and watched them swoosh her view clear. Headlights kicked on in the gloom as the air conditioner blasted to life. She knocked that off without a second thought. As she secured her seatbelt and shifted her car into reverse, her eye caught water trickling in silver-line streams across the windows. She hadn't bothered to look back at Everett, to see which direction he headed.

Do I care?

The afternoon was nothing like she anticipated. But what was even normal for the day of a finalized divorce? How was she supposed to feel? Her coworkers had said she'd be thankful when it was all over. Her attorney had said she would feel relief. Danica, trying her best to be a friend, said she was entitled to feel whatever feelings came. But her emotions were a blur, like her vision at the moment. It was hard enough to see in front of her through the pouring rain. Visibility was harder still because of the moisture building in the corners of her eyes. She had barely pulled out of the grocery store parking lot when the waterworks began. All the way to the day care, she kept the napkin close, wiping at her tears that spilled steady as the rain.

It was the first time all day that she lost it.

The rain storm and the safety of being alone in the car provided the blanket of security she needed for a therapeutic, quiet cry. She had to drive, but she also didn't have to keep up appearances for this brief window of time before she

AUDREY WICK

resumed her role as mother. For this space, Paige was alone. Vulnerable.

And maybe because of that, she needed to lose it.

Allowing herself that time, Paige then transformed herself as best she could into a presentable, got-it-together parent before stepping foot into the day care. The rain was an excuse for her soggy look, and she apologized to Nathan's caregiver for her appearance.

To her credit, she dismissed with, "I'll be soaked too by the time I make it home." She followed with small talk of the weather. "That storm came out of nowhere, you think? We had a blink of an outage, but the lights came back on within seconds." But Paige didn't respond since her attention was diverted to the center of her world. She reached for Nathan, those sweet tiny arms of his outstretched to meet her own.

Truly, she lit up inside and out every time she saw him. "There's my boy!" She squeezed him close, him babbling "Mommy, Mommy" and something she recognized as his word for *crayon.*

"Sweet boy!" She cooed, pivoting at her hips to give him a satisfying rock. He immediately lay his head on her shoulder, the move that melted Paige's heart. He was at an age where he could exchange these displays of emotion that made Paige swear he understood more than his two-year-old brain always conveyed. He knew people. He knew places. And he knew her.

Maybe her son was one of the only people, lately, who did.

Nathan was her entire world, and she owed it to him to

always be her best self. Around Nathan, she tried hard to be the mom he deserved.

"Any problems today?" she asked his teacher.

"An angel."

Just what she wanted to hear.

But his teacher wasn't finished. "You may want to take a look under his diaper when you get home." The admission halted the joy in the mother-son mini reunion. "Some diaper rash developing."

Just my luck.

"It's probably best to treat it this weekend." His teacher waved goodbye to them both.

Diaper rash was normal in children, but that logic was lost on Paige. After her rough day, it took every ounce of composure she could muster to avoid another cry right there in the middle of the day care. Why couldn't she catch a break?

Chapter Four

RAINDROPS PLUMMETED THE windshield of Everett's black Tacoma pickup in sheets. The skies emptied more heavily outside of town than they seemed to do inside the city limits. As he drove along the farm-to-market road to his parents' property, he tried to fit the puzzle pieces of what he knew of Paige together.

He had been too shy in high school to ever pursue her. Everett wasn't a loner back in those days, but he also never needed to feed an ego like some of his classmates. So he wasn't front-and-center at gatherings and parties.

But, then again, neither was Paige. And he liked that.

Her quiet beauty and her kindness shone, even as he watched her from a distance. She had a kind word or gesture for everyone she met and was always involved in some community service project through one school organization or another. Her concern for others was genuine, and even as a teen he recognized it. He thought maybe summer after senior year he could approach her. But that never happened. She moved—college, he assumed—and he stayed close to attend in nearby San Antonio.

Still, Paige left an impression, for it was her personality that Everett longed to find in a woman. And he did. He had that, found a romantic partner in his early twenties. He had Catherine, the woman of his dreams.

But not for good.

"Enough," he mumbled, squaring his jaw and aiming his focus straight ahead as he drove. He didn't need to start feeling this way, not again. He shook the memory of Catherine because compartmentalizing was best. He let himself think about her. It would have been unnatural not to think about a woman with whom he devoted five years of his life. Catherine had taught him to love, and Catherine had shown him what it was like to be loved. That was the gift she had given to him. And he wasn't going to waste it.

It had been two years since he had loved. Two years too long.

Seeing Paige was an unexpected and refreshing rewind back to feelings he thought were lost for good.

Did Paige know Everett's recent past or present circumstances? If she had, she didn't react that way in the grocery store. There were some telltale tip-offs that he learned to recognize through the years that communicated who knew and who didn't know. Those who did know his situation would often begin a conversation with "*I'm sorry to hear . . .*" followed by some borderline inappropriate admission veiled as consolation. Others would try an "*It's got to be tough*" line, but rarely did that go any further than scratching the surface of true feelings. That was because no one really understood.

Paige hadn't led with any of those after he approached her in the grocery store. So maybe she didn't know.

And that was why a lunch date would be perfect.

35

"Date." He snorted the word aloud. How long had it been since he had been on one of those? Not since courting Catherine.

The pounding rain drowned his thoughts, and he eased his foot from the gas as he entered thicker showers with less visibility. Even in the wide-open rolling hills outside Seguin, he could barely see a car's length in front of him.

Everett cranked his truck's wiper blades to more aggressively combat Mother Nature. "She's angry about something today," he mumbled. Rain could be pretty, lithe, and light. But this rain was thick, permeating, and obstinate. Like a surprise encounter with an alleyway criminal, this rain packed a punch.

He squinted through the glass, but even so was unable to avoid the potholes he couldn't have seen anyway. Without warning, his Tacoma bounced through a series of three as he steadied the wheel. A rush of adrenaline surged from his core to his fingertips, and he gripped the steering wheel hard as his knuckles turned white.

An expletive of frustration escaped his lips. First the grocery store blackout, and now these annoying sheets of rain. How many inches had already fallen? And would there be electricity on for his parents at the farm, or might that have been knocked out too? He silently chastised himself for not checking for blackout provisions like flashlights and batteries before he went into town.

The rain was relentless, making no apologies as it continued to pour. Redirecting his eyes from the road for a split second, Everett checked the wiper speed and was about to click on his high beams when the truck started to fishtail. The truck's tires took on a life of their own, hydroplaning in a momentary loss of control across rain-slicked asphalt.

Another expletive, this time louder and angrier, spliced the sounds infiltrating the cab from outside. Peeling tires and cutting rain mixed with his loud gasp before he held back his breath. There was no protocol for loss of control, and Everett was at the mercy of physics and force.

The truck spun round and round—how many times he couldn't count—because all he counted instead were the flashes of images he saw of Catherine.

PAIGE'S MIND WAS awash in parenting. Tips, tricks, and techniques were at the forefront of her existence from morning to night—and, depending on how Nathan slept, sometimes through the night. There was so much to know about being a parent.

And Paige was a parent in singular form. She didn't have a choice. So, like she did in most cases, she tried to find the bright side as best she could. When she couldn't, she turned to reading.

A recent addition to her home library was giving her some ideas. It was a self-help book Paige ordered online and had been using as her unofficial guide. One of the chapters was on benefits of being a single parent. The first advantage listed was the freedom of choice. It was a stretch, but Paige tried to understand the author's point. After popping two ibuprofen, she flipped open the chapter ironically titled "Pleasant Surprises" and began reading.

Single parents have the unique opportunity to be the undisputed household authority. She moved her finger under each line, focusing on interpreting the words in light of her situation. *A single-parent household can flourish under centralized power, with the head of the household in full freedom to manage the space and the children.*

Geez, was she managing a house or an army squadron? Since when did child-rearing cross into "centralized power" and "full freedom" territory? She continued.

With no partner to second guess or question decisions, a single parent can independently set rules and encourage boundaries, sometimes with greater consistency and success than two parents.

Weren't two heads better than one? Maybe that adage was just ignored by the writer. She tried again to focus on the overall message instead of the individual words.

In short, the author stressed, *one parent can be a success.*

As Paige considered the advice, she tried to forget the author, according to the biography at the back of the book, was a smiling, twenty-year veteran of marriage. So she wasn't exactly writing from experience. When she offered this advice, then, what did she have to lose?

Paige shut the book. There was a self-help selection for everything, and reading was one way to adjust. True, certain tidbits from this book had proven helpful, but other times reading advice from other people simply frustrated her.

But that was one thing the book also made clear—a single parent could easily get frustrated and overwhelmed.

"No kidding," Paige snarked aloud at the memory of an earlier section from the book.

She tossed the book on the coffee table, already covered with a messy collection of others—some hers, some Nathan's—along with odds and ends. Her whole house, actually, had gotten like that. Some people had homes where everything had a place. Lately, in Paige's, it was as if nothing had a place.

And the self-help handbook on single parenting didn't exactly cover that.

Yet she looked over at Nathan, completely absorbed in play with his farm animal set, and she couldn't help but smile. He was a happy kid. He was a healthy kid, diaper rash aside. And he was loved.

Paige shifted to the edge of the couch and leaned down to where Nathan sat on the carpet.

"Cow!" He palmed the plastic animal between chubby fingers and offered it to Paige.

She accepted the toy as if it were a precious gift. "Thank you." She lifted the cow between them. "And what does the cow say?"

Nathan tilted his head as his lips puckered into an exaggerated, "Mooooo."

"Mooooo." Paige joined in unison. Their duo of playful voices echoed through the house, louder and louder as they upped each other's call. Nathan's forceful sound and insistent lips made Paige start laughing. Nathan responded with the same. Then, mom leaned into son to tickle him, both collapsing in utter delight.

If only every day—every interaction—could be so easy.

EVERETT LIFTED HIS head, his neck tensing with the strain of movement. As if a sack of concrete had been tossed onto his back, pressure weighed on every muscle. Everett rolled back his shoulder as best he could as he straightened. Still held in place by his truck's seatbelt, his movements were confined, which heightened the intense discomfort. He blinked hard.

Rain continued to empty from the sky, heavy droplets illuminated by still-shining headlights. Beams pointed not in the direction Everett had been heading but instead perpendicular to the road. Barbed wire, pasture land, and a rain-blurred landscape washed into view between windshield wiper swipes.

Everett wiggled his fingers, reawakening his body to awareness of each part in quick succession before he released his grip on the steering wheel.

"Where . . ." Everett stared through the windshield then turned left to get his bearings. The slight pivot was enough to send a shot of pain further from his neck into his shoulders and upper back. He winced.

"Brake . . ." Everett's muscle memory jolted him back into logic of what to do. His right hand dashed to the gear shift, placing the truck into brake mode as it continued to idle. The gentle reverberation of the engine rocked through the single cab.

He turned his head right. A limited view provided just enough for him to determine a next move. From his swift survey of where the truck was positioned, he couldn't have been off the asphalt, at least not completely. And staying put inside a truck that was half on/half off the road wasn't wise. "Got to move." He willed, readying his hand again to change the truck from park into drive.

But he needed his foot to cooperate. He kicked it forward to wake it up, his body resuming manageable control of the vehicle. Still, careful and slow movements made him feel like a cautious sixteen-year-old rookie driver. But it worked.

The truck responded to Everett's maneuvering as it eased from the shoulder of the asphalt back onto the road. When he had judged he was parallel again—and facing the proper direction—he realized he must have hydroplaned. The truck was running, nothing felt lopsided, and he couldn't have been unresponsive for long. Vehicles weren't racing by, and if even one had passed, he wasn't aware of it having done so. No sounds. No lights.

"Hydroplane," he murmured, as if doing so would convince him that was what really happened. But he had seen more than water.

He had seen her.

Catherine's face was as clear as if she had been right beside him. But how?

She couldn't have been. It had been two years since he had seen her face.

Two years since anyone had.

Everett pressed harder on the gas pedal as he resumed the route to his parents' farm on the FM road. With hands firmly on the ten-and-two position, he drove well under the speed limit and with heightened attention to his surroundings the whole way, basking in the experience of having seen Catherine, if only for such a brief and harrowing instant.

Once he arrived at the farm, Everett swung open the screen door on the wraparound porch, stepped into the dimly lit interior of his childhood home, and called to his mother. "Is the electricity off here too?"

The door sprang closed behind him, snapping into place from a gust of wind. The rainstorm's breeze made the interior of the home fresher, alight with circulating air that, even in the absence of overhead bulbs, created an inviting atmosphere.

"Mom? Dad?" Everett called again into the home.

"Up here." His father's voice echoed from a room upstairs. The scene could have been a repeat of his life from over a decade ago, but time had forced changes through them all.

"I got some cough medicine." Everett held the plastic bag with two fingers, debating if he should take it upstairs or leave it in the kitchen.

His father made the decision for him. "Bring it up."

Everett tossed his keys on the table by the front door before striding toward the wooden stairs, ascending the second story where his mother had been spending most of her time, in bed. Everett had talked to his father about converting the old-fashioned sitting room downstairs into a bedroom, at least temporarily. He worried about his mother having to

42

climb up and down the stairs, especially as both his parents aged. Everett had been born to them later than most couples had children.

But his father would tell him not to worry. "Keeps us young and limber," he'd joke.

Maybe to some extent, but "limber" was relative. Everett took the stairs two at a time, a feat he was sure his father couldn't still do. Certainly his mother couldn't. Not with all the recent radiation. Every time they returned from a session, the laborious task of ascending to her bedroom sent his mom, Ruby, into a breathing frenzy. She'd march in slow pace taking each stair a step at a time, catching her breath after only three or four. If she wouldn't let Everett or his father help her, then the banister would be her lifeline. "Good reason," she'd joke, like Everett's father, "to tire me out so I'll sleep well." And she would. After, of course, she made it up the stairs and around the corner to her bedroom.

Everett took the route she did, the plastic grocery bag still swinging from his arm as he arrived in front of his parents' open bedroom door. Raised windows and pushed back curtains allowed shadowy light to fill the room, while a battery-powered Coleman camping lantern lit her bedside table. The rain stopped, but it still looked as if the world had turned off half its lights.

"Hi, Mom." Everett's gaze immediately found her face peeking out from her covered body inside the sheeted cocoon of her bed. "Snug?"

A faint smile spread across her lips before she replied with "Power's off," as if Everett couldn't tell. He was surprised she could since she was keeping her eyes shut, even as she spoke.

"I see that." He stepped into the room and held up the bag. "Got the cough medicine you wanted."

His dad was seated in a rocker in the corner of the room, a stack of *San Antonio Express-News* near toppling at the side of the chair. He had always been a daily reader. "Bring it over here," he instructed.

"No," his mother redirected, surprising Everett with the strength of her request. "I want some of it now." His father didn't protest. "Plus," she continued, "there's something I need to tell you, Everett."

He wasn't going to mention the little mishap with his truck on the road. No need, after all, to make his mother worry. But as he stepped nearer, he wondered if she would ask about the conditions outside or the state of the roads going into Seguin, given the storm. "Yes?" he prompted.

His father interrupted, his voice stern. "He doesn't need to hear this."

Everett's gaze shot to him. "Hear what?"

His father just shook his head as his mother insisted, "Dale, don't tell me what to say to my son. He most certainly does need to hear this."

"Hear what?" Everett repeated, worry about his mother's health filling his thoughts as he prompted again, "What do I need to hear?"

His mother's eyelids lifted, her deep gaze commanding Everett's as he leaned over her to hear. "Your Catherine," she began, the two words as crisp as if Everett were saying them himself, "she was in my dream today."

Chapter Five

E VERETT WIPED THE back of his hand across his forehead
as a headache took hold. Maybe it was the pain of
memories about Catherine, or maybe it was from the
hydroplaning. He was lucky the truck wasn't damaged, but
his head was beginning to feel like it bore the aftereffects of
all that roadway centripetal force and dizzying recollections.
"Mom, I told you—"

"And I told you the moment you stop talking about her
is the moment you lose her."

Everett was tired of having conversations about loss. He
had been through this with everyone from coworkers to
friends to every member of his family. He wasn't going to get
into a deep conversation about his past with his mother. This
wasn't the place, and now certainly wasn't the time.

He did his best to give as dry an answer as he could to
keep the conversation from taking off. "She's been gone two
years."

"Let me tell you about my dream." His mother inched
back against the headboard. "Grab that pillow, will you?"
She pointed to one with a floral sham that had been tossed
on the floor.

Everett pinched it by the corner, fluffed it, and helped

his mother angle it behind her. Then he sat on the foot of the bed, perching with one leg bent to keep the mattress as still as possible. His mother didn't feel good with sudden movements, especially after a nap. And his head wasn't reacting well to jolts either.

His mother started again. "So in the dream . . ."

Everett was trying his best to feign attention. The last thing he wanted in his mind was a fake memory to contend with all the real ones he really was trying to hold close when it came to Catherine. His mother's animated retelling was punctuated by hand gestures and facial expressions as she raced to verbalize a mental story that wasn't even complete in her own head. "Now let's see . . ." She brought a finger to her chin when she couldn't quite finish a sentence or complete a scene. "Oh, yes! So then what happened is . . ." She'd pick up at no place in particular. At least no place with any regularity of a storyline that Everett could follow.

"Yes. Um, huh." Everett obliged his mother with requisite head nods and verbal cues that he was listening.

But I'm not. Not to this. I've had enough.

When his mother finally quieted, she gestured toward him as if they were playing cards and it was his turn. "Well? What do you think about all that?"

Everett leaned forward and grasped his mother's hand. So frail, the skin was drawing loose. The meat seemed to separate from the bones like an overripe peach whose fuzz wrinkled away from the fruit and pit. His mother's once youthful, full hand had lost all firmness in its grip, a sad effect of the cancer which was monopolizing her life as well as Everett's.

Still, he raised her tender hand to his lips and placed a loving, gentle kiss on top. Then, he sandwiched her hand in both of his as he looked her straight in the eye. "Mom, Catherine will always be mine. Don't worry about me forgetting. I remember her. I do." Some days, even when he didn't consciously force it, Catherine found a way to weave into his subconscious. And then there were other, less frequent moments—like his near slide off the highway—where she bound her way back in, reminding Everett in force that she couldn't be forgotten.

"Ruby." Everett's father folded the section of the newspaper he had been reading and placed it on his lap. "That's enough for Everett to hear."

"I haven't even told him the message yet, Dale," she snapped. Ruby Mullins had always been a feisty, strong-headed farm woman.

His father waved his hand as if it were a white flag of surrender. "Go on."

"Like I need permission." She huffed. "Anyway," she emphasized, placing her opposite hand on top of Everett's so their full grip was on one another. "She said in my dream that you needed to stop using snuff."

Everett felt his face scrunch. "I don't chew tobacco." He had never been a smoker and, though he tried the smokeless variety a couple of times in high school, its use didn't stick.

"Then why did Catherine say you did?"

Because it's a dream.

"Ruby," his dad interjected into the conversation, "let

47

Everett chew tobacco if he wants to chew tobacco. He's a grown boy."

That's an oxymoron.

But his parents didn't let Everett interject. His mother talked over both of them. "I just don't want him to end up with cancer of the throat. Or gums. Or get sick to his stomach." She continued with resolve. "You know, if you swallow too much of that stuff, it ends up in your stomach where it can burn a hold straight through—"

"Everett's got a strong stomach anyway so the last thing you should be worried about as a mother of a grown—"

"That's enough." Everett dropped his hands, separating from his mother and silencing his father.

Are you both not hearing me?

There was a fine line between being softhearted and iron willed with his mother. Letting her go on too long, especially about something that could have been more of a hallucination from all her medicine than an actual dream, wasn't going to do either of them a bit of good. And Everett's father wasn't exactly operating with unbiased logic. Since his wife's diagnosis, even Everett could tell the normally still waters of his father's heart were running deep with worry.

Everett did his best to lay to rest any concern of a talking figure in a dream. "I do not. Chew. Tobacco. Period."

"Like I said," his father snapped a new section of the newspaper open with both hands and spread the pages wide to keep reading. "I don't think you have to worry about Everett."

But I have to worry about you. Both of you.

DUTIES OF PARENTING never ceased. There was joy in that, and there was plenty of exhaustion too.

Diaper rash was treated. Dinner was completed. By day's end, Nathan was ready for bed, but not as much as Paige. She seemed to tire before her two-year-old did.

She tried her best to establish a nighttime routine that would suit both and make the process of laying down for bed a smooth one. The sequence began with bath, then a pajama change, and then selecting a good book. Before the story was read, either Paige or Nathan would have to find his blue snuggly giraffe, the toy he received as a gift from Danica during her first visit to the hospital after his birth. When the giraffe was in hand, her son was soothed and ready.

Paige clicked off the overhead light in Nathan's room as the nightlight in the corner kicked on in response. "Night time," they'd exchange before Paige would settle in to the rocking chair and Nathan would climb atop her lap. "Our nest," she would say in gest, snuggling him close like a baby bird.

Nathan loved animals. Perhaps it was a stage with every kid. Regardless, Paige enjoyed feeding Nathan's excitement for learning about animals any way she could, and that included working them into his nighttime routine.

"How about this one?" She reached for one of his favorites from the small stack of well-loved books on the bedside table. Nathan nodded his approval.

Paige pointed to each word as she read the title. "*Guess How Much I Love You.*" Taking her index finger from the book, she repeated the final word as she teasingly poked Nathan's tummy. "You!"

He giggled and repeated the word. When he stilled enough, she let him turn the page to begin.

The pictures of cartoon rabbits in vivid colors and the easy turn of the board book pages made it one of Nathan's favorites. At least, it was whenever he would stay seated long enough to finish the whole story. But Paige had to admit the tale of Nutbrown Hare and the care of the baby rabbit in the book was one of her favorites too. Rich with love and full of the message of a parent/child bond, it was a sweet book through and through.

Nathan settled deeper into Paige's lap, snug in his footed pajamas and clutching his stuffed toy. She took her time reading, steadying her voice and lowering her volume as bedtime grew closer. By the time she read the final line, her voice was barely above a whisper. She added her own special twist after the treasured ending for Nathan. "I love you from your toes to your nose." She spoke into Nathan's ear, capping it with a kiss atop his head.

Through his weariness, Nathan pointed hard against the final picture and repeated "Love you." It made Paige's heart melt to see him happy and advancing. She squeezed him close as she shut the book. "The end," she announced.

"De end," Nathan repeated.

She had read the book to Nathan more times than she could count. But tonight, the image of the rabbit in the story—with one parent, not two—stayed with her. She never quite thought of the classic children's tale as a reflection of single parenting. Yet, as she sat with Nathan perched in her lap, the two gently rocking back and forth, all she could think about was single parenting.

Nathan was hers to teach.

Hers to comfort.

Hers to quiet.

Hers to put to sleep.

And when she woke up in the morning, it would again be the two of them. Nathan would need to be changed, dressed, fed, cleaned. And she was the only parent around to do it.

"Oh, baby," she whispered atop Nathan's head, mentally scrolling the list of tasks that happened day in and day out. "Oh, baby," she repeated again, tucking Nathan's giraffe closer to him as he settled into her chest. A mother's work, indeed, was never done.

The sweetest time of the evening was this period of stillness right before Nathan nodded off. She could hear his breathing, touch his soft skin. His warmth and her warmth intermingled as they rocked, mother and son together.

Eventually, as Paige was lulled into her own bit of peace, Nathan would drift to sleep. Ever so carefully, the delicate dance of transitioning him from lap to bed would begin. Each night, there would be a new challenge—floor creak, body startle, arm movement. But ultimately, drowsiness would triumph, and Nathan would be asleep for the night. Paige would tiptoe out, and, as the bedroom door closed behind her, she could finally exhale.

Lately, she had breathed in deep relief once the door closed, relief that he was asleep and well. Nathan would stay sleeping ten hours, and she was grateful. That was one sweet bonus of age two to balance the temperamental challenges. But tonight, instead of relief, she blew a breath of exhaustion. Exhaustion for the end of her day. For the end of her week. For the end of her marriage. The state of Texas said so, as did the quiet in the house. It was her and Nathan. Like the storybook, just the two.

She would love him, of course she would. To the moon and back!

But Paige couldn't stop tears from welling in the corners of her eyes as she asked in the dark empty of her house, "So who will love me?"

THE BUZZING OF the phone as it rattled against the kitchen counter caught Paige's attention on her final pass through the kitchen for the night, after she treated herself to a bowl of Cheetos and a glass of wine. Her best friend's name flashed across the screen. Paige answered it with a thankful, "Hey there."

"Hey, girl." Danica's voice was sweet. "I called because Nathan's got to be in bed by now, right?"

Paige held her hand over the receiver to muffle her response. "Yes, but I never know about that little pistol. He could fire up a cry at any minute."

Not unlike how I'm feeling.

But Danica cut in. "Understood. Did he go down all right?"

"Yes." Paige breathed, thankful for a low stress evening. "That part was pretty smooth."

"Maybe a positive sign of things to come?"

Like a good friend, Danica could be counted on to see the bright side to every situation. "Maybe. I hope so, at least."

"Well," Danica concluded, "you made it through the day. I was thinking about you all afternoon. How did the courthouse go? Any hang ups with the paperwork?"

"Thankfully, none. But I was waiting for it just in case." She was grateful to have her friend as an honest sounding board. "So many things can happen during divorce proceedings, even when the case isn't contested."

"I bet," Danica agreed, though she really had no way of knowing. She had never been married, and her experience with divorce proceeding protocol started and stopped with Paige.

The magnitude of emotions was so overpowering that it was still taking all of Paige's energy not to fall apart during this short conversation. Danica filled in her silence instead.

"I knew you could handle it. You're a strong woman, Paige, and getting through this on your own terms today was important. Are you sure you don't want me to come over?"

Danica had offered yesterday, and she even texted this morning to be sure. But Paige was sticking to her original intention to be by herself. She was having to learn how to be alone again, and the transition could best be accomplished in private. That way, when she cracked, faltered, or had a tearful breakdown, no adult friend would be there to see her. She wanted to keep as positive and strong a composure in the company of other people as possible.

And that included her best friend.

She blew out a breath she hadn't even realized she was holding. "I'm sure. But how about tomorrow? Want to come by and we'll grab some lunch?"

After all, it will be good practice for when I see Everett. She mused, half in reality, half in sarcasm. Talking to Danica would be like a dress rehearsal for carrying on a conversation with another adult over lunch on Tuesday when she and Everett got together at Chili's for their—what exactly was their meet-up supposed to be? *Am I supposed to call this something?* She didn't even want to tread into couple territory with naming it. And she had no real basis for what this was, this grocery store surprise appearance of a high school friend whom she agreed to meet for a midweek interstate café meal. Not exactly a fetching first encounter—or second, for that matter.

With no certain label and no energy to generate one, she shook her head to refocus her attention on Danica. Her momentary mental fog cleared just enough so Danica's conversation took center stage. Paige could sort labels later.

Danica resumed. "Meeting up tomorrow would be perfect. I've got some errands to run in town in the morning, so I'll be by around eleven. Anything you have to do?"

"Absolutely nothing." And that was the truth.

Danica responded with a warm offer of "Takeout or go out? Your choice."

"Maybe we'll just order takeout?" Paige wasn't exactly in the mood for any more public appearances.

"Totally understandable."

"Thank you." She smiled through the phone, wishing Danica would see the appreciation she felt. It was good to have a friend.

Danica dispensed a final dose of personal prescription for the evening. "Get some rest tonight, okay? You deserve it."

Paige brought her hand to the back of her neck, massaging the tension that had built up throughout not just the day but the months leading up to it. "I'll try. I'm so tired as it is."

"Well, go get some sleep." Danica hurried her along with an audible "Chop! Chop!" followed by a reminder of "I'll see you tomorrow."

"Sounds good. Bye for now."

"Bye for now." And the line went dead as Paige brought the phone down from her ear.

She walked to the edge of the bar that separated the kitchen from the living room, stopping at the wall's edge to plug her phone into the outlet charger. As she secured the port and smoothed the wire, it dawned on her that Danica hadn't asked the one question she expected would have been at the forefront of her mind. "Did your ex show up in court?"

Not knowing if he would a source of anxiety for Paige the past week, and she had expressed as much to

Danica. Why wouldn't she ask about that?

Fatigue trumped answers, and Paige allowed herself to succumb to the demands of her body, one worn with exhaustion and racked by responsibility that desired nothing more at the moment than a long, satisfying slumber.

PAIGE AWOKE THE next morning to Nathan's babbling. Most mornings, Paige was up before he rose, but Saturday morning was the lone day of the week where she might be able to steal a few extra winks. When she did, Nathan teetered in to the open door of her bedroom with an announcement of "Mommy! Mommy!"

There were worse ways to be roused.

"Morning, sweetie." She beckoned him to the side of her bed, embraced him, and then hoisted him onto the mattress. "Did my big boy have a good sleep?"

"Morning!" Nathan answered instead, burrowing playfully into the sheets like a prairie dog. "Morning!" His voice rang again.

"I know." Paige rolled over, the queen size bed in the master suite now occupied by one instead of two. She still hadn't gotten use to sleeping in any location but the right-hand side of the bed, even without a partner next to her. Old habits, it seemed, really did die hard.

Nathan kicked his feet against the covers, the plush comforter cushioning under his weight. "Time to get up, I know." Then reality hit her in the form of a potent smell. She pointed to Nathan. "And you need a diaper change."

Nathan nodded his head, rubbing the back of his hair against the bottom sheet as he agreed. If only potty training would be as smooth as his recognition. Alas, there was a lot of progress to be made there.

"Come on, big boy." She sat up as he did the same, crawling into her arms for a bear hug. She squeezed him tight, unpleasant aroma and all.

After a morning change and more diaper rash ointment, she busied Nathan with some blocks in the living room where she could watch him while she poured cereal and brewed herself a cup of coffee. Her single shot machine had become her household best friend ever since she treated herself to its purchase a few months prior. It wasn't cheap— and an expense she wasn't sure she should make—but it was a simple morning luxury she now couldn't imagine doing without. She always had one cup in the morning that she sipped in between getting herself and Nathan ready, and then she'd often make one cup to drink on the way to day care drop-off.

Before Nathan was born, her only morning commute was one she could handle on her bicycle. She absolutely loved riding her bike to the land and title office when the weather was pleasant, a long-standing hobby that turned into a practical mode of transportation during certain seasons of the year in Seguin. But now, with a child to transport to day care, morning bicycle riding just wasn't practical.

However, she made a concerted effort to not give up her

rides, even after Nathan's birth. Now that he was old enough, she'd strap him into a ride-along that Barry attached to her bicycle and off they'd go.

That was one good thing her ex had done. Maybe the only.

Mother and son would take advantage of the charm of Seguin, bicycling to the library, to a park, or through the square. Mostly, they would ride just to ride.

But even morning caffeine couldn't give her enough energy to ride today. Plus, she didn't want to risk being seen by prying eyes. There were so many of those in town, especially on a weekend.

She had to be discreet about everything. That's what life in a small community called for post-divorce.

Chapter Six

P AIGE SWUNG OPEN the front door to find Danica all smiles as she held up two paper sacks and announced, "I brought Dixie Grille." Paige smelled the southern fried comfort food the moment the takeout came within inches of her.

"You're an angel," Paige cooed, ushering her in.

"Thought you'd like this." She stepped just inside the entryway as Paige closed the door behind her. "I got us both chicken clubs with bacon—"

"Mmm, you just said my favorite food group."

"Oh, it gets better." She handed one sack over as Paige unfurled the top. "Fried okra for me, fried pickles for you."

"You didn't!" Paige reacted as if she had won the lottery.

"I did." She beamed with the pride of a chef who had cooked the meal herself. But being thoughtful enough to order and deliver it was a worthy source of pride too. "And each of us is having banana pudding for dessert. Nathan's got one in here too."

"Yum. My stomach is going crazy already." Paige walked the sack to the kitchen bar and started unpacking the contents.

Danica joined her, pulling out a stool to have a seat at

the counter. "Well, with all these calories, that's expected."

"I'm not on a diet." Which was a good thing as Paige sat on a second stool next to Danica and eyed the generous club, with its buttered toast, thick cheese, crunchy bacon, and creamy avocado. She also unclasped the Styrofoam container of her fried pickles side dish, settling it next the ranch dressing that was sent to accompany it, creating a salty-savory combination. "And pickles are low calorie anyway, right?"

Danica stole a small, crispy one from the center of the pile. "Not when they are battered and deep fried." She bit into it, her mouth puckering at the sour taste. "In oil," she emphasized.

"Don't knock the Dixie Grille. Oil is their secret ingredient." Paige pinched a circular dill chip covered with crispy, golden coating and popped it in her mouth whole. She savored the strange and delicious concoction. "Who was the first person who ever thought to deep fry a pickle chip?"

Danica shifted her hips and settled into bar stool. "Probably a mistake. I bet someone accidently dropped one into a deep fryer or something."

Paige grabbed another, this time dipping it into the ranch dressing. "If so, that was a good mistake."

Danica smoothed out her paper sack to create a make-shift plate for her club sandwich. "Or maybe it was genetic modification. Done on purpose."

Paige followed Danica's lead, making her own place setting from the content of the sack before pointing to the fried okra. "Think those are genetically altered?"

Danica popped a few bite-sized pieces of okra into her mouth. "I don't care if they are."

"They're no better for you than the pickles," Paige reminded. "But deep fried anything is so, so good."

"Agreed." Danica shook her head. "So what should inventors concoct next?"

Paige paused before giving a thoughtful response, one that ceased their playful exchange and turned her attention back to the life that concluded yesterday with a gavel pound and a judge's announcement that her divorce was granted. "I think someone should invent a substitute husband."

Danica stopped eating and wiped her hands on a napkin. "Oh, Paige." Then she put her hand on her friend's shoulder. "Do you want to talk about yesterday?"

"I don't know." She absently tucked a lettuce shred back into the folds of her sandwich. "There's not much to say."

Danica pivoted to give Paige more of her attention. "How are you feeling?"

"Some days I'm not," she said quietly, staring at her food. It was the truth. Some days—yesterday included—her whole body seemed devoid of emotion. Even when she did cry, it was as if the tears were drawn from a well of absence somewhere inside of her she couldn't quite tap into in a meaningful way. The tears just came, but real feelings didn't.

Danica squeezed Paige's shoulder in support. "That's perfectly understandable."

"Is it?" Paige didn't want her words to sound tart, but she had no metric for how to measure what were proper reactions and no tool for helping to calibrate her feelings into ones she could manage. She thought about the grocery store yesterday. "You know I bought Cheetos? And wine?"

Danica removed her hand and waved it dismissively between them. "Honey, that's a normal weekend snack for me."

Paige broke into a slight grin. Danica was trying to cheer Paige up, and she was certainly grateful to have a friend who could do that. And because Danica was such a good friend, Paige could look her straight in the eye and ask the raw and direct question she had wanted to ask someone she could trust. "Am I going to be okay?"

Danica tilted her head, her face alight with sympathy. "Oh, girl." She leaned forward to bring her into an embrace. "You're going to be just fine." Her words were measured, with the soothing tone of a coach consoling a player after a loss. But Danica knew Paige's life wasn't a game, so to underscore her next step, she added, "You just have to believe that."

They were simple words Paige needed to hear. "Thank you." She hugged Danica tight before releasing her.

Danica gave a reassuring smile, and then suggested they both turn back to eating. "Because I still want that banana pudding to be cold by the time I get to it."

"Understood," Paige agreed, resuming her meal as well.

After a few moments of silence where the glories of bacon and deep-fried foods drowned their words, Danica repeated, "Paige, you are going to be okay."

Paige chewed on a bite of her sandwich before responding. "I hope so." Because in addition to being a new divorcee, she was now carrying another label of liar. She still had the matter of Everett to attend to on Tuesday, but she didn't have the strength to launch into the reason why she was having lunch with him to Danica. If she could keep the white lie confined to Everett, she might just be able to weasel out of causing any serious damage to her own reputation.

PAIGE MANAGED TO keep a low profile through the rest of the weekend and even into Monday. If it hadn't have been for Danica, she wouldn't have seen another soul. She did have a pleasant phone conversation with her mother and father, who had moved to Angel Fire, New Mexico, for winter contract jobs and for what they hoped could eventually be early retirement. Further south in Santa Fe, her only older sister, Mallory, settled as well for a job. Her sister offered her a futon for whenever she wanted to visit, and her parents offered to set Paige and Nathan up in a rental house in Angel Fire as soon as she told them her marriage was over.

"It's a great escape from Seguin," her mother explained of the city set high in the Sangre de Cristo Mountains. "Close proximity to Taos. Great shopping and skiing."

"I don't ski," Paige reminded her mother.

She still enumerated other reasons she should consider a move post-divorce on one of their routine phone calls. "The mountains are so beautiful, even if you just look at them. And our trees! Plus it's a lot cooler in temperature."

Paige could think of one drawback. "What would I do for work?" Full-time year-round jobs weren't exactly ripe in her parents' small mountain town.

"I'm sure there's something you could do." Her mother volleyed back, though with nothing close to a commitment to assure Paige of anything. "You could ask at the chamber of commerce office."

"Moving without a job is not a stress I need," Paige deadpanned.

But more than career considerations, there were personal ones. Even Paige's parents didn't understand that nearly her whole adult life—and certainly her whole life since becoming a parent to Nathan—was wrapped up in the town where she was living. Work, day care, the doctor's office, local parks, friends like Danica. These weren't easy things to leave. And starting over in a brand new location—in a whole other state—would present its own set of challenges. Paige simply wasn't ready for any more of those.

Her mother passed the phone to Paige's father. "It's a standing offer, buttercup," her father reiterated, using the adoring nickname he called her ever since she was a little girl. "You know that."

"I know, Daddy," she acknowledged in as much gratitude as she could convey through a phone line. "Thank you."

She was glad to have a supportive family, even though they lived a state away. And, in some ways, distance was a blessing. There were days she didn't want her parents to see just how much she was struggling, how much she fell apart at the slightest event or encounter. Appearing strong for Nathan's sake in the eyes of her parents was something she could more easily control with geographical space between them. And while she would have loved to share some of Nathan's everyday events with both her mom and dad, there were frequent enough visits and technology to help them manage the times where they weren't face to face. They did get to see Nathan and be part of his life in lots of capacities, and he very much knew his grandparents and his aunt.

So a weekend with no agenda in order to adjust from Friday's courthouse end to her marriage was just what she needed. It was hard enough to stay in the home she once shared with her husband, but she had Nathan. Her personal compass pointed to a new family; Nathan was her family now. Paige took comfort in him and the fact his surroundings remained the same, which was important to minimize the impact of divorce on him. She would deal with personal effects herself and work hard to find her new normal.

Monday came and went without fanfare as she tried her best to resume ordinary weekday activities of day care, work, and evening chores around the house. There was comfort in routine.

To her coworkers' credit, when she resumed work, no one asked about the events of Friday. Paige had taken off, and although she categorized it as a personal day for human resources' purposes, she was pretty sure her coworkers knew she was attending court. Working in such close proximity to the town center and having easy access to legal paperwork didn't leave much room for secrets among her coworkers.

But the people she worked with could be discreet, and she could be too.

She was going to have to be, after all, to steal away and meet Everett for lunch without anyone asking what she was doing.

THE TOWN'S ONLY Chili's Grill & Bar sat at the Interstate 10 frontage road just north of town. The major interstate ran the length of the southern United States, all the way from the Pacific coast to the Atlantic. Santa Monica, California, to Jacksonville, Florida. If a traveler threw a dart at a map of the interstate stretch, Seguin would be dead center. Perhaps it was a crossroads in that way, but, for Paige, it was home.

Because of its location to the interstate, the restaurant served mostly out-of-towners, both Texans and those passing through from states away. It was rare to run into locals there, which was why it made a perfect setting for a quick, discreet lunch with Everett. Away from prying eyes and gossip, Paige could simply eat, pay Everett the cash she owed him from her blackout grocery store bailout, and be on her way.

That, as least, was the basic plan.

So when Paige spent a few extra moments getting ready for work Tuesday morning, she found herself asking aloud, "What am I doing?"

Already two outfits had been discarded on her unmade bed, and she couldn't decide between flats or heels. Normally, getting ready for work was easy. The past few months, there were only a few outfits that fit because she had actually lost a bit of weight. It wasn't a conscious loss, more of a stress loss. Responsibilities of work, home, and parenting converged in ways that didn't always allow lavish meals. Or even many meals at all. She met Nathan's needs, but her own attention to cooking was taking a backseat to everything else that needed her care.

She picked up a pair of thin cigarette pants she had discarded on the bed. The classic black style had a side zipper and an inside adjustable snap that made them fit perfectly on her slim frame. They were a good go-to option, and even though she had worn them last week, they were a staple of her rotation she hoped no one else was tracking. *Why are you worried about what to wear?* She talked herself into this original choice of pants and added a crisp white blouse and leather ballet flats.

There. She judged her appearance. *That looks fine. Nothing fussy, nothing to attract attention.*

And that was her intent: to blend in, not stand out.

She fastened a simple, silver chain around her neck, a gift from her mother on a birthday long ago. It was the only bit of glamour in an otherwise forgettable outfit.

She grabbed her travel mug of coffee and purse before corralling Nathan and heading out the door. After a smooth Tuesday morning drop off at day care, Paige arrived at the land and title office.

"Morning, Paige," Liz greeted Paige as she passed by her cubicle when she arrived.

Paige was stowing her purse and spun to meet her. "Good morning."

Liz stopped in her tracks. "Hot outfit today."

Paige could feel her face puzzle in confusion. *Me?*

"You look like a sexy Audrey Hepburn."

Not what I was going for. "Thanks—I guess?"

Liz added a wink, followed by a lowered "glad to have you back" wish before she continued to her own cubicle.

Even though no one outright said the words "divorce" or "official," her coworkers had their own way of reacting to her situation based on what they knew from whispering when she wasn't around and seeing public record notices. That wasn't something Paige could control. Though she could control how much she revealed in the open to them, and she was keeping her mouth shut there.

When her lunch hour arrived, Paige simply told her boss, Miguel, that she'd be stepping out instead of eating at her desk today. When she did, there was always a phone call or email interruption anyway, so this way Miguel would know not to transfer anything.

"No problem. Go enjoy the sunshine," he encouraged.

"Something like that," she mumbled on her way out.

The drive to the Chili's from the town square was short. Once she passed under the interstate, there it was, with a wide entrance and ample parking. She pulled down her visor mirror to check her reflection as she applied a bit of lip gloss. It wasn't so much for color as for the practical reason. Texas sun was hard on skin, especially her lips. A simple gloss filled in the dryness and made her appear less of a zombie when she talked.

She left her car and scurried across the asphalt and through the heat radiating from it. The midday sun was already baking concrete-heavy areas like this. Luckily, a cool blast of air conditioning greeted her the moment she swung open the entry door to the restaurant. Also greeting her was a perky young hostess. "Table for one? Or are you meeting someone?"

"Meeting someone," she confirmed, glancing as best she could given the limited view she had from the restaurant entryway.

The interstate location usually meant people were in and out. Not many people actually met there. "There's a man waiting in the bar." She gestured to a pub table with two high-backed bar stools. "Is that him?"

Everett waved as he spotted Paige, flashing a grin and triggering his left dimple.

"That's him." Paige couldn't decide if she was glad he was already seated or if that indicated something else, perhaps an eagerness with which she didn't want to deal.

She pulled her purse close as she maneuvered through the tight aisle to the table in the corner. Everett greeted her first, standing up to welcome her to the seats he had chosen. "Hi there."

"Hi." She sounded sheepish. The word "date" that Everett had used in the grocery store still hung heavy in her memory, and it wasn't a word with which she had any level of comfort. Plus, seeing him standing made the meet up more formal. *Just sit down*, she wanted to say. Instead, she hung her purse on the back of the chair.

"Glad you made it." He eased Paige's seat from under the table and gestured toward it.

This move was something a man did.

On a date.

Paige reminded herself this wasn't one but did not forgo a requisite, "Thank you."

Everett sat in turn and then uttered something indistinguishable while clearing his throat.

"What was that?" Paige prompted.

Everett tried again. "Um . . ." He stalled some more before he verbalized an admission that hit Paige from left field. "Seeing you just made me forget the line I was going to use."

Paige didn't know whether to laugh or cringe. "Is that a good thing?"

Everett shook his head and looked down, his nervousness obvious. "Maybe."

"Well, then, this was a good idea." Although, the verdict was still out for Paige.

Everett was quick to add, "I agree."

Paige wasn't sure if Everett was complimenting his own invitation or her acceptance of it. Still, she had to admit he was trying his best to make their meeting pleasant by carrying most of their conversation. And his attempt at fusing a greeting and a pick-up line worked at lightening the mood. Maybe it was because Paige was woefully out of practice at male to female one-on-one dialogue. Nathan made fine company, but her toddler wasn't exactly a conversationalist. Paige shook her bangs then brushed her finger across them.

"Glad I can solicit that kind of response."

Everett passed her a menu, moving on from his flubbed opening. "So how much time do you have?"

"Not much." Which was a true admission.

She tucked a loose strand of hair behind her ear then opened the menu. Paige relayed her typical noonday habits during the week, which consisted of lunch on the run if she had errands or a working meal spent at her desk.

"Don't worry about being short on time. I'll watch the clock so you get back to work without a hitch." He pointed to his watch as confirmation that he would, indeed, be keeping an eye on it. "It's still nice to steal away and get a good bite to eat." He opened his menu to scan the offerings as he continued to steer their talk. "So any problems at your place after the power outage on Friday?"

"No." Paige wasn't comfortable revealing much of anything about her true home life, so if she avoided detailed answers all together, she might be able to sidestep her whole widowhood lie. She wanted to clear the air, but doing so wasn't as easy as she thought. She swallowed her plan along with some of her pride as she answered Everett's question. "Just an electricity hiccup that made me reset the microwave clock. You?"

"Well, at my parents' property, we stayed without power for a good two hours. But I heard the east end of the county had it worse."

If Paige could keep Everett talking about his family, the focus would be off hers. And she wanted to consciously prevent any reference to Nathan, keeping her personal life private, especially since Everett thought her private life involved widowhood. Talking about Nathan and her divorce would choke her up too much anyway, and she wasn't ready for that. She aimed to keep Everett speaking. "How is your family farm?"

"Same as it's always been. A little rougher around the edges because my dad's getting up in age and can't tend to the little things as much as he'd like." Everett flipped the page of the menu. "But good."

A waitress came by to take their drink orders and reminded them of the restaurant's fast delivery lunch specials. Paige pounced on the time-shortening option perhaps a bit too quickly. "Yes! I'll have one of those."

"Oh. Okay . . ." The waitress renegotiated her typical lines of delivery. "We can have our salads and burgers out quick too. Are you ready to order then?"

She looked from Paige to Everett, whose attention was squarely on the menu. "Um, sure thing." Paige saw his eyes dart through the options. "But ladies first." He nodded toward Paige.

Her weekend junk food binge and Danica's Saturday delivery of fried food fare left little desire for something so calorie-ridden. "I'll have the grilled chicken salad. Dressing on the side."

"To drink?"

"Blackberry iced tea."

"That sounds good." Everett chimed in. "Make that two for the drinks?"

"You got it." The waitress committed Paige's order to

memory, not even relying on a written ticket before turning to Everett. "And what would you like to eat?"

"Old-timer," Everett answered. "Plain and dry. No vegetables, no condiments. Just meat, hamburger bun, and cheese."

"That's simple enough." The waitress obliged with a courtesy smile.

Everett turned his gaze to Paige. "I'm not that complicated." But something about the way he spoke combined with his attention made Paige certain the line was not a reply to the waitress so much as it was an admission to her.

Chapter Seven

EVERETT ENJOYED THE distraction of adult conversation with someone his own age. Since returning home to care for his mother, both she and his father were the only face-to-face partners for conversation. Unless he counted the doctors.

He didn't want to count the doctors.

Conscious, too, of what he was sure was a delicate emotional state, he purposefully avoided any questions about Paige's widowhood. That part of her life wasn't his to ask about. Instead, he enjoyed hearing a bit about her work and then reminiscing about simpler times from high school.

"Remember the Matadors homecoming game our senior year?"

"It's a bit of a fog." Paige speared a piece of grilled chicken with her fork.

"Did you go to games?"

"Some of them. Not always the out of town games, but most of the ones on the home field I did. That's just what people did."

"I know." Everett agreed eagerly, taking swift bites in between his fast talking. "Everywhere you go in Texas, football is king. Probably now more than ever. Up in

Amarillo, you should see the fever on Friday night."

A parade of stereotypical football images marched through Paige's mind. "Kind of ridiculous sometimes, isn't it? I mean, all this focus on a single sport, especially in high school."

"Don't talk like that." Everett wagged a playful finger. "Anything anti-football is sacrilege in Texas."

Paige lifted one eyebrow. "Is that right?"

Everett signaled to the heavens above as if someone were watching them.

"What's the mascot in Amarillo anyway?" Paige mused, "Probably something yellow." Everett knew conversational Spanish, and *amarillo* for the color *yellow* was but one of many Texas cities whose names could be translated. It sounded like Paige knew a bit of Spanish too.

Everett shrugged. "Depends what high school you're talking about."

"How many are there?"

Everett held up fingers on both hands.

"No way! You've got to be kidding."

"Amarillo's a lot bigger than Seguin." But, then again, lots of places were.

"I figured that much."

"Ever been? Up to Amarillo?" It was a good eight-hour drive from where they were in central Texas.

"Been through, but I've always sort of skirted around it. Never spent time there."

"Fair enough." Everett resumed his bites of burger. What started as reminiscing about high school wove its way into a talk on football then mascots and finally travel.

As if on cue, Paige urged, "You said you went to the Netherlands? Tell me about it." And just like that, their conversation took yet another turn, organic and comfortable.

And easy.

The hour lunch flew by, and before Everett knew it, the check had arrived. He glanced at his watch. "I told you I'd keep track of time, and you've got about ten minutes to get back if you want to make it by one o'clock."

Paige dabbed the corner of her mouth with a napkin. "I do. I really should be going then." She pivoted to retrieve her purse, fishing inside of it.

"What are you doing?"

"Looking for my wallet." She raised her head with a proud "There!" when she found it.

"Oh, no you don't." Everett's hand was already on his own in his back pocket. "I'm getting this."

"But I owe you for my—groceries." The word caught as she said it, her comeback sounding more pathetic than she intended.

"Nonsense." Everett waved his hand. "I want to. I enjoyed this. And I think I'm the one who asked you anyway." Everett stopped short of overdoing it with compliments, though the truth was this distraction was exactly what he needed to feel normal again after so much devoted attention to his mother's cancer. It felt like the disease was a fourth member of their family, so being at a lunch where he could talk about anything but blood cell counts and chemotherapy was refreshing.

You made it so, he wanted to tell Paige. But even though he didn't know details of her being widowed, he knew enough to not make it a topic of conversation. This much he knew—anyone who experienced loss needed opportunities to just be normal.

And I feel normal today too. Everett hadn't felt that in far too long.

One lunch could be enough to do that, to help resume normalcy. His mother and father, however, had their own ideas of what was normal for him, which was the precise reason Everett didn't tell his parents he was meeting someone. He didn't want their prying, and he didn't want to open himself to questions that would put Paige on the spot either. Plus, his mom needed to conserve as much of her energy as possible for the sake of her health, without wasting it worrying about Everett.

Paige stood, not extending her hand and not bending in for a hug. Instead, she offered a simple compliment. "This was nice."

Everett grew warm in hearing her sincerity, repeating the words because he agreed with them. "It's good to be distracted from my mother's illness, you know?" But as soon as the honesty escaped, Everett wished he could suck it back in. He didn't want to end their lunch on a depressing note.

Paige tilted her head, offering a genuine, "That must be hard for you." The thoughtfulness in the simple words struck Everett, for most people said cliché remarks whenever cancer was revealed. Well-wishers would offer condolences, thoughts, and even apologies—but those were empty. Here,

Paige was reacting not to Everett's mom but to Everett.

And he noticed.

A rush of intense appreciation and admiration swirled with something Everett couldn't quite identify. *Curiosity?* Not exactly. *Allure?* That might have been part of it, but it wasn't all. *Ease?* More than that. *Attraction?*

Maybe.

His mind was invigorated and his heart raced in a way it hadn't since he was with Catherine. And just the taste of this reminder of being alive in the presence of another person and enjoying the company of a woman was enough to drive Everett to a hasty parting line that came out as more of a command than a request: "Have lunch with me again."

His mounting joy, however, was momentary. For the way Paige flinched at Everett's words communicated more than anything she could say.

PAIGE'S TUESDAY LUNCH hour was one of her more enjoyable ones in recent memory. Rarely did she ever go out without Nathan attached to her hip, and she couldn't remember the last time she carried on an actual conversation with another man in such a way. As Everett waxed poetically about traveling, Paige wondered if she'd ever get a chance to take Nathan abroad on a trip. She considered mentioning her son then to come clean about her hasty lie, but doing so in that context seemed just as hasty.

To Everett's credit, he didn't pry about her personal past. He seemed completely focused on her in the present. Because of that, she could just be Paige with him.

Not a mom.

Not a divorced woman.

Just herself.

She glanced at her bare ring finger as her hand steadied on the edge of the table.

Everett must have perceived some hesitation for his lunch request, so he filled the silence. "No pressure." He angled his head to will her eyes toward his. "Look, if we're being honest . . ."

Are we? Paige bit her tongue.

"I just really enjoyed your company today. I like talking about high school." Everett, standing too, skimming a hand across his hair. "Geez, I haven't done that in forever. It's fun to be with someone I know."

He was getting ahead of himself. It was time for Paige to pump the brakes. "Everett, we really don't know each—"

"I mean that I used to know. And now I'm getting to know." He placed his hand close to hers on the table, in parallel space that was both friendly and intimate. How was that even possible? Paige's legs went weak beneath her cigarette pants, her knees practically giving way to the weight of Everett's words that landed on her. She rocked her hips to prevent her whole body from locking in response.

"I just like talking to you. And I'd like to do more of that while I'm in town."

How could Paige say no to such a simple, heartfelt request? Everett hadn't made any move toward something romantic, and he hadn't made her feel uncomfortable either. Instead, something about their time spent together was satisfying and uplifting.

Plus Everett paid for their meal, even though she still owed him for the groceries. And she intended to pay him back.

"So I'll be in town another few weeks," Everett clarified. "I've got more medical appointments to see my mom through the worst of her chemo, but it would be nice to have a distraction again."

And hearing him talk even in this limited way about his mother reminded Paige of the awful stress he must be under, having to swoop in to provide care, transportation, and put his own life on hold. No doubt he, too, was struggling with feeling normal. *Why didn't I consider that before?*

"Would you be up for a lunch next week?" The request was so meek, so simple. "Same time? Same place?"

One hour of the week carved for a little conversation with another adult didn't seem like a heavy commitment, especially to spend it with someone whose time in town was limited. Everett would be back in Amarillo before she knew it, and that would be that. A second lunch might help both of them.

Paige grabbed her purse from the back of her chair. "As long as you let me handle the check next Tuesday."

A smile spread across Everett's face and he raised both hands in the air in a mock hold-up pose. "You drive a hard bargain. But I think I can let you do that."

"Good teamwork." The short distance between them could have been bridged by a parting hug or a playful punch in the shoulder or even a pat of the hand. But nothing seemed appropriate. They parted instead with agreement to meet in a week, which gave Paige plenty of time to think up conversation starters that would keep Everett away from asking about her personal life.

EVERYTHING IN DAILY life was an adjustment post-divorce.

Meal preparation was different. Paying bills became a stretch. There was no one else on whom to rely for help remembering dates and assisting with responsibilities. For Paige, there was also some loneliness when it came to those quiet moments when Nathan slept or played independently. Being the only adult in the house, there was less human contact all around. The tenor of day-to-day life was an entirely new tune.

But some things were turning into a beautiful song.

There was more closet space. Laundry was less. There weren't as many dishes to wash. Someone else didn't have a monopoly on the television. There was more room to maneuver her car and her bicycle in the garage. The refrigerator was stocked with only the things she liked to eat. And Paige could track every penny of her expenditures without surprise. There was a silver lining to everything.

Paige's ex had a custody arrangement in place as the

noncustodial parent, though he wasn't acting on it. She telephoned her attorney on Wednesday to clarify her role and prepare herself for what to expect from Barry as visitation kicked in. Paige wanted to be sure she understood the reality of what had previously been more of placeholder paperwork prior to the finalized divorce. Paige cradled the phone to her ear as she received her attorney's advice that her ex's right to see his son trumped his responsibility.

"And what exactly does that mean?" Paige reacted to the blunt statement with tartness the moment she heard it.

"Rights versus responsibilities," her attorney reiterated, keeping her tone level and her vocabulary measured. "That means that a father can invoke his right to see his biological son on the dates set forth by the court. In Texas, that's every other weekend and Thursday nights for two hours. Regular contact with both parents is in the best interest of the child."

Paige tried to keep pace with legal language and not let her emotions get the best of her. "And when Nathan's father doesn't take him? When he doesn't invoke that right?" Talking about parenting in such an antiseptic way still didn't sound natural.

"Then it's your responsibility. You can't make a father see his son. Neither can a court system, even with the divorce now finalized. All that can be done is to lay the groundwork legally for making contact between them a possibility." She spoke with the precision of someone who had this conversation with clients all day long. As an attorney who specialized in family law, she probably did. She concluded with the words that now seemed completely at odds with one another:

"rights versus responsibility."

Paige still wanted to clarify. "So this upcoming weekend, when it's my ex's custodial weekend, there's no legal basis mandating him to see his son?"

"That's correct."

"So I don't have to drop him off at his residence?"

"Right. You and your ex can come to whatever personal agreement you decide, as long as it's mutually understood and not at odds with the courts."

But that was the rub. She and her ex weren't mutually deciding anything. She was the full-time parent, and he was living a single life. "And if he just doesn't call?" The tension that had been confined internally now externalized through an elevated pitch of her voice. "If he doesn't reach out? Doesn't express any interest in time with Nathan?" Frustration heightened with each question.

Her attorney remained matter-of-fact. "Then that's his legal right."

Paige placed her hand over the speaker of the phone so her attorney wouldn't hear her grit her teeth and grunt in aggravation. When she finished that brief moment of verbalizing her anger, she removed her hand and resumed the conversation. "So I carry on? Just keep Nathan home, and then if his father calls and requests visitation, I take him there? And if he doesn't, he doesn't?"

"That's the course of action I recommend. Look, Paige . . ." Her attorney's voice swerved ever so slightly. Taking on less of a legal tone, it had the hint of a friendlier one, like a phone call between almost-friends. "You're a good mom. Don't doubt that. You're staying in your domicile, which keeps familiarity for Nathan. He's settled in a good day care. His life is fine. Now, you need to concentrate on making sure your life is fine. Don't try to live your life around court orders that your ex is not going to invoke. This is a new opportunity, a new chapter."

The last time she heard advice like that was at her wedding. There were smiles, congratulations, and advice aplenty there. Hugs and toasts commemorated the special day. Decorations, presents, and photos dotted the reception hall. At the center of the celebration of happiness was a giant, triple-layer wedding cake, replete with pristine frosting, edible flowers, pearlized sugar, and a figurine of a happy couple topping the highest tier. The entire celebration of their wedding was like icing on the cake of their relationship, sealed together on that day both legally and with the shared joy of their family and friends.

Now, her marriage had turned from an expression of joy into a sterile one of legalese facilitated by lawyers and a seemingly endless volley of paperwork. The sweet cake that symbolized so much promise was now revealed for what it hid. It was an appetite-spoiling, stomach-churning pit of sugar and calories that was as devoid of real joy as her marriage with Barry. The cake masked the truth. Paige and her ex were not meant to be together. They had enough in common to make a relationship work, but not a marriage.

And her ex clearly had no interest in being a father.

The cake of her marriage crumbled after Nathan's birth. She wasn't sorry to have him—not in the least. His presence just illuminated her ex's weaknesses and inability to commit to responsibilities. Maybe he wanted cake, but he wanted it on his terms. For him, those terms didn't involve a son. He couldn't step up to be a father when Nathan arrived. So Paige did what she could, fulfilling the role of mother but trying to be as much of a protector, provider, and comforter as she could be to fill the gap of a second parent.

She took a similar role on the call with her attorney. Nathan wouldn't be visiting his father, and the court paperwork would sit idle. "Thanks for the advice. I'll manage." And she would. Paige clicked off the call, resuming her role as a single mother.

SOME DAYS, SHE had it all together. On those days, she gave herself a lot of credit. Other days, she faltered. It was as if metaphorical cake crumbled all around her.

When it did, she handled it as best she could. What else could a single parent do? And when she needed it, she headed to the great outdoors, dialing back into one of her stress busters that worked like a charm—bike riding. That was on the agenda for Friday evening, a type of celebration for getting through the week.

With a safe view and a secure strap-in on his ride-along, Nathan could enjoy an outdoor adventure just as much as Paige. She could whisk them away on quick outings through their neighborhood and to close parts of town.

And Nathan knew when it was bicycle time. Paige just had to make a motion toward strapping on her own helmet, and he would eagerly call for his. He looked so cute tottering around with his safety gear in place, the chin strap holding up a wide, beaming grin and framing a face that brightened every time he went outdoors.

"One minute, Nate." She needed to make sure she filled her water bottle and grabbed her wrist wrap so she could stow her house key. "Mommy's got to make sure we've got what we need."

Nathan's enthusiasm was contagious, and Paige was pleased he enjoyed riding as much as she did. She looked forward to the day when he'd be old enough to pedal his own two-wheeler. They'd make more sweet memories together that way.

"Let's go!" She clasped her hands, Nathan bubbling with such excitement that he couldn't get out the door fast enough.

Days before, Paige wasn't ready to bike ride and be seen. But she didn't want to be a prisoner to her fears of encountering neighbors and being back in the public view forever. She had to live her life. And she had to provide a normal one for Nathan.

As they rode, the wide Texas sky practically swallowed them, their presence but a tiny speck along an otherwise vast landscape of everything she considered her home, her town. But instead of focusing on the beauty of her surroundings and the connection with her son, a new sensation tugged, something she could only describe by the image she saw in her mind when she dialed in to the feeling it caused. That was the image of Everett.

And he was making her question everything.

Chapter Eight

"**I**'M NOT A liar." Paige repeated this to herself as she pedaled, cresting over gentle slopes in the asphalt and across smooth, well-worn sections of the shoulder on which she rode. "I'm not a liar, but I lied."

Principles were important. Even if it was to save face, she still didn't like the charade. She could keep it going, as long as Everett didn't ask anything. And, so far, Everett didn't seem to be the wiser. She didn't have a follow-up phone call, nor did he text. They just planned to meet again at Chili's on Tuesday, a low commitment and an easy one to uphold.

Paige told herself not to worry so much about Everett's perception. What was done was done.

So why are you still thinking about it? She jerked her head as if to snap the thought from her consciousness as she and Nathan enjoyed this Friday evening ride. It was exactly a week since her finalized divorce, and she was feeling ready to make more appearances as she resumed some semblance of a life routine.

And that involved bike riding. Glorious, carefree pedaling around charming city streets did more for her wellness than any multivitamin or vegetable smoothie.

Or any bag of Cheetos. This was just plain healthier.

It was also stimulating for Nathan, who pointed to animals he saw and cars that caught his eye from his position behind Paige's seat. He laughed at loud noises and clapped in glee when she leaned to make a balanced turn. His kiddo sensations were on overdrive, and Paige was glad to witness him so engaged with his surroundings.

Rides were exciting for a toddler, and they were fun for Paige too. It was something they could share together, and in some ways she could be reminded of what it felt like to be more of an adult than a mother. Nathan's responsibilities never evaded her, but in moments like this, where he was perfectly satisfied and she could fix her focus on the world in front of her, she experienced pure contentment.

"Maybe I should clap my hands like that." She called to Nathan as he congratulated her for completing a right turn. She eased upward, her posture a bit straighter than her normal curve when pedaling so she could raise one hand. "Oh, Nate, the tricks Mommy can do . . ." She released her other hand from the handle bar, momentarily steering with no hands as she fired the muscles in her abdomen to balance.

"Still need to lay off the junk food. No more weekend binges like last Saturday." She abandoned the trick after a couple of seconds, tapping her stomach with one hand as she placed the other back on the handle bars. Even though she had lost weight in the last few months, she hadn't been toning her body. Maybe now was the best time to get back into a routine. Some strengthening moves at home, a few sit-ups before bed, maybe some invigorating morning lunges and curls. These could be her new routine.

"We'll see," she concluded of the possibility of implementing the exercises.

Paige continued pedaling down a low traveled road. This entire area of central Texas—from San Antonio to Austin—was one of the fastest-growing in the nation. People were moving for jobs, commerce, land, and quality of life, which were all the reasons she and her ex decided to settle here. Plus the town high school was her alma mater. Seguin was going to be her forever home, and maybe it still would. There was so much for Nathan, and Paige adored the proximity to all of the culture, history, and recreation in San Antonio. Plus, here in Seguin, she still had space to move. Stretches of unoccupied roadway like that which curved into pasture land and the rest of Texas' wide-open plains gave her the best of both worlds, the urban and the rural.

Some subdivisions, though, were already popping up in large tracts that sat undeveloped for years to keep pace with the fast-growing area. Land for livestock was turning into land for new homes as the market demanded. She saw one such change in front of her as she rode. An imposing "For Sale" sign caught her attention on several flat acres, though her eyes were quickly diverted away from the message and onto the parked car she noticed as she pedaled closer. Someone had stopped, and as she squinted she could see a figure walking the fence line in front of the property. The individual's back was to her, but she didn't need to see the front to know.

The car was his. Those shoulders were his. That gait with a little bounce to the left as he took each step was his. And as he shifted his posture a bit to one side, she could see what looked like a rolling surveyor's wheel that he pushed to measure square footage. That tool was his.

Paige applied the brakes. The last person she wanted to see was him.

Her ex.

Paige made a U-turn, diverting Nathan's attention with a "Look over there" signal to a natural pecan tree grove on the opposite side of the road. "Do you see any birds? Any squirrels?" The possibility was slim he'd recognize his father, especially at such a distance, but Paige didn't want to take any chances with an unplanned surprise from Barry Van Soyt. She leaned lower and pumped her feet against the pedals, increasing their speed. She pressed on, faster and faster to close the gap between her and the ex whose very sight still made her uncomfortable.

But more than just seeing, she questioned what he could be doing. As a home inspector, he had a portable wheel for measuring distance around houses and lots, but he didn't survey raw land. That wasn't in his career jurisdiction. Not that he couldn't, of course. Paige's mind trailed with possibilities.

What was he doing on these open lots? Why was he measuring this undeveloped area that was for sale?

Pumping and pumping, she transported Nathan faster than before, sustaining speed until she veered left onto the road that took them out of sight. He laughed and clapped as the wind hit his face and roadway views whipped past, a toddler completely absorbed in the joy of the ride. But Paige felt none of his shared enthusiasm, for the pit of possibility in her stomach churned in sickening rhythm. She'd have no energy for starting core exercises tonight since the surprise sight of her ex made her feel more like puking than anything.

DANICA CAME BY again on Saturday, just for a quick stop while she was running errands. She stood at the bar while Paige cleared away the breakfast dishes and wiped down the counters. Nathan was absorbed in cartoons.

"Want to head to the farmers' market?" she offered. "I've got to get some ears of sweet corn." She sounded so serious.

"Like it's a matter of personal necessity?" Paige jabbed.

"Exactly." Danica played along. "If I don't pump my body full of golden kernels, who knows what will happen."

"I know what will happen." Paige ran water from the tap, dampened the sponge she was using, and wrung it clear to give the counters a final wipe.

"Oh? And what's that?" Danica drummed her fingers on the counter, waiting for Paige's reply.

She sponged in a tight circular motion across the laminate. There were vegetables and fruits aplenty at the farmers' market. Especially popular around the late spring in Texas were melons, cucumbers, tomatoes, zucchini, and lots of wonderful greens. There were fresh eggs. Beekeepers brought honey. Some sold plants or packages of seeds they harvested. It was easy to eat well with access to a local outdoor marketplace with homegrown foods.

"You'll buy so much healthy produce at the farmers' market," Paige continued, "that you'll reward yourself with something far less healthy later in the day."

Danica mocked offense. "Well, I never—"

"Spare me. After filling up on organics, are you telling me Haribo won't come calling?"

Danica had a weakness for gummy candies, especially the colorful bears in the gold package from the Haribo company. "Now, there's nothing wrong with a fat free candy . . ."

Paige snorted. "Fat free? How much sugar do those have?" Though she remained privately aware of the irony in questing her friend's habits after her own junk food binge the previous weekend. To lighten their banter, Paige turned the knob of the faucet and flicked her finger under the steady stream to send a few drops of water in Danica's direction.

"Hey, watch it. I'll melt." She shook the droplets that landed on her arm.

Paige shut off the water then dried her hands on a nearby kitchen towel. "If the humidity outside hasn't melted you, a little water won't hurt."

"You aren't kidding about that. I can barely walk out the door without breaking into a sweat." Central Texas weather could be beautiful, but it could also be stifling. "Have you been riding?"

Paige flashed to her bike ride yesterday and her surprise stumble onto her ex at the property that was for sale. She wasn't in the mood to add paranoia to her list of problems she shared with Danica, so she simply answered, "A little.

Trying to ease back into it slowly, you know?"

"Yeah." Danica offered sympathetic eyes. "But it's good you're getting back out there."

Paige shrugged, hearing a double meaning in Danica's words whether it was intended or not. "Something like that." Should she tell Danica about meeting Everett? But what was there to tell? This was her best friend, but Paige had already leaned on her so much that she didn't want to burden her with miniscule encounters of a high school acquaintance and her ex, even though they felt very big to Paige. "Besides"— she swerved from the subjects—"I still have cleaning to do around here. You know Nathan's father still never picked up those boxes I packed away?"

"What boxes? Did he leave some stuff here?"

Paige rolled her eyes. "More than you would think. I don't know how people can accumulate so much stuff." She had spent the last few weeks digging through the attic and garage, putting aside things Barry had left behind when he moved out of the house.

Then there were little things she kept finding—old mugs of his taking up space in a kitchen cabinet, half-used toiletries stuffed away in the bathroom vanity, extra electronic chargers tangled in a junk drawer. Paige stowed all of these in boxes in a corner of the den, but he never retrieved them.

Danica answered Paige's query with her blunt conclusion. "Men can be pigs."

"Here, here," she seconded. "My advice to you? Purge what you own while you can."

Danica paused, her finger poised against her chin in contemplation before she turned the words back on Paige. "Why don't you take your own advice?"

"What?" Paige didn't follow.

"Purge," Danica said simply. "Look, if he's not going to come get his stuff, don't worry about it. Get it out of the house. Donate it. Sell it. Whatever. It will probably help you feel better to do that."

Paige hadn't thought about an alternate means of disposal until now. The idea of purging was immediately attractive. "He has had plenty of opportunity . . ."

"See!" Danica held up a finger, checking off his chance with a motion through the air. "Time to clean house!"

But Paige wasn't sure about tackling another project solo. "If I do a garage sale—"

But Paige couldn't even finish her thought before Danica jumped in with "I'll bring the signs!"

Priceless. Paige smiled at her friend. Danica was already one step ahead of her.

EVERETT BUSIED HIMSELF with chores in between meeting his mother's needs and his father's avoidance of anything to do with the word "cancer." Whether it was to keep his mother's spirits high or whether it was a result of Dale Mullins' own discomfort with the disease moving in to his life via his wife, Everett wasn't sure. He just did what he could to pick up the slack of responsibility for the remaining few weeks he was able to stay in Seguin.

His work leave would expire at the end of the month, and he'd need to be back in Amarillo. But he had two and a half more weeks to try to make both his parents' lives easier, amid their struggle.

His mother's needs were relatively easy to assess, for her expressions communicated her level of pain or comfort. His father, though, wasn't as easy to read. Everett had seen his father slow since he returned to the farm. Signs of aging were hidden remotely with Everett living in Amarillo, but now that he was temporarily back home, his father couldn't camouflage the truth of his health so easily.

"Need me to carry that up?" He pointed to a laundry basket his father stowed at the bottom of the stairs.

"I'll get it," he dismissed.

Everett noticed his father being more conservative with his stair climbing. Whereas Everett could dash up to the second story of the farmhouse without hesitation, his father took each step more warily as he leaned onto the handrail for support. He also had the routine of not making a trip up the stairs unless necessary, so putting away the laundry, for instance, could wait until he ascended for another reason.

"Knees bothering you?" Everett sensed pain in his movements, not just on stairs but in other instances, such as standing after being in a seated position for an extended period.

"They're fine. A little rusty, but it's just age." His dad wasn't one to complain.

And neither was his mother.

As much discomfort as she must have felt due to the chemo, she refused to complain. She handled her nausea and her weakness as if they were her albatross to wear, suffering in silence by putting on a brave face.

Everett picked up the basket anyway when his dad rounded the corner. Then he ascended the stairs and slid it on the inside of his parents' bedroom wall when he poked his head in to find his mother awake, sitting up in bed. "Hey, there."

"Hey." She blinked hard, stirring to his presence. "Guess I dozed off."

"Your body needs rest." A body fighting cancer always needed rest.

"I just feel like the day gets wasted when I do that too long." His mother had always been one to be as productive as possible. Even though she was retired, her propensity for hard work never changed. Between farm chores, volunteerism, and even church duties, she was the busiest retiree Everett knew.

But that was before the cancer.

"You're entitled," Everett reminded her.

His mother huffed, her breath blowing loose bangs that framed her face in silver. "Hardly."

He stepped to the headboard and grabbed a pillow she wasn't using. Kneading it between his hands, he fluffed it before instructing her to lean forward, and he swapped it for the flattened one behind her back. "Mom, you can tell me what you need." Everett wanted her to be honest so he could help her as much as he was able.

Aside, though, from cough syrup for her dry throat, a box of tissues nearby, a romance novel on her bedside table, and a bottle of moisturizing cream within easy reach, she didn't ask for much.

"Are your feet better today?" Everett prompted. His mother's feet had swollen with the treatments, and even her toenails were reacting to the chemicals by becoming brittle. "Those feet have to take you through your Monday appointment."

"Well, they'll be fine by then." His mother knew the routine well, as did Everett. "Got the weekend to recover. Not that weekends and weekdays are much different," she added dryly.

"Sundays have been good days," Everett reminded her. And since Sunday was just a day away, he was hoping she had more energy, perhaps even enough to venture from the bedroom and sit on the porch. Maybe he was being overly optimistic, but he wanted to seed the idea. "If you're up for it, we could go for a drive? Get a little sunshine?"

"I'm not a plant." She wriggled her toes. "You don't have to check my roots. You don't have to give me sun."

Maybe Everett had gone a little overboard. He toned down his approach. "Sorry, Mom. Just want to make sure you're not uncomfortable."

"I have cancer," she retorted. "And cancer has a monopoly on uncomfortable."

"Fair enough." Everett wasn't going to win the battle of appeasing her today.

"There is one thing you can do." Her mother added an afterthought. "You can try to relax. Maybe enjoy your time off a little more."

He had reminded her that his time away from work was not so much time off as it was medical leave that he devoted to her care. Everett wasn't expecting a vacation out of his return to Seguin.

"Doesn't matter." His mother contended. "You've got to do something for yourself, so you don't go stir-crazy."

Everett folded his arms across his chest and leaned back. "I'm not anywhere near stir-crazy."

"Wouldn't know it if you were." Now his mother was just edging for an argument. But before either of them could take it further, she counseled, "Listen to your mother, Everett. Mother knows best."

There was no arguing with that. He uncrossed his arms and leaned in to kiss her on the forehead. "You know I love you," he whispered.

"Love you too." She closed his eyes to accept his kiss and his words. Then, while he was still close, she opened one eye, pinched the fabric of his shirt to keep him from pulling back, and urged, "But you've got to do something for yourself while you're in Seguin."

Everett considered spitting out Paige's name right then, telling his mother he was doing something for himself. He was learning how to have conversations with a woman again and be in the company of one without his emotions stalling. But what could he really say about Paige? He bit his tongue, deciding he might mention her if their second date went well.

It was a date, after all, wasn't it?

Chapter Nine

EVERETT ORDERED ANOTHER Sprite as he waited for Paige to arrive. He didn't want to be late, yet he didn't expect to have so much time before she arrived either. A quarter before the hour gave him an opportunity to sit, study the menu, and get nervous about seeing Paige. Even the Sprite didn't soothe his butterflies as much as he hoped. And, disappointingly, it was having the opposite effect.

"Here's a refill." The Chili's waitress set down a frosty mug of ice cold soda. But Everett stifled a burp as he gestured a "thank you" that looked more like a move-it-along signal. He raised the palm of his hand when he saw her frown. "No, I mean," he swallowed another burp. "Thank you."

This was not going to do.

"Actually," he called for her attention before she moved to the next table, "can I have some crackers? Or bread or something?"

Starch appetizers were not Chili's protocol, and he should have known. But he needed something to calm his stomach before Paige arrived, or he'd make a gassy fool of himself.

"I can bring you some chips and salsa."

"Tortilla chips?"

"Yes." It was probably all she could do not to add, "This is Texas," where Tex-Mex was defined by appetizer chips and salsa.

"Perfect," he agreed. "That would be—good." He narrowly edged another embarrassing burp.

He felt like he was back in high school, not only experiencing odd bodily functions but also with his sometimes awkwardness in general interaction with others. His trouble with getting words out in front of the waitress came as a surprise. But he also experienced the same problem earlier in the morning with his parents. He simply avoided direct answers to his mother's questions about his so-called errands for the day so, admittedly, he could meet Paige on the sly. Granted, it was a timed lunch at an interstate café, but it was still exciting for him to be able to see Paige—and to keep his private life hidden from his parents.

Plus, as much as he enjoyed a little getaway, he hoped being out was good for Paige as well. Losing a marital partner required massive life adjustment, and he wanted in some small way to assist her with that, even without knowing details. Yet he wasn't going to bridge the topic to find them out. It wasn't his place, and he was sure Paige needed to focus on something less personal anyway.

Five more minutes passed, which was enough time for Everett's talkative stomach to quiet and not quite long enough for him to order a third soda.

Again, like a teenager. He swirled the straw around the near empty glass, reminding himself to act his age.

The waitress brought chips, salsa, and two appetizer plates. "Still waiting on your guest?"

"Yes." Perhaps as much to convince himself, he added, "But she'll be here soon."

Everett waited some more, snacking on the appetizer, though nervousness mounted. Had he asked for too much? Maybe Paige really wasn't ready for routine outings. Widowhood came with so many mixed emotions, and though lots of people claimed to understand it through writing books about it, there wasn't a true manual for proper dealing or response from outsiders.

Interrupting Everett's worry, however, was the reality of an approaching woman whom he now recognized with refreshing clarity.

"Paige," he whispered under his breath. He watched her hips snake their way around obtrusive chairs and her feet sidestep furniture legs to arrive at their table, the same one as last week.

Paige looked fresh and feminine in a dusty pink top and slim khaki skirt. He couldn't remember her shoes from last time, but he noted sexy, strappy heeled ones this time. Bright bubblegum-colored polish peeked out at him from pedicured toes. "Hi there." He could sense a wide grin spreading from ear to ear.

"Hi. Again." Paige's emerald irises peeked from beneath her bangs as she tucked a loose strand of hair behind her ear. She bit her lip yet still gave a halfway grin. "Sorry I'm a little late." She pulled back her chair.

"Oh, no problem at all," Everett dismissed.

"Have you been waiting long?" She settled into her seat after hanging her purse over the back of it.

"No." Everett fumbled with his straw, churning the last bit of liquid in his mug around and around in the remaining ice, most of which had melted.

Paige looked at the near empty mug. "Is that right?" She raised an eyebrow as her gaze shifted to half eaten chips and salsa.

Everett leaned back and slumped his shoulders in a dramatic "guilty as charged" admission.

Paige clicked her tongue in a "tsk, tsk, tsk" admonishment. But then a wider smile—a seemingly genuine one—broke across her face as she snapped open the menu, creating a playful barrier between Everett and herself.

He stayed silent as she studied the choices. *No ring.* He noticed as he eyed her left hand. To Everett, that was a sign she was healing from her loss. *Good.* He still wasn't going to ask her anything, but it was a green light sign of moving forward.

And that bit of go-ahead was all he needed.

He cleared his throat as she lowered the menu enough to see him. Their eyes met. "That color looks good on you."

"This?" She turned her head and leaned into her shoulder, pointing to the fabric of her blouse with her chin.

He nodded. "It reminds me of a flower."

She gave a spirited seated curtsy using just her upper body. "Why thank you."

"What exactly would you call that? Maybe rose-colored?"

She shrugged. "Maybe."

Everett had seen that color on a flower somewhere before. Very recently, in fact. *No, rose is too dark. But some other one . . .* "On my drive in," he remembered. "In the fields. Those buttercups." Now he could place the color, likening it to the pink of the tender-leafed buttercup native to Texas. Mingling with bluebonnets and especially prevalent after a rain, native Texas Buttercups were nothing like standard yellow ones that grew in flower gardens elsewhere. These wild ones had bold, rounded leaves of pink, framing a bright yellow center. "Buttercup pink," he concluded, settling on a name for the color.

Paige looked down and whispered something.

"What was that?" Everett couldn't detect a clear tone one way or another.

Speaking just a hair louder, she looked up and said, "That's what my dad calls me." She repeated, "Buttercup."

"That's cute." Everett tilted his head. "And it fits."

Paige shifted in her seat and tucked another strand of hair behind her ear. If she were nervous, simply shutting down this part of the conversation was best. He didn't want to be the cause of nervousness for her, so he decided to steer the conversation to lunch.

He leaned back in his chair, conscious of creating breathing room for her. "What are you thinking of ordering?"

His redirection to their reason for meeting at a restaurant worked as Paige perked up. "Tex-Mex something. I've been craving that. Plus I have a little more time today." She glanced at her watch. "Though I'm sure the staff will serve us quickly anyway."

There weren't as many people in the restaurant today as compared to last Tuesday, by Everett's judgement. And he had plenty of time to assess while he waited for her.

"I'm thinking about an enchilada plate."

"Enchiladas do sound good," Everett agreed.

As if waiting for that exact time, the waitress appeared. "Are you two ready to order?"

Everett gestured toward Paige. "Ladies first."

Paige made a quick scan of the photos to accompany the dishes she was most interested in from the menu. She pointed to the colorful photo of ones with citrus-chili rice and black beans. "How about the green chile chicken enchiladas?"

"Good choice." The waitress accepted her menu as Paige folded it. "Those are my favorite. And for you?" She turned to Everett.

His mouth watered at the possibilities. Taking Paige's lead of deciding by pictures, everything looked good. He expressed that, but decided on a classic. "Beef enchiladas."

"Good choice as well." She opened her hand to take his menu.

"I'm simple." He winked at Paige. "Remember?"

She nodded. "I don't tend to forget things."

EVERETT LOOKED EVEN more handsome than Paige remembered in a button-down plaid work shirt and dark denim jeans. The top two buttons were undone, revealing a "v" of skin slightly tanned by the sun that likely smelled as delicious as it looked.

Maybe I'm just hungry. She bit her lip so as not to communicate any of her lascivious thoughts aloud.

But Everett was attractive. Fit. Presentable. Polite.

Why isn't he taken? Surely some lucky woman should have snagged him by now. Maybe it was his work responsibilities. Or perhaps it was travel, both domestic and foreign. He hadn't just made one trip to the Netherlands for his job, but the way he explained it during their last lunch was that there were several which took him away for a couple of weeks at a time. He was part of some group that assisted with water management projects there, so surely the duties must have been all-consuming.

Or maybe Everett wasn't in a relationship because of the move to Amarillo itself. Settling in a new place always came with challenges. It could be that having a romantic relationship just wasn't a priority.

Which would be a waste for someone like you, Everett. Paige had to consciously still her dreaminess so her musings didn't tumble onto their table like an accidental salsa spill.

"So have you heard what's going on in Amarillo? Weather or anything?" It was a weak conversation starter, and Paige knew as much the minute the words escaped her mouth.

Weather? Really? She wanted to kick herself.

Everett was kind in his reply. "Not as much rain as we've had here. Especially that downpour Friday before last."

How could she forget?

But even as Paige silently chastised herself for being so pedestrian with her questions, Everett had a way of making any topic interesting. Perhaps it was his general charisma or his unexpected humor when he made a joke or stumbled into a pun and offered a cute facial expression that exposed his left dimple. Whatever the reason, the result was pleasant. And, as she reflected on how he made it so, her thoughts shifted again to what she imagined to be his personal life.

No wife.

No kids.

At least not that he had revealed.

A girlfriend? If so, he would have found a way to work her into the conversation. *Right?*

But that hadn't been the case. So, suffice it to say, there was no girlfriend. Maybe women in north Texas were just different from those in central Texas. Either way, Paige was glad to have this opportunity to reconnect, at least in these small ways, with someone from high school.

She tried again to start a more pointed conversation, asking about Seguin instead of Amarillo. His eyes lit when he talked about his hometown and his parents' farm.

"The circumstances aren't the best for being back," he started. Paige didn't press about his mother's illness or how treatments were progressing. "But it's so refreshing to see the ole stomping ground. You know, time away can give a new lease on a place. You appreciate it more. See it for what it is." He grabbed a chip and crunched through it before he chose his next words. "Really understand why it feels so much like home."

Yes! She wanted to scream. *That's it!* Why couldn't anyone else understand that was why she wanted to stay in Seguin, at least for the immediate future? "It's a security blanket."

He nodded. "Exactly."

Then, as if they had rehearsed the line, they both said in near unison, "It's home."

A smile broke across Everett's face, and Paige's cheeks flushed from the coincidence.

Everett, to his credit, made conversation easy. He talked about chores on his parents' farm as well as errands around town he did on behalf of both parents in the weeks he had before he returned to Amarillo. But he didn't carry himself with the smug look of someone wanting attention or recognition, nor did he seem hurried in how he operated. On the contrary, in both the grocery store and in the restaurant, Everett exhibited immediately recognizable characteristics—kindness, generosity, agreeableness. He seemed to be genuinely interested, too, in Paige, in what she had to say, in sharing conversation. Encounters were surprisingly easy between them.

"So tell me about work. How long have you been at the land and title office?" Everett volleyed conversation to her. "And what do you like best about it?"

Paige crossed her legs under the table and tried to angle her body against the back of the chair to get more comfortable. She swung her foot in tune to her talking.

"Let's see," she began, still wanting to avoid any mention of her ex or son as she answered his questions with, otherwise, as much honesty as she could.

She was proud of her job, and she relayed the types of everyday duties she did. After a few moments of outlining the basics, she surprised Everett with, "Now, can I tell you a little secret that just happened? Yesterday, in fact?"

"Sure thing!" He seemed baited by her leading question. "Fire away."

She stilled her foot and uncrossed her legs. With both feet firm on the support of the chair, she confessed, "I got a promotion."

Everett's eyes grew as wide as their appetizer plates. "Paige, that's fantastic!"

She couldn't hide her excitement, but she was keeping the news relatively quiet. "I haven't told people yet. I mean, of course my coworkers know. And then yesterday after it happened I called my sister. And my parents."

"Where are they?"

"Mallory is in Santa Fe. My parents are in Angel Fire."

He nodded. "Beautiful locations, both." He beamed. "I bet they are so proud of you!"

"Yeah." She brought her mug of iced blackberry tea to her lips and swallowed a thirsty sip. "I have one friend I told." But what reeled through her mind was the truth. *I don't have anyone at home to tell.* Telling people over the phone just wasn't the same. She met Everett's gaze over the rim of the glass. "You're the first person I've told face-to-face." The magnitude of sharing filled her, and she felt more proud of the promotion today after verbalizing it in this way than she did yesterday.

And she didn't know that was possible.

"So, let me hear all about it." He cleared away his plate, as if doing so would give her the table as a stage to spill details. "Don't hold back."

Paige eagerly obliged, telling Everett that, while her cubicle size wasn't changing, everything else was. She would have new responsibilities, new reporting oversight, and new signing authorization. She would also have to learn some additional software duties, and she was most excited about the continuation of building her skill set in that way.

"But my hours are going to remain the same. And that's good." She stopped herself before she mistakenly added, *for the sake of Nathan's day care.*

Only when there was a lull in the conversation on Paige's end did Everett suggest, "That's fantastic. You have every reason to be proud."

She did. And she took his comment to heart. "Thank you."

"Anything else?" He prompted. "I mean, that's all such a big deal, but do you think anything else might change for you?"

Paige replayed the conversation with her boss yesterday. "I nearly forgot!" She punctuated with a single finger in the air for emphasis. "My paycheck!"

Everett raised his drink, his chiseled face glowing in shared joy to Paige's news. "Well, cheers to that!"

THE HOUR FLEW by for this lunch faster than last week's.

"I'm sorry I did all the talking." Paige glanced at her watch.

"I like listening to you," Everett replied simply.

And it was true. Watching her enthusiasm, seeing her animation, witnessing her pride and professionalism. These were treats of an intimate, two-way conversation.

And of attraction.

Everett couldn't help himself. The more he was around Paige, the more he remembered not only what he liked about her back in high school but why there was so much more to like now. How she had built on all of her good characteristics, time making them even better.

They exchanged smiles. "It was nice to share my news."

It must be. And hard, considering your husband isn't here to share it. I'm sure he would have been so proud. Everett wanted to acknowledge the pain Paige must have been experiencing as a layer underneath all of the happiness, but it wasn't his place. The best he could do was be the ear she needed and share the joy of her news rather than rain on her parade with questions about her personal life. She could deal with any contradictory feelings in private.

"I'm glad you told me," he said instead.

She tilted her head. "Me too."

As much as he wanted to linger, it was best to send Paige on her way. "I don't want to make you late, now that you're a big shot and all."

She rolled her eyes. "Not exactly." She pushed back her chair, stood up, and grabbed her purse. Fishing inside, she found her wallet. "And I'm paying, remember?"

Everett followed her lead in standing up before he raised his hands in mock surrender at her comment. "Hey, you're the one making the big bucks. Who am I to complain?"

Paige leaned into him with her shoulder, giving him a playful bump. The slight bit of contact served as a taste of what more they could share. Like a meal where he was only allowed one bite, her brief contact with him left him wanting more.

She righted her posture, and placed cash on the table. "Tip included," she clarified, perhaps so Everett wouldn't make a move to add any additional bills.

"Well"—he gave a tight nod of his head—"I thank you."

She stowed her wallet, slung her purse across her shoulder, and pivoted to lead them out of the restaurant.

But as they wound their way around tables and through the aisles to exit, Everett had a hard time fixing his gaze on anything but the gorgeous woman walking a step ahead of him.

Chapter Ten

MIGUEL CALLED PAIGE to his desk first thing on Wednesday morning. Now that news of her promotion to Title Officer had two days to sink in, it was time for her to roll-up her sleeves and get started. Miguel planned a morning of duty shadowing along with introduction to original documents and online access she would need to perform her new role.

"I'm going to get you set up so you can start working the actual closings," he explained.

The prospect excited Paige. Before this promotion, she had attended mortgage closings that were scheduled at the land and title office, and she often acted as the unofficial hostess for the buyers and sellers of lots and homes who met together to sign the paperwork during a sale. Those were just part of her administrative duties. But she wasn't the actual one signing documents or facilitating the meeting. Now, however, she would be doing those tasks and trusted with more of a leadership role.

Miguel thumbed through files in a pull-out drawer. "And I want to make sure you enter into these real estate closings comfortably, so I'm going to give you more responsibility with researching title documents." He procured a manila folder and handed it across the desk to Paige. "Are you ready for a few more trips to the courthouse?"

Paige balanced on one leg, elevating her foot to where Miguel could see she was wearing her comfortable leather ballet flats today. "I've even got good shoes for it."

Miguel pushed his desk drawer closed. "Well, I don't know much about women's footwear." He grabbed another folder from the top file tray of his desk. "But I do know you'll be wearing a pretty thin path between here and that giant pecan."

Paige chuckled. Most people did whenever the municipal landmark of the bronzed pecan was mentioned. Erected a half century earlier, a single fake pecan the size of a bathtub sat atop a concrete pedestal on the Guadalupe County courthouse lawn, immortalizing the area's nuttiest export. And nutty was just the way to describe the look of the pecan, poised like an oblong rocket in the shadow of the courthouse.

But there was also something to be said for local, eclectic statues, landmarks, and traditions, especially in small towns. It was a sight, but it was Seguin's sight. That pecan was the people's.

It was Paige's.

When no one was looking, Paige would sometimes walk by and thump the pecan, for no other reason than just to do it. It wasn't made of actual bronze so much as caster, but who was really going to argue with the way it was described in chamber of commerce brochures?

She also wouldn't admit this to anyone from out of

town, but she had taken Nathan's picture by the pecan—every six months. There was a whole, goofy set of photos she treasured of Nathan by the town landmark, growing like the tree which bore the fruit. Again, it was something perhaps only locals could appreciate.

For how many more years would she snap a photo? She stood about at the pecan's height, and one day Nathan would too. But, oh, how many, many more years he had before he grew that tall! For now, he—and she—needed to enjoy the toddler stage.

Miguel led the two of them out the front door of the land and title office, calling to the administrative assistant that they'd be back in half an hour. He held the door open as Paige stepped through, into the midmorning white-hot Texas sun.

"Shade on the sidewalk," he directed, as Paige stepped into the shadows of the surrounding buildings as best she could.

For deed and public record research, she'd need to visit the county clerk's office. She knew a few of the employees, though she prepared to reintroduce herself as Paige Fredrick, not Paige Van Soyt. Reclaiming her maiden name involved jumping through hoops of bureaucratic paperwork, but her identity was hers again. It did mean she and Nathan would be under the same roof with different surnames, but there was a pride in reconnecting with her family identity that was important.

The last time she had been in the courthouse, though, was as Paige Van Soyt. Now, with her divorce finalized, she could step in as her new self. Armed with her new-old name and this old-new job, the journey really did feel like a fresh start.

PAIGE AND MIGUEL arrived back in the office with skin sticky from the heat. "This is why I can't ride my bike to work anymore." She twisted her arm to expose the crease inside her elbow as she simultaneously inventoried the skin at her wrist, moist with perspiration. "I would be absolutely soaked."

Miguel pinched the fabric of his shirt and tented it up and down to fan his chest. "Tell me about it."

A little heat from outdoor trips seemed to be the only drawback to her promotion, so far at least. And if that was the absolute worst of it, she'd take it.

"Go get a drink if you need it, and meet me back at my desk in ten minutes." Miguel split from Paige, but the administrative assistant stationed at the front caught her before she passed.

"You got something," she played coy, "while you were out." Pointing to a bright floral arrangement atop her desk, she announced, for Paige and for anyone within earshot, "It's for you!"

Paige froze in mid step. "Me?" The flowers were perched in a simple glass vase at the edge of the desk, as if they had just been delivered. *But why would they be for me?* "Are you sure?"

The assistant pointed to a card peeking out from the greenery. The envelope held her first name. "Take 'em." Paige squared her stance in front of the arrangement, but she was still too shocked by its presence to even touch. "Unless you want me to keep them."

With that playful urging, she bent her knees and grasped the water-filled vase between both hands, steadying it as if it were made entirely of porcelain. She could smell the sweet fragrance of lilacs and peony before she identified their buds, which comingled with various carnations, fern leaves, and baby's breath for a vibrant, lively mix of colors and textures. A thick, pink bow encircled the waist of the vase, tied in prim and fluffy perfection.

"Thank you," Paige uttered on the way back to her desk, not entirely sure if she was aiming it at the administrative assistant, the long-gone florist who delivered the arrangement, or the mystery individual responsible for sending it.

She walked with gingered steps to her cubicle, admiring the beauty of the compact and appealing sight. *Is this why Miguel wanted me to take ten?* Sending flowers in honor of her new duties seemed a little outside of his character. *And what must my coworkers think?* The last thing she needed was for them to speculate she somehow had curried favor and won the promotion with anything other than hard work and dedication to her duties.

Swerving around the corner and into her cubicle, she set the arrangement next to her computer before rolling back her desk chair. She sank into it, giving her feet a break. In this slightly more private setting, she could react to the message on the card.

She plucked the envelope from its plastic holder, fingering it as she contemplated her next move. She wanted to read the note, but she also needed to be smart about this. Their office space was not large, and she was sure at least a few others had seen the flowers—and were likely already drawing private conclusions.

Twisting in her chair toward her computer, she struck a few random keys to bring it back to life. Then, she poised her finger on the mouse, clicked twice, and opened her email, preparing to send Miguel a message rather than meet at his desk as intended. She could react professionally in writing to the gesture, nothing more.

She pivoted to look again at the flowers and placed the envelope face down as she slid her finger underneath the back flap. Shadowing Miguel to learn the rest of her new duties would have to wait until the afternoon, when perhaps news of the flowers wasn't as fresh. She'd email, but she wouldn't race back over to him. A little bit of distance and perceived autonomy as she learned her new role might work at keeping coworkers' possible thoughts of impropriety between the two of them at bay.

Just what I need. She now regretted being sent the flowers.

She opened the flap on the miniature envelope and slid out the rectangular cardstock enclosed inside. She knew Miguel's handwriting, and this wasn't it. But whose was it? She didn't recognize the script on the front of the card as a giveaway pattern.

It didn't take her long to identify the voice behind the words, for when she read them, she could hear as if they were being delivered from across a lunch table:

> *To Paige—*
>   *Congrats on the promotion. Sorry there are no buttercups.*
>   *—from Everett*

Miguel was off the hook, but this gesture now waded into impropriety of another kind.

Just what, exactly, was Everett trying to convey by sending these? He had already expressed congratulations over lunch yesterday. So why did he feel the need to do more?

Paige chewed on the possibilities and her bottom lip as she tapped the card against her desk. But as she lifted and lowered, a bit of writing on the back caught her eye. Even more interesting than the front message was the writing here, for a surprise series of digits stared back at her, shifting the power of a possible next move to her.

Everett had included his phone number.

EVERETT'S FATHER WAS flipping ground beef patties, trying not to let the grease sizzle and pop out of the pan.

"Dale, don't flatten those when you flip them." His mother coached from her position in the living room recliner.

"Don't you worry, Ruby, about what's going on in here. Watch your show." His father didn't look up from the pan.

But *Wheel of Fortune* was already muted, which was just as well. "I like solving the puzzles without all those buzzers and talking." His mother leaned over the arm of the chair toward Everett, revealing her guilty pleasure as if it were a national security secret. Everett simply nodded. "And have you started the gravy?" she called back.

"You'll have gravy," his dad assured, sidestepping her question.

After forty-five years of marriage, Dale and Ruby Mullins had their pulse on the exact way each other operated. They also understood each other's quirks and faults. "I finally have an appetite, and I don't want to eat dry meat tonight." Everett's mother was having a remarkable string of good days, with her energy level higher, her mental state clearer, and even her humor taking an upward turn. "You know?" She pointed to the television screen and lowered her voice as she directed the words to Everett who was nearer to her. "That contestant looks like your father does when he makes that spoiled milk face of his."

"Ruby!" Dale snapped from the kitchen, though he probably only heard half of what she said anyway. Then he said an expletive as he pulled his hand back from the pan.

"Told you to be careful," his mother said without looking at him, winking instead at Everett. "Mother knows best."

"You're not my mother," his dad mumbled from the kitchen.

"I still know best," she insisted. After such a long and

comfortable relationship, she had a propensity for finding the exact statement that would jab her husband. Everett just shook his head in response to this old, married couple banter.

After his father ran a bit of water over what sounded like a minor finger burn, he said, "That's a line you can't use when he leaves, you know."

"I know." She suddenly grew quiet, patting her hand on the arm of the recliner and rocking back and forth in dedicated thought. The subject now shifting, she couldn't help but ask Everett, "And just when do you plan on going back to Amarillo?"

"End of the month. Like I told you I would." He came with a plan. It wasn't that he wasn't flexible in changing it, but he did have to complete leave paperwork and set up his water service crew with a temporary supervisor in his place during this absence.

"But I'm feeling better." She curled her biceps in a playful pose, pumping them in and out. "Like Popeye!"

Everett shook his head. "Not quite, Mom."

She turned her head into one of the bicep curls and kissed her muscle. "Suit yourself." She was much more animated and comical the last couple of days, but especially tonight. And since she asked for a specific meal, that was certainly a good sign as well that her body was processing things better. Everett enjoyed seeing his mother in such a pleasant state. It was good for everyone in the house not to have an evening spoiled by cancer.

His mother noticed a change in Everett too, turning her

focus to him. "You've certainly had a smile on your face these days."

"Oh?" He played dumb.

"Oh!" She mocked. "Yes, you, the prodigal son of Seguin. Returned, but insisting you're going to be the stay-quiet-and-not-do-anything-around-town guy." She angled toward him. "Like Amarillo is going to be offended if you so much as crack a smile or have a little fun while you're here."

His mother was exaggerating, and he called her on it.

"No, I'm not," she countered. "But the last week, you've finally loosened up. Maybe all the rain we had shook off the seriousness of you. Livened you up a bit."

Indeed, Everett had changed since being home, but the change wasn't due to the weather. And it wasn't due to his parents, as much as he loved them and appreciated being able to care for his mother. It was due to someone else entirely.

Paige. He made the silent admission to himself.

She was occupying his thoughts in a wonderful way, giving him a renewed avenue for thinking about interactions with another person. Even their two lunch meet-ups had punctuated an otherwise tiresome week of doctor appointments, home care, medicine administration, and evenings like this that consisted of nothing more than silent *Wheel of Fortune* and chopped steak patties.

"Food's up," his father called with the pep of a short order cook.

Everett stood then stretched his hand to help his mother do the same. She led them into the kitchen, with Everett following a short way behind. He flicked off the television and tossed the remote on the coffee table. Then, he reached into the side pocket of his jeans when his phone vibrated with the notice of an incoming message. He slid his finger across the screen and a bright bouquet of summer florals in a glass vase stared back at him.

Paige had gotten his flowers. And she was using his number.

He was a teenager all over again.

PAIGE DEBATED CONTACTING Everett all day. Ultimately, the simple gesture of acknowledgement won out. She decided it best to give him the courtesy of knowing his surprise arrived, but she didn't muster the courage to text him until after she and Nathan had dinner and were getting settled for the evening.

She stared at the picture she had taken with her cell phone of the flowers, which were still at work. They occupied a clear space of her desk, adding vibrancy to the otherwise droll landscape of file folders, Xeroxed copies, legal pads, and pencil cups. She planned to keep the flowers at work for the remainder of the week. On Friday, she could bring them home and allow them to brighten the house instead. She hadn't received flowers since . . .

Nathan's birth?

She tucked her feet beneath her as she relaxed on the

couch. Had it been that long? She recalled Mallory sent a bouquet to the hospital when Nathan arrived, a cheery token of baby blue florals that did little to numb the pain of actual childbirth but was kind nonetheless. Her sister never had any children. Otherwise, she probably would have sent codeine.

That was the last gesture of flowers she could remember receiving. Aside from flowers at her wedding, there weren't any she received during her actual years of marriage. It was a shame to admit, but her ex wasn't the type and never had been. Barry Van Soyt spent money on garage gadgets and technology gizmos, not flowers.

So the rarity of the occasion might have been part of the reason for the magnitude of surprise, but it was also the knowledge of the sender.

Paige sorted through the several snapshots she'd taken of the flowers, choosing the best one. The lighting was pretty, and the bow around the middle of the vase was centered. The flowers looked so fresh she could almost smell their fragrance through the phone.

She added the picture to a message and then typed a few characters. No words looked right. Every expression she drafted came across as trite or wooden. So, with the right words eluding her, she simply typed in Everett's phone number and hit send.

Tossing the phone onto the cushion next to her, she would see if Everett made any move. While she did, she called Nathan over to the couch, welcoming him into her arms. They exchanged a big bear hug before he climbed into her lap, showing off an action figure he carried.

As Nathan generated noises and pushed the figure's

jointed limbs up and down in mock movement, her phone screen lit, diverting her attention. She looked at the incoming message, a text reply from Everett.

That was fast.

She palmed the phone and read his two-word response. "*Pretty enough?*" It wasn't so much a reaction from him as a solicitation for more communication. She sensed that, but she also didn't want to ignore a question by leaving it unanswered.

As Nathan wiggled on her lap, she held the phone to the side and poised her thumb above the keypad, trying out responses in her head. Deciding on the best one, she entered, "*Prettier than any buttercups I've seen*" and hit send before she could talk herself out of it.

He replied with a wink.

Her stomach tingled, and it was from something greater than the weight of Nathan's wriggly body. She was already invested in this cute conversation, wanting more from Everett. She waited a minute's time for a further reply, but nothing more flashed on the screen. After the short delay, she decided to cast a few words, keeping the message short but ensuring further interaction by now asking him a question. "*Having a good day?*"

The screen stayed lit, hardly a time delay in his swift response. "*Not as good as yesterday.*"

Oh. Paige was sure her face flushed in flattery. Those words made the tingle move from her stomach into her chest, the chitchat turning into something flirty.

And fun.

He followed with a smile icon.

Casting a few words at Everett from afar worked. She reeled him in.

Throughout the rest of the evening, texts pinged back and forth with random evening comments. Everett offered a playful meal commentary about the dinner his father cooked as Paige chastised him for using technology at the table. Later, they invented a quick trivia game of sharing lines from movies and making the other guess the name of the film. It was fun to have a time delay, too, because he mentioned he was clearing the kitchen, and she used it to start Nathan's bedtime routine.

But she didn't mention that.

When he asked about her living arrangement with text guesses of "*House? Apartment? Treehouse in a live oak?*" she had to tread especially lightly to keep things general. She had no problem sharing a little bit about her home life, but she needed to remember Everett's perception of her was as a widow.

And childless.

She was glad for texting and not an actual call so she could keep her life under wraps, at least for the time being. Plus, there was a giddiness she experienced in waiting for the next ping of her phone.

Paige might not be an actual widow, but she sure felt like someone she wasn't. With their lighthearted banter, shared humor, and ease of corresponding, she was carefree in a way she hadn't been since probably a decade ago.

She was a teenager all over again.

Chapter Eleven

THROUGH THE END of the week, Everett continued correspondence with Paige through texts. Aware of the rude message overreliance on technology during conversations could send, he tried not to use his phone in the presence of his parents. Instead, he dodged around corners or ducked into rooms for privacy so he could read or respond.

He felt an inner jab of guilt at his keeping the messages—and his growing attraction to Paige—out of sight. But, like a teenager hiding things he didn't want to explain, he was simply tucking their interactions away in private, under wraps so he didn't have to field his parents' questions or distract his mother. She needed to conserve all the energy she had and shouldn't waste any, even on Everett.

He was a grown man. He knew what he was doing.

Also, if he mentioned Paige at all to them, he'd have to reveal she was widowed. They would both have strong opinions about that.

It was easier, then, just to keep Paige out of sight.

But not out of mind.

Quite the contrary, he couldn't shake her from his thoughts, and he looked forward to every bit of interaction they had, no matter how mundane. They spent Thursday night sharing their "to do" lists, commenting randomly on things they needed to accomplish, from chores to grocery store purchases. Out of the blue, she pitched, "*Know how to tighten a leaky shower head?*" Everett did. Not only did he work with water, but he could make it run—and not run.

But Paige backtracked when he offered to come by and have a look over the weekend. Maybe she didn't want to put him out, or maybe it was the more pressing nature of other things she enumerated from her "to do" list that just outweighed. She mentioned yard work and errands and even a garage sale she and her friend were hosting. That girl stayed busy.

Everett hadn't even realized how, in the span of two days' time, he had already gotten used to hearing from her. Their texts weren't constant, but they had become routine. So much so that by midmorning on Friday when he hadn't heard from her, he texted, "*All okay?*"

A reply arrived about ten minutes later. "*Yes. Just BUSY. Land sales = crazy!*"

"*I hear ya.*" Everett typed back.

He only went by what he saw in the newspaper, but it did seem that land prices were soaring around town, compared to just a few years prior. Maybe it was the influence of San Antonio putting the squeeze on smaller, outlying areas. Maybe it was just part and parcel of twenty-first century development. Or maybe Seguin's secret had gotten out. Whatever the reason, more and more people wanted to own land in the area.

So he could imagine Paige's life must be a whirlwind,

especially with the promotion and her new work responsibilities. And then to add weekend chores and a garage sale on top of that, he told himself not to pressure her too much with messages.

But he wanted to see her.

"Headed to Walnut Springs Park," he texted.

Everett planned to scope out the park to see recent renovations for a possible weekend outing for his mother. When he last strolled the scenic property, he hadn't paid attention to benches and shade, and he wanted to make sure the park had plenty before he brought his mother there, if her body was up to it.

"Want to join me for a stroll over your lunch hour?"

Paige's reply took about ten minutes, but his phone's eventual ping made Everett's emotions stir in excitement when he read, *"Yes."*

As much as he wanted to give Paige space to attend to her responsibilities, spending time together, even if it was only in a city park, would be a lot more fun.

WALNUT SPRINGS PARK was a pearl of a place nestled around a tributary of the Guadalupe River just off the square. The gorgeous spring-fed emerald waterway was one of the area's natural jewels. Tanned bodies and sun-streaked hair were tell-tale signs of locals who turned into river mermaids for six months out of the year. Further down, the full river carried recreationalists who lazed in inner tubes and kayaks. That used to be Everett.

But that was back in high school.

His toes hadn't touched the river in years. He had no desire to do so until he stepped foot back in the park and strolled along the pedestrian trail waiting for Paige, who had promised to join him during a thirty-minute slot on her lunch hour. He was content with that, but the babbling of the current over the stone dam downstream talked him into imagining more than a walk.

Everett's pulse quickened as he indulged in a fast fantasy, one that involved his reunion with the water as he waded in with the company of someone he trusted.

Paige.

His heart did a somersault just thinking about what it would be like if he and Paige could go for a refreshing dip—and what Paige's body might look like in a bikini. It wasn't characteristic of anything Everett had allowed himself to dream of in two years, a playful afternoon spent in the company of another woman, but today the thought refreshed him as much as he was sure the actual water could.

Forward motion from his past felt good.

Today, though, he'd have to fight the urge to take Paige for a dip. He was getting thirty minutes, tops. She had been clear about that.

"Hey there," he called when he saw her approach along the pedestrian trail.

She waved, a bounce quickening her stride. Sunglasses shielded her eyes, but her wide smile was on full display.

"Hey yourself." She fell into step with him, the proximity of their bodies sending an unexpected sensual charge through Everett.

To snap himself out of petrifying, he kept his feet moving, asking if this stretch of the trail parallel to the springs was all right for a walk. Paige nodded, staying close as their feet locked in comfortable, shared footfalls. She started the conversation first, asking about his mother. He obliged with an answer of "day by day with her," although sometimes it was more like hour by hour. "But can we talk about something besides cancer?"

Paige didn't hesitate. "Of course. Some topics we'll just keep off limits."

If perhaps it was a passive way to steel against prying into her personal life, Everett would respect that. They continued to walk side by side as he asked about Paige's work, a topic where there seemed to be no shortage of stories to share. The longer she spoke, the more animated she became, with cute hand gestures and verbal quips.

When there was a lull in their conversation, he side-stepped it back to their surroundings. "I forgot how beautiful this place is." Textures and colors only Mother Nature could create extended from the river to the sky.

Paige slowed their pace, following his lead to look across the water. "Let's stop for a minute."

Standing shoulder to shoulder, Paige didn't speak. Everett couldn't even hear her breathe. Instead, it was her proximity which communicated for her, filling him with a completeness of being he hadn't experienced since standing by Catherine . . .

He stared ahead, letting old memories lap in rhythm with the current against the bank as new memories rose inside of him. Being with Paige was exactly what he needed.

He pivoted, turning to face her. "Thank you for coming today." She slid her sunglasses up, her bangs lifting to reveal eyes that were meeting his for the first time that day. Their sparkle stole his breath, for he hadn't realized the full reach of their beauty until they met the natural light.

Paige's eyes were the same emerald shade as the river, a cooling sight through an otherwise tepid atmosphere. He held her gaze, one of depth that gripped him to his core. Stillness seized as he told himself not to waste the moment. Something felt so right. *Kiss her. Don't let this moment—*

Paige broke away, diverting her gaze.

Pass.

She wasn't ready. A woman like her needed space. Everett was ready to close the distance between them, solidify whatever was developing with a shared expression of meaning. But the timing would have to be on Paige's terms.

And Everett could wait.

DANICA PLOPPED A stack of four garage sale signs onto Paige's coffee table and balanced wooden stakes against its edge. "If we put these out tonight," she advised, "that will be one less thing to do in the morning."

"Is that mine?" Nathan toddled over, his hand outstretched toward the signs.

"Sorry, buddy." Danica intercepted him, hoisting him onto her hip. "These are Mommy's. Because Mommy"—she poked his shoulder—"is going to make you some m-o-n-e-y."

"That's the plan." Paige stepped out of the kitchen and into the living room to join the two of them.

Danica gave Nathan a one-handed tickle as he laughed and tried to escape her grasp. She bent at the waist to put him down. He ran into his room in a hurricane of indistinguishable toddler noises that prompted Danica to ask, "Are those happy sounds?"

Paige nodded. "Oh, yes. That's Nathan being happy." Even though she couldn't identify with any certainty the words he was using. "You'll know when he's not."

"So . . ." Danica resumed her reason for coming in the first place. "I think these need to get out tonight."

"Remind me again why I agreed to this?"

"Because . . ." Danica stepped forward and poked Paige's shoulder as she had done to Nathan. "We're going to make you some m-o-n-e-y."

Except Paige didn't squeal with delight as her toddler had done. "Yeah," she feigned, already exhausted at the amount of work she had done over the past week with gathering, sorting, and pricing everything from housewares to power tools. She launched into the biggest source of her struggles as she prepared to purge her house—and her life— of all kinds of things she didn't need, mostly left behind by

Barry. "I don't even know how to tag some of this stuff. Or even what some of it is."

"I'll take a look," Danica assured her. "Is it all in the den?"

"Yes." Paige held a hand to her forehead, massaging one of her temples with her thumb. "Permanent marker, stickers, and hanging tags are on the windowsill. Mark what you want," she instructed. There was still progress to make. Noticing the outdoor signs needed to be labeled with her address, Paige called after Danica, "Do you want me to bring these signs in there?"

"Sure," she replied from a room away. "And then when you do, you can tell me why you are selling a fresh bouquet of flowers."

Busted.

Paige said an expletive in her head, racing to Danica. Since it was Friday, she had brought Everett's flowers home with her and stored them on a side table in the den—not one that she was selling. She made a little progress after work with tagging and labeling, and she wanted her flowers there to keep her company where she could see them, to remind her both of Everett and their midday walk in Walnut Springs Park where she sensed there was something building that neither of them acknowledged. She was keeping her feelings private, and she forgot to do the same with the flowers by moving them into her bedroom and out of sight when Danica came over.

"Okay, missy." Danica spun to face Paige, her hand on her hip. "Spill it. Who sent you flowers?"

Paige couldn't lie to her friend. But she did try being as vague as possible. "A guy."

Danica's mouth dropped open as her eyes popped. Paige had never seen Danica so characteristically shocked. "Say that again?"

Paige flexed her neck, trying to snap the tension from it. "I said a guy sent them to me."

Danica wasn't going to let that slide. She placed her other hand on her hip, angling one leg in a complete face-off with her best friend. "You better start from the top. No details left out, got it?"

There wasn't any getting out of this. Paige pushed her bangs to the side, blew out a breath, and started to tell Danica about Everett. "There's this guy who I used to go to high school with . . ."

Danica listened with intent, Paige moving from box to box and trying to get some of the labeling done as she spilled emotion and her giddiness about the past two weeks.

When Paige paused, Danica asked, "And why haven't you told me any of this before now?"

Paige shrugged, being blunt with Danica. "Because I don't know what this is." It was true. She hadn't been able to sort her swirl of feelings. "I'm flattered. I'm flustered. I've been—"

"Found."

"What?" Paige snapped her head to attention.

"Found," Danica repeated, in no less confusion to Paige. "Look," Danica explained, noting her friend's muddled look. "It's okay to have a male friend. It's fine to enjoy someone's company." She gestured at the bouquet, like a trophy in the midst of all the cast-off chaos of her garage sale preparedness. "It's perfectly fine to get flowers."

"I'm a divorced woman," she reminded Danica. And then, as if Danica forgot, Paige emphasized, "a *newly* divorced woman."

"So?" Danica dismissed, shrugging her shoulders. "Divorced women can't enjoy things?" She rested a hand on the cradle of her hip again, taking in Paige with her stare as she rendered a firm and definitive opinion. "I call your bluff on that."

"Oh, do you now?" Paige challenged. She widened her eyes as she returned Danica's gaze. She took her turn in the impromptu match of verbal sparring. "And I'm just supposed to enjoy this and think moving on is okay? Is that it?"

"Yes!" Danica raised both her arms as if to make Paige see the magnitude of her one-word response. "Yes," she insisted, "that's exactly what you're supposed to do."

Paige couldn't believe it was that easy.

Sensing her skepticism, Danica posed a rhetorical question. "Why do women think it's not okay to enjoy things after a divorce?" Though from what experience she was speaking from, Paige was completely unclear. "Look, I'm not married . . ."

I know that. Paige open a shoe box to check the contents. Danica had completely stopped any chores related to garage sale preparation as she instead used the room as a platform for sharing her advice.

"But I've been in relationships. I have feelings—and I've

had my feelings broken completely apart, just like any other woman." Danica's tone was filled with fervor Paige hadn't glimpsed before. "We do what we need to do to move on, to feel human again."

Maybe.

Danica followed up with, "That's just the way I see it."

Paige was listening to Danica's every word, even privately beginning to agree. But she still needed more clarity than that. "And, precisely, what way is that?"

And that was why Danica finally chose words with which there was no debate, for the words were true. Summarizing all she heard and all Paige revealed she had felt, Danica leveled her verdict. "Everett is making you feel alive."

Her observation was simple and true. Paige knew as much.

Still, giving her friend time to react and absorb the words, Danica added, "Maybe more than that, he's making you feel alive and comfortable."

Danica was right about that. Everett had made Paige feel more alive in two weeks than she had felt in a year. She was brought back into joy with simple pleasures—a surprise run-in, lunch meet-ups, two-way text conversations, a stroll in the park. She looked at her flowers. Even those, whether with her in her office or here accompanying her at home, made her feel bright and beautiful.

All of the awareness of the impact Everett had on her slammed into her consciousness with hurricane force. But the sad truth that she now required Danica's help with was something Paige needed to find a way to rectify. She took no pleasure in admitting what she did to her friend, but she was obliged to make this first step of being honest. Her attempts to deceive Everett were going to have an expiration date at some point. So if she wanted anything more than interstate lunches and funny text messages, she was going to have to muster enough confidence to be honest with him and deal with her lie head-on.

And verbalizing it to Danica was a positive first step.

She drew strength from a heavy inhale, and then admitted to Danica, "I lied to Everett."

PAIGE PLACED AN ad in *The Seguin Gazette,* which was the best money she could spend in driving customers to her Saturday morning event. Along with the signs, all arrows would be pointing toward sales, sales, sales.

At least, that was the idea.

Danica helped her tag and sort items until nearly midnight, several hours after Paige put Nathan down for the night. That took a little more time than usual because he was pretty riled up at having a visitor in the house. But, to Danica's credit, she worked steadily through Paige's absence until all was quiet in Nathan's room.

Then, they cooperated on laying things out on tables in the garage, making sure everything had a price sticker, and gathering plastic grocery bags and extra boxes they could use to help people haul their purchases.

Heaving boxes out of the house, standing on concrete, bending over tables, and working in an un-airconditioned space left both of them beat by the end of the night.

Seeing Danica's exhaustion and being completely in touch with her own, Paige convinced her friend it was silly to drive home just to get six hours of sleep and return, so she invited her to crash. They went inside, careful to tiptoe as they passed Nathan's room and convened again in Paige's bedroom, where she helped Danica get set up as if they were having a slumber party. Danica borrowed a set of pajamas from her closet and used one of her elastics to tie back her hair as she scrubbed off the day's makeup using cleanser at Paige's bathroom sink. Paige even had an extra courtesy toothbrush from her last dentist visit she found in a vanity drawer.

"This is better than a hotel," Danica chided. "Treated like royalty around here!"

Paige tempered her exaggeration. "It's Crest. Not Cartier."

"Still"—Danica waved the brush handle like a magic wand—"I feel privileged."

Paige brought Danica back to earth, letting reality hit. "You won't when we're two hours into this garage sale tomorrow, out of grocery bags, low on change, and stuck with all of these ridiculous tools of Barry's that we priced too high."

She jerked her body in defense. "You think we overpriced them?"

Paige had no idea, not only about cost but even about

what so many of his cast-off gadgets were. Danica had helped
identify a few, and Paige was grateful. But with the others,
they just took a gamble and labeled some at one dollar, some
at five. She wasn't interested in recouping the value of what
those things were worth so much as her priority was for
complete removal of her ex's footprint from the house. These
things had to go. "Who knows? We'll find out tomorrow."

"Treat it like a purging," Danica's voice rang with joy.

"A purging that's going to net some money," Paige reminded her.

Danica rubbed her hands together in comedic greed before Paige responded in kind with her own version of
drama—jazz hands that turned into a quick mime of imagi-
nary money grabbing.

If only hosting a garage sale would be so fruitful.

Danica stopped her theatrics to repeat Paige of one final,
practical bit of advice. "Be open to negotiation."

"After getting divorced, I think I've got that ground covered." Between her experience in court and her constant
research to clear deeds at the land and title office, *negotiation*
felt like Paige's middle name.

Danica ignored the tinge of bitterness in her reply, instead asking about linens for the extra bedroom.

"Already made." Paige stayed prepared.

"Perfect."

"You know Nathan's going to go crazy when he sees you
in the morning," Paige warned. She could already imagine
Nathan teetering into the guest bedroom in curiosity about
Danica's overnight stay. "He's my little alarm clock on

weekends. No sleeping in for that kiddo."

"Good." Danica shrugged. "We can use an early riser. He can help with the sale."

"Doubtful." Nathan was adept at making messes and hoarding things, not organizing and getting rid of them.

"Give that kid some credit." Danica clearly had a plan. "We'll strap a sandwich board on him and let him toddle through the garage with a tin cup soliciting handouts."

Paige cringed. "No way."

"Suit yourself." Danica turned on her heel to head down the hallway. "Get some sleep tonight, okay?"

"You too." Paige smiled.

Tomorrow would be cathartic, a chance to recalibrate her life. Getting rid of things that no longer mattered to her along with others that held negative emotions would be a purging indeed, a way to work through her past to focus on the future. Her marriage didn't have a happy ending, but, at this point in her life, Paige was more interested in happy beginnings anyway.

Chapter Twelve

P AIGE AND DANICA tag teamed at the garage sale check-out station, alternating who would make change and who would help customers bag their items. Nathan played on the concrete nearby, sitting inside the track of a push train with his blue stuffed giraffe. The toys had been occupying him for nearly an hour. He watched as cars came and went, and some people stooped to talk or coo close to him.

Smooth operating, for the most part, was happening at the actual sale too. Items moved steadily, and customers were polite. Parking was being handled well enough, with ample street space.

Occasionally someone would need help carrying something to a vehicle. There were small pieces of furniture that required two people to help move. When Nathan needed something, whether it was a snack or a different toy, either Paige or Danica would retrieve it while the other stayed in the garage. There really was no way one person could have made this work.

"So glad you're here," Paige said as she collapsed with early fatigue into the lawn chair behind the card table and tackle box which doubled as their cash register. Change stayed organized in the dividers that were designed to hold different lures while smaller bills were easy to stack in the bottom compartment. Beneath that, larger bills could be hidden and secured.

"Any idea how much you've made?" It was just shy of ten o'clock, but there was still a steady stream of customers.

"I told myself not to calculate anything until the end." Paige clicked the lid of the tackle box closed until the next customer arrived. "I'll certainly be rich in quarters, if nothing else."

It seemed like every customer came shopping with available quarters, and now Paige was the keeper of them. Granted, she and Danica had labeled quite a few things with twenty-five cent stickers. A water bottle, a gallon Ziploc bag of men's socks, random barbeque tools—these all looked like bargains at just a quarter each, and anything marked a quarter seemed to move faster than anything else.

Looking out at the expanse of items, what remained was mostly Barry's. What would he say if he were here? Were there some things he would mind Paige profiting from, if only in change? Or would he throw a fit and start grabbing his old wok that he never once used for a meal, those desk drawer notebooks he never cracked, his winter gloves barely worn?

She hadn't advertised the garage sale in any nefarious way, although there was a tinge of temptation to do so. A funny headline in the newspaper or a classified ad with "ex" in the sale might make a few people laugh. But when it came time to advertise, she opted for just the basics—the words "garage sale," the starting time, and a quick overview of items. After all, she remained a part of the community, and whether she liked it or not, her ex did too, at least as far as she knew.

"I don't know how Barry thought he could fit all of these things into his new house."

"He didn't." Danica corrected. "Isn't that why he left this stuff behind?"

Paige slumped further in the chair, relaxing her legs in a long stretch in front of her. "I don't think he thought much."

"Maybe he didn't want to burden you."

Paige turned to where Danica stood, questioning her response with a quizzical look. "Is that supposed to be funny?" She waved an open hand to gesture to the makeshift sale that consisted of ninety percent his stuff.

Danica straightened her posture. "I'm just saying that maybe leaving this behind was easier than him bothering you to retrieve it."

Are you sticking up for him? Paige bent her knees, ground her heels against the concrete, and sat up in the lawn chair. She needed to understand Danica because these were not words of friendly support she had long received. Something about them had an edge. It didn't sound like casual musings on the circumstances but rather words tinged by a desire to convince.

"So he did me a favor?"

Danica heaved a sigh of frustration, then quieted her voice to keep it low so customers didn't overhear. "I don't know. I'm just saying there might have been more thought—more kindness—into leaving the things the way they were."

Where is this coming from?

"Not that I know, or anything. I'm just trying—um, maybe if you put a positive spin . . ."

"There's no positive spin." Paige couldn't help but to spit the words. "Barry hasn't hedged on the side of positive in months, years even." She glanced at Nathan, absorbed in play with his train. "The only positive in Barry is that kid." She pointed to Nathan, whom she loved with a completeness of her being she didn't know she had in her. "I got the best of him. He just has leftovers for anyone else."

If Danica wanted to say anything else, she bit her tongue instead. Maybe they were both tired. They had worked late last evening, so the edge and crankiness of little sleep was now just catching up to them. That was her way to chalk-up an excuse for Danica's otherwise out-of-character remarks. After all, if Paige took them at face value, she'd have to concede that perhaps Danica was trying to stand up for Barry in some way.

And that couldn't be right. Could it?

PAIGE PROFITED ABOUT four hundred dollars, which wasn't bad considering the real prize was the removal of items she didn't care to see anymore. She offered to split the proceeds in some way with Danica. "At least stay for a pizza?" she urged.

"I really need to get home. I've got laundry to tackle, and I can't remember the last time I pushed a vacuum around the carpet. Seeing you purge like this has put me in the mood to clean—something."

"You look exhausted," Paige observed. "I know I do too."

"I'm fine," Danica dismissed. "I hope this has been a good day."

Paige flashed back to their bit of a verbal spat from midmorning, but she decided not to dwell on it. Whether Danica was really trying to defend Barry or whether the words just didn't come out quite right, it didn't matter. Paige was moving on.

All things considered, Paige concluded, "Yes, it's been a good day."

"What are you going to do with the stuff that didn't sell?" There were random items left, but the majority of things had sold.

"Donate," she replied simply.

"I figured." Danica nodded. "Do you need help boxing?"

"No. You go on. You've already done so much." She opened her arms for a hug.

Danica reciprocated, but with a warning. "I'm kind of sweaty."

"Me too." It didn't matter. They had worked hard and, with the garage sale complete, she had one more reason to move forward and feel refreshed in her new life post-divorce. The spoils of her ex-husband were behind her.

Before Danica pulled away, Paige whispered, "I appreciate you." Danica squeezed Paige's shoulders in acknowledgement. They had been friends for a long time, and even with a few strained words now and again, their friendship never faltered.

Paige felt a shift in balance coming from below. Nathan slammed into her leg, latching on like a firefighter to a pole. "Oh, you want a hug, too?" She looked down at him.

Danica bent and scooped him up instead. "How about me, Nate?" She embraced him in a twisty bear hug, as he laughed and laughed.

Paige opened the tackle box and took out a twenty dollar bill. "Well, I'm still going to call in a pizza."

"Pizza?" Nathan called through the air as he twisted in Danica's arms. "Pizza!" he cried again.

"Yes, pizza." Paige soothed.

Danica stilled and lowered Nathan to the ground. "I'll let you two get to that. Call me tomorrow?"

"I will," Paige agreed.

Danica retrieved her purse, and Paige and Nathan waved to her from their garage as she got into her car. She would call Danica tomorrow to check in with her, but Paige also thought of someone else with whom she was itching to communicate.

PAIGE HADN'T REALIZED until all her ex's items were removed just how much space they had occupied. His footprint now gone from the interior of the house, it took on a lighter, more airy feel. There was less clutter, less furniture, and more room to breathe. It was the same structure, but it felt like a new home.

Already Paige was content with what she was building, a renewed space and a fresh start for both her and her son. Small changes could indeed make a big impact, and there was satisfaction in the house being theirs in a new way.

Paige had received a few morning texts from Everett about the status of the garage sale, and she had jokingly responded with her estimate of the percentage of items removed. She didn't reveal the types of items she was selling. For all Everett knew, it was just her stuff, not an ex's.

She struggled with what to reveal and what to keep hidden. Everett wasn't a total stranger, after all, and if their correspondence continued, there would be a time when she'd have to level with him. But did it make sense to do that now? Everett had so much to think about with his mother and with his job. He'd be headed north to Amarillo in another couple of weeks, back to his home. Just as confusing as navigating the road to divorce was now navigating life after divorce. There was no easy route to take.

But, thankfully, there was an easy route to deciding on lunch.

A quick trip for takeout pizza was a perfect reward for all of the hard work during the morning, a success in Paige's book. She also picked up the four garage sale signs Danica had staked at various intersections. With the signs removed, the garage sale was officially over.

The warm smell of melty cheese and sweet marinara swirled through her vehicle's interior the moment she closed the door on the pizza. Her stomach rumbled with hunger. Two cups of coffee and a yogurt on the go during the garage sale hadn't done much to satisfy her appetite. Pizza—and solitude—would be her comfort this afternoon.

She was in for a bit of a motherly treat with the latter, as Nathan feel asleep on the way home. It was typical for a sunny car ride to lull him into a snooze, and Paige was grateful for the timing. She carried him into the house first, settling him in his bed for an afternoon nap. He could eat when he awoke, which would give Paige time to relax.

She returned to the car to retrieve her purse and the pizza, positioning both on the kitchen counter as she arrived inside. The side pocket of her purse buzzed with the indication of a new message on her phone. She plucked it, held it up, and saw Everett's inquiry. "*100% gone?*"

Resuming the percentage guesses from this morning. Paige smiled. She was proud of what she and Danica had accomplished and wanted to communicate that. But would a text or photo be best?

She could reply with *yes*, but that was boring. Maybe she could step back into the garage and snap a quick photo of the interior as evidence. Or she could fan out her cash from the tackle box to illustrate her success. Both of those photo options, though, would involve reveals and the chance Everett might notice something related to her ex in the background of the garage or even question her owning of a tackle box which, yes, had been Barry's.

She sighed at the charade she felt compelled to continue. She still wasn't ready to show Everett too much. A picture wouldn't do, but words she could safely send instead. She settled on a simple, two-word text. "*Good enough!*"

She hit send and placed the phone on the counter. Grabbing a plate from the cupboard, she balanced it in one hand as she lifted the box of the takeout pizza with the other. Diving in to the comfort food concoction, she chose the biggest slice from the pie. Mozzarella stretched from the box to her plate as little wisps of heat escaped from the crust.

"Come to Mama!" She settled the pizza onto the plate.

As she reached for a paper towel, she leaned across her phone, which signaled again. "*Need a final customer?*"

Everett wants to come by? Oh, boy.

Paige tore the towel, tucked it beneath her plate, and suspended her first bite a bit longer. Contemplating a response, she lowered the top of the pizza box and drummed the fingers of her free hand on the cardboard.

"You are not making this easy," she spoke aloud toward the phone, knowing Everett couldn't hear her.

Her garage sale was over, and it would be simple for her to communicate that in truth. But what was Everett's intent behind asking to come to the garage sale? This had to be about more than rifling through someone else's trash, hoping to find a treasure.

This must have been about him—fishing.

That was it. Everett cast this line of an innocent way to meet again, and he wanted to see if Paige would bite. Her first inclination was absolutely to do so. Sharing more face-to-face conversation with Everett in her home over a meal—even if it was takeout pizza—would be a lot of fun. She could tell him about the strange things that sold during the garage sale, she could brag about her bartering skills, she could show off the cash she earned and jab him with a promise she'd never go to the grocery store without emergency cash in her purse ever again.

But if she did that—any of that—she would be revealing her life. She would have to share the impetus for the sale was her ex-husband. She would then have to come clean about being divorced. And then there would be the matter of sharing motherhood, that she had a son. Would she just point to Nathan sleeping in his room and expect Everett to be okay with that? Over two weeks of avoidance of her truths made the discovery of her secrets carry more weight. Being caught in a deceitful web was a sickening reality.

She suddenly wasn't hungry.

She felt more ill at ease than anything.

Whatever this relationship with Everett was—or wasn't—how could she now back track and casually fill in these segments of her life she had kept hidden?

Paige couldn't stall on a reply to Everett's latest text forever. She needed something to keep him at bay . . .

"*Signs are down. Register closed.*" She typed. Then, she poised her phone over the plate of pizza and snapped a photo, following with another text. "*Having a late lunch now.*"

Everett's reply was near instantaneous. "*May I join you for a digital meal?*"

It sounded like Paige had avoided a visit from Everett at

her home, but she still wasn't certain what he had in mind. "*How's that going to work?*"

He replied with a photo of his hand on a half-eaten sandwich.

"Cute." Paige reacted aloud, to the sight of the sandwich—and to seeing even a sliver of Everett.

Back and forth texts and images served as a way for them to have lunch together, connected only by technology. The ease and safety of it helped to still the churn in Paige's stomach as she regained confidence as well as her appetite.

That afternoon, Paige and Everett ate together without ever seeing one another, each in silence and comforted by the other's presence.

SUNDAY TURNED INTO DIY day.

Paige hadn't planned it that way. Sometimes home renovation projects were just like that. But she felt a yearning for a few minor do-it-yourself improvements now that the house was less cluttered and the garage sale was over.

Plus she had some cash. And just holding it reminded her of why she tended not to carry much. It was too easy to spend.

But the home improvement store allowed her to make some attractive changes to her home, while staying on a budget.

She had been wanting a new switch plate for the light in

the kitchen.

An improved welcome mat for the front door.

A few solar lights to line the front walkway.

Some perennials to add to an empty flower pot she found in the garage.

Mulch.

Lightbulbs.

Batteries.

Epoxy.

And she talked herself into a discounted gallon of sky blue paint for an impromptu update to the hallway bathroom that Nathan used. She was tired of the drab floor to ceiling eggshell in there.

Good thing she had cash.

She didn't expect her cart to be so full. Even Nathan knew something was different when Paige had to slow the speed at which she pushed the cart when she added the second bag of mulch.

"I can help you out with that, miss." An employee who looked no older than sixteen but who probably had more dexterity and endurance than Paige at the moment offered his assistance, and she was happy to accept.

Nathan kicked his feet playfully as the boy took helm at the handle of the cart, Nathan facing him in the child seat.

"Hey, buddy." He tried easy conversation, though Nathan hid his face in his hands. "Are you going to help your mom today?"

Paige smiled to herself at the idea. One day, indeed, Nathan would be old enough to help. He could replace a lightbulb. He could wield a paintbrush. He could spread mulch. Those days were coming.

Just no time soon.

If Paige wanted something done, she'd have to do it. She mentally crafted an order for tackling all of the things she wanted to do. "I'm going to be updating." Paige resumed conversation with the home improvement store worker in the absence of a reply from Nathan. "He'll probably watch." Which she knew was wishful thinking. He'd never stay still. More honestly, she admitted, "Or he'll pick at the flowers."

The worker pretended to dodge Nathan's kicks as he pushed the cart through the store exit and onto the sidewalk. "Sounds like a gardener in the making."

"We'll see." Who knew what Nathan would grow up to be? Or do?

Nathan found his voice once the cart shifted. "Woah!" His whole body rattled as the metal clanged and vibrated, moving from the smooth concrete of the sidewalk to the rough asphalt of the parking lot.

The boy exaggerated his steps from side to side as if they were in an earthquake. "Bumpy road ahead." He seemed to be having fun with such a little customer.

And Paige had fun watching them. She always did when Nathan was in a good mood and someone else could share his company. "My car's that one." She pointed.

"Just lead the way," he insisted.

She arrived first, popping the hatchback of her silver Mini Cooper. It was small, but mighty. "Think that mulch will slide in there?"

"Won't be a problem." Then, as if he were playing human Tetris, he organized everything in tight precision. Nathan even clapped when the worker said, "All done."

Both Paige and the employee laughed at that. Then, on cue, Nathan did too.

The worker closed the hatchback for Paige as she unbuckled Nathan and lifted him out of the cart. He grabbed the edge and swung it around to grip the handle again. But before he made a move in the direction of the store, he offered Paige a surprise compliment. Pubescent boys aren't known for their wisdom, yet these words gave her hope for teenage boys everywhere. The simple words were delivered with such sweetness and sincerity she had to blink back tears when she heard them. "Your kid's happy."

She squeezed her eyes as if doing so would help her hold onto the words.

Savoring their strength of meaning, she turned to kiss Nathan on the forehead. "Yeah," she whispered, admiring her son's complete contentment in that moment. "I guess he is."

Then, with the characteristic breeziness of a teenager, he put one foot on the cart and pivoted it like a skateboard. As a near afterthought before he headed back into the store, he added, "You must be a good mom."

Hands down, that was the best compliment Paige had ever received.

Chapter Thirteen

EVERETT JUMPED EVERY time his phone buzzed. He was still getting work calls and staying in touch with his professional life in north Texas, but he now had a renewed reason to enjoy random calls.

His reason was Paige.

Their communication came easily. Their exchanges were fun. They stirred in him an awareness of life and a carefree joy that had long been absent, at least since Catherine. Paige wasn't a replacement, but she was showing him he shouldn't be scared of opening his heart and letting in what might come.

So, just what was coming? Everett still couldn't quite put his finger on it.

But rather than worry with a label, he instead enjoyed the unexpected tidbits of conversation, the fun exchange of a joke or two, and the security in having someone with whom he could communicate openly.

But am I? At some point, he was going to have to tell Paige about his past. *But when?* Timing just didn't seem right. And there was no good way he could perceive to do so without potentially destroying everything she was trying to build for herself. She was fragile, and there was danger in overstepping boundaries. As a widow, she was experiencing a level of pain and loss unimaginable to most people. The last thing Everett wanted to do was contribute to that.

So communication at a distance while letting her set the pace seemed like the best arrangement. He'd continue that for as long as—how long? He would be returning to Amarillo in less than two weeks. And then what? Could he expect she'd be happy with daily text pings on a phone?

Everett leaned over the bathroom sink early Monday morning, preparing to wash his face before he got dressed and ready for the drive to his mother's medical appointment in San Antonio. "I am so out of practice," he admitted aloud in the mirror.

Dropping his head, he twisted the knob on the faucet, splashing his cheeks with the cold water which poured out of it. Their farm's water supply was fed via a rural well, which sourced water deep from under the rolling hills outside Seguin. The depth of the underground table beneath their land provided a bounteous supply of cool, fresh water. That couldn't be said for all of Texas. In many areas, tables were drying, and long droughts were resulting in shifts to availability of water. Water rights themselves were becoming a politically divisive issue.

Worry kept some land owners up at night.

To alleviate the stress, many counties—including Guadalupe—formed water management groups and governing boards. Their groundwater conservation district helped preserve this precious natural resource and protect landowners as well. Taxes levied to the rural residents helped ensure their access to water flowing in tables beneath them, insulating them from developers who wanted to tap into them just to fill vanity ponds and from fracking, now their biggest threat.

Water. A simple resource and Everett's livelihood.

He turned the knob off, raising his face and drying it on a nearby towel. He was thankful his parents were water rich. Dale and Ruby Mullins had nothing to worry about when it came to their water supply.

Still, the threats and horror stories they heard from others in the county didn't keep Dale from asking. His father expressed to Everett his concerns about losing their water, but through Everett's expertise in the field, he was able to alleviate those worries.

And, if anything did malfunction, Everett could fix it.

"Not when you're up in Amarillo you can't." That was his dad's biggest complaint—the distance.

But Amarillo afforded him a different lifestyle, one at a pace he enjoyed with a low cost of living. Amarillo also had more going on than most people realized. It wasn't just honky-tonks, rodeos, and ten gallon hats. There was culture, sports, a college, outdoor recreation. He had taken advantage of all of those things, but only with Catherine . . .

Stiffening his posture, he attempted to tip the memories back into the corners of his brain. He didn't want to think about them, not now. He had recalled them far too much, and he needed to look forward, not back.

He didn't have a happy ending. But he could still have a happy beginning.

He grabbed his phone from the bathroom counter and scrolled through the messages he'd exchanged with Paige the previous night. He had gotten a near play-by-play of her home improvement projects, her ambitious attempts at seeing how many minor renovations she could accomplish in one day.

There was a photo of a new light switch plate.

A crisp new welcome mat at the front door.

A row of installed solar lights lining the front walkway.

Shiny, white epoxy applied as a seal around a bathtub.

She also texted a picture of an unopened gallon of paint with the line *"My Monday evening date."* Paige was certainly ambitious, not a woman who shied from hard work. That alone was an attractive characteristic.

She had other attractive characteristics as well. He let memories wash ashore in his brain with images and experiences over the last couple of weeks, small events and encounters that had a big impact.

Paige was like that.

He scrolled to the final picture she sent, a cheery one of freshly planted flowers filling a clay pot. She juxtaposed that picture of her green thumb project with the cut flowers Everett had the florist deliver to her office. He was glad she liked flowers and was pleased at his ultimate decision to send her some.

The bouquet was pretty, and the fact she had snapped pictures was confirmation she was enjoying them. And, it appeared, she snapped more than one, for the one he received on Wednesday was of the flowers on a desk. Here, however, the location wasn't the same. The background was homelier.

Paige had taken the flowers home with her. He smiled at the realization.

Indeed, there was a glimpse into her personal environment he could now detect as he looked more closely at this second photo. He could make out the shade of a lamp, the top of some type of table, the corner of a window with a billowy white curtain, and a blurred background of colors that didn't reveal much clarity . . . except . . .

He leaned over the screen, pinching and dragging the corners of the photo to enlarge the image. He scrolled with his finger across the upper corner he hadn't examined before. *That is a strange looking water bottle.* A squat, plastic container perched on the edge of the window sill, nearly hidden by the edge of the curtain. The container was far smaller than most. It clearly wasn't an ordinary water bottle, nor did it seem to be a shaker or blender bottle. Something about it was characteristic of an entirely different purpose. The colors, too, were bright, a cartoon image wrapping around the base. But the dead giveaway was the popped spout. Even though the item was muted, a bit of focus resulted in certainty of his guess.

That wasn't a water bottle; it was a child's sippy cup.

PAIGE WORKED FAST and furiously through Monday. There

weren't enough hours in the day at the start of the week, though the time flew by in a flash at the land and title office. She covered what needed to be done, completed paperwork she couldn't do on Friday, and even staged two afternoon closings back-to-back. Miguel complimented her efficiency.

She surged with a productivity she hadn't expected, especially after a busy weekend of handling the garage sale and the DIY projects she started around the house. Maybe, though, her industriousness was just what she needed. She was accomplishing things, sleeping better, and awakening for the day not with dread but with a start.

Thanks to her successes, she planned to ride the momentum of work responsibilities and use the energy to paint Nathan's bathroom that evening. There wasn't much prep work. She had already applied painter's tape around the baseboards, vanity, and ceiling the previous night, so as long as she could corral Nathan out of the space, she'd have easy access to her sheetrock canvas.

And one coat should do. She hoped.

To Nathan's credit, he was not as curious as Paige thought he might be. Maybe day care tired him out for the day. Or maybe he just sensed this was his mom's project. Either way, he seemed to gift Paige with uninterrupted time in order to work even more efficiently.

Aside from minor splatters and a bit of a fume high before she thought to switch the exhaust fan, painting turned out to be liberating. Wielding a brush, transforming the space, being engulfed by the new shade. It was an experience that was at once exhausting and invigorating. The color was just right, minimal cost for a major impact. It made the space new, and it made the space Nathan's.

For her, these mini DIY projects were a source of pride, producing a joy in home ownership she hadn't felt before. Freshening the space created opportunities for her to put her mark on the house, unencumbered with having to ask another person's opinion or compromise on a plan. Singularly, she could freshen the space however she wanted, and there was a type of emancipation in that. So much of the house held memories and experiences with her ex, but just a few minor updates were making it her space, a location that would hold unspoiled memories and markers from her life now, not her life then. She was making a new life from old parts.

Paige wanted to share the feeling and the result. And rather than friend or sister, parents or neighbors, one person came to mind. He was the same person who was in her mind lately.

A lot.

Everett Mullins had seemingly taken up residence in her thoughts. He had moved in, and Paige was sharing mental space with him, sometimes even edging him over so she could focus on tasks. But he was there, keeping her company, almost like an invisible cheerleader and confidant.

She wanted to reach out to him tonight. She wanted to text him. But virtue held her back.

This wasn't right.

She wasn't right.

Maybe it was the fumes clouding her judgement—or

maybe it was clearing it instead—but she couldn't text Everett. Not tonight.

The charade with Everett had to end.

Paige wasn't a widow, and she didn't like pretending to be. She needed to come clean, painting the picture of her life to him that was true, unclouded by secrets or simple omission of details. She had been coating the surface of her life ever since the day they met in the grocery store, but she couldn't keep the façade any longer.

Whether it was for her own stability or whether it truly was because of her blossoming feelings for Everett, the underlying reason didn't matter. The truth did.

How Everett would react, though, wasn't something she cared to predict.

Like ripping a bandage to minimize the pain, she just needed to lay it all out, get it over with, be completely honest with him. If Everett was worth his salt, he'd hear her out. He would understand. And he would have some compassion for what she had done, how a simple white lie had slipped and she just rolled with it.

He will understand, right? Self-doubt knocked, and she questioned her own ability to do so, if she were in his shoes. Could he overlook a lie? Even so, could he forgive the continuation of it for weeks?

There was only one way to find out.

She did send a message that evening, nothing comedic, nothing cutesy. It was straightforward and pointed, at least more so than she had been. *"Can you meet me at 2 p.m. tomorrow?"*

"*Where?*" He pinged, a short time later.

She didn't need much of a commitment. But she did need the venue of a public space. She needed an out.

"*The courthouse lawn. By the pecan?*"

So it wasn't the most comfortable location. That was the point. They couldn't stand there for long. She'd say her piece, and then she could disappear back into the land and title office, letting Everett react on his own.

"*A bit nutty,*" he teased, though he followed with a single word agreement. "*Yes.*"

IT WASN'T AN interstate café lunch date. It wasn't a courthouse lawn picnic. It wasn't even going to be an afternoon stroll. Everett wasn't sure how to categorize this bizarre rendezvous in the shadow of the town's landmark pecan. But he was game for anything, and Paige must have had something in mind.

The mystery alone perked him up all morning as he cared for his mother, who was having a particularly nauseous reaction to the previous day's chemo treatment.

Her body needed rest, and she told Everett as much. Clearing her room and not fussing over her condition helped her feel more personally in control and did help her make strides. He made sure she had what she needed nearby on her bedside table—cough syrup, lotion, tissues, and her romance novel. "Try to get some rest, Mom," he wished as he closed her bedroom door.

His father was in his shop, preparing to shape a trio of table legs using his lathe. He had always been a skilled woodworker, and Everett was pleased to have some of his hand-built pieces in Amarillo. There were even more, though, throughout the farmhouse, beautifully timeless pieces that were fashioned using local lumber. He had such a talent, though his slowed movements and the overall pace of retirement made projects take much longer than they once did.

Everett didn't have the same success in making furniture as his father, but he enjoyed assisting and picking up a few tips and tricks where he could. Today, he asked his dad if he wanted any help, but he insisted, "It's a one-person job."

"I'm going into town then," Everett announced.

He had a little time to kill before he was scheduled to meet Paige, whom his parents still didn't know about. He even managed to sidestep their two o'clock secret since he did have to run a few errands.

Everett revealed those instead of mentioning her or the courthouse. "I'm going by the bank. Then the post office. Need anything?"

"No." His dad's attention was on preparing the lathe.

"Well"—Everett backed out of the shop and waved— "good luck with your project."

His father nodded, the thin walls of the shop reverberating as the machine thundered to life.

Everett walked across their dirt driveway to his pickup. As he settled inside, he lazed in the feeling of anticipation, for seeing Paige was going to be the highlight of his day. He had to depress his lead foot the whole way into town, careful not to burn the asphalt. Every fiber inside of him was aching with desperate anticipation at seeing her.

I hope she feels the same about me.

The radio kept him company as further thoughts of Paige, some from back in high school and some more recent from the past few weeks, collected together in a mental album of memories. He enjoyed flipping through, recalling what she wore in clothes and expressions. These were snapshots of Paige, ones he could index and organize, to recall whenever he needed.

More particularly, whenever he needed—her.

He arrived in Seguin, easing through the thin streets that pulsed with a quiet rhythm of a workday. He pulled up to the center of Guadalupe County, securing a parking spot parallel to the courthouse. Unlatching his seat belt, he shifted to check his reflection in the rearview mirror. As he skimmed his hand across the side of his hair, daylight illuminated a change in color he hadn't noticed until now. Spring and early summer Texas sun had already lightened the tips. If he didn't find a barber soon—or head back to Amarillo for a cut—he risked turning blond. He shook his head and tousled his hair at the possibility of that.

Satisfied, though, with his look, he opened the door of his Tacoma, swung his legs out, and stepped into the possibility of the afternoon.

He had dressed for the day in a charcoal t-shirt, his favorite light-washed jeans, and a black leather belt to break the contrast of color. The square toe boxes of his boots and a small portion of the heel were the only pieces of his footwear visible beneath his pant-legs, the designer scallops at the top of each boot covered.

Paige had work responsibilities, but aside from playing a guessing game until he turned blue in the face, he was just going to roll with whatever the afternoon brought.

Under the shade of pecan tree limbs beneath an otherwise clear sky stood Paige, right where she said she would be. She held a manila folder tucked to her chest, and she shielded sun from her eyes with her other hand poised like a visor as Everett approached.

Breezy in a summer wrap dress, she looked even more gorgeous than Everett had seen her.

He spoke first. "Hey there."

"Hey," she replied.

"Some nut, eh?" He had been wanting to make a joke about the landmark pecan, but when Everett registered Paige's serious reaction, he wished he hadn't. Her entire countenance lacked the sweet calm he had come to expect from her. Instead, her downcast eyebrows and the tight corners of her mouth revealed a seriousness to their meeting Everett hadn't anticipated. "What's wrong?"

Paige's eyes darted, her focus uneven. Like a deer in headlights, every bit of movement either from across the street on the opposite sidewalk or above in the gently swaying leaves of the trees competed for her attention. Everett didn't know whether to reach out to her or stay distant as she searched for her bearings. All he could do was lock his feet into place on the concrete where they stood, bracing his stance for Paige's bombshell delivery. "I'm not a widow."

Chapter Fourteen

PAIGE'S WORDS MUST have stung like a bite from a copperhead snake. Everett stood rigid, paralyzed in his inability to react to the admission. He was but inches away, yet he seemed a world apart.

She had committed to redeeming herself with honesty, as uncomfortable as it was to do. Her body reacted in confusion. Tension swelled in her shoulders, fear paralyzed her throat, and the only thing stilling her hands and fingers was the manila folder she now clutched in desperation. Her knuckles paled as they clenched, her hands the one outlet for her uncertainty as she waited in limbo for Everett's next move.

In extreme cases of anxiety with which she dealt in the past, Paige remembered the moment of action, the turning point where she had to choose fight or flight. But a response here wasn't so easy as a coin toss between two. This situation, complicated as it was, did not fit the conditions for her to have a choice. She wasn't entitled because she wasn't the one on the receiving end of the surprise.

That was Everett.

Instead, she was the one dealing the shocking blow. And this situation was entirely her own making.

She couldn't fight. She couldn't flee. She had to own her mistake and wait for Everett's next move.

An otherwise windy day might have blown Everett over. His face washed pale as his arms hung limp. His stance lost all casualness, the words pulling the rug of security on which he stood from under him. His shoulders remained back, perhaps his attempt at controlling one part of his body enough so he didn't completely lose it.

But Paige knew better. The blankness in his stare alone told her he was losing it.

"Say something," she willed, whispering. She internally braced for whatever Everett might say.

Everett just shook her head, not looking so much at her as through her. The previously fresh air now smelled stale. The heat, warmly sunning her exposed skin earlier in the day, now stifled her. Her entire budding relationship with Everett took a nosedive, and if there was a way to recover, Paige couldn't see through the haze of the present situation enough to know how.

How words came were a mystery, yet sounds were the only sense that seemed to function. "I'm not widowed, but I'm alone. No relationship," she clarified, if the words even counted as that. She nearly choked on the next sentence, but she knew it had to be delivered. "I'm divorced."

She expected him to ask—something. Anything. Maybe a "*How?*" or "*Why?*" or "*When?*" question. Instead, there was silence.

No questions.

No comments.

No verbal reaction of any kind.

Silence spoke between them, her heart thumping in anxious rhythm for some next step, any next step.

Desperation for feedback now overcame her, though she couldn't make Everett talk. All she could do was continue to talk herself, honesty leading the way as the words spilled out. "I married several years after college and had a son. Nathan is two." This wasn't the life she expected, but it was the life she had. "I'm divorced. And it was official on the day we met in the grocery store."

She had been through difficult days, one of them inside the very courthouse in whose shadow they stood. This was a difficult place for her, but it was a meaningful one too. She needed to face that, yet she struggled with the way to convey that for Everett—because this meeting wasn't about her.

It was about him.

And Everett was not himself in this moment.

Owning her mistake and swallowing her pride in front of Everett pushed Paige back to a level of angst she hadn't experienced since the day of her divorce. With no one on which to lean then and now, Paige mustered every ounce of courage just to keep standing. "Say something," she pleaded again.

Any response would give her something to work with, dialogue rather than this awkward monologue. Everett could have asked a million questions. Maybe he should have done that. Instead, he chose to respond with a sentence that slapped Paige's heart out of rhythm, sickening her to the core.

With a stony expression, Everett dwarfed Paige's surprise line with one of his own. "I can't do this anymore."

EVERETT WASN'T ONE to play games. He was past that in his life. He wasn't one to live in memories of former glory. He was past that too. He had no agenda, no ulterior motive in the relationships he fostered with people around him. He valued certain things. And he valued people.

Paige was a woman he valued.

He didn't need much time to determine that.

But what have I overlooked? He flashed through the album of memories that were green, new snapshots of their encounters which were so fond just moments before. Now, fond turned to foul. So many questions . . .

Even so, Everett didn't care to ask any of them. Emptiness fell instead into the space between them where fullness had been.

Paige was making peace with her reality, and Everett could understand that. He was someone who had made peace with his own reality, accepting it only after time allowed past wounds to heal. And Everett was venturing into a time when he could share that reality, with those in whose company he felt safe. Paige had made him feel that way. She had that effect.

Until now.

In that split second where she revealed her truth, Everett

was glad he hadn't fully revealed his. He couldn't show his cards to her; he couldn't best her hand. He held a poker face, his head straight but his stare blank.

What could he do in public? Here they were, at the center of the town, prying community eyes likely all around, and the two of them stood on display. Any move he made could be seen by someone in a building or in a car, and any word he spoke could be heard by a pedestrian or an eavesdropper. Paige was bold to bring him into this public setting, her steeliness evident as she stood within an arm's reach.

He could touch her, but he didn't.

He wasn't going to make a scene. He also wasn't going to hurt Paige in what was undoubtedly a situation that caused some level of private pain. Whether that, though, was through what she had lived or was more a manifestation of keeping her true life a secret, Everett wasn't sure.

And it didn't matter.

He repeated his line, keeping the blame on himself. "I can't do this."

Everett couldn't get caught up in drama. An ex-husband? A child? And what else? If a device could measure his confusion, it would be off the charts. As much as he relished rediscovering his high school crush, he didn't relish this surprise into something so far from left field he couldn't catch it.

He had a sick mother. He had an aging father. He had a life to resume in Amarillo, a job and a residence. He couldn't play games here. Even with a woman brave enough to come clean face-to-face, he didn't know how to deal with someone who purposefully concealed her truth.

No parting words seemed appropriate.

But Everett, shocked as he was, couldn't just leave her. Not like that.

He didn't think the move through, which also didn't give him time to stop it. Compassion for maybe nothing more than her fragility at the moment outweighed. He rocked on his foot from heel to tip, leaned forward, and grazed Paige's cheek with a single, parting kiss. He closed his eyes as he pulled away, turning from her. He pointed the toe boxes of his boots toward his pickup, resolute steps carrying him away from a woman who couldn't possibly know the ways in which she had opened him.

Over the last few weeks, Everett didn't think beyond each day he was spending with Paige. He didn't have to. What worked with them just worked. Yet she was a woman with a life he didn't know. Although he couldn't have imagined turning his back on her, here he was, adding distance between them with every footfall.

When he finally reached his black Tacoma and climbed in the cab, he willed himself to look out the windshield. Space and location now separating them, he expected to see Paige one final time. But when his gaze lifted, there was only emptiness where the two of them had stood, the scene more like a dream than reality.

EVERETT LEFT PAIGE in waves of disappointment, sorrow, and regret. Temporal joys that stirred her back to life now disappeared with him. Everett Mullins turned his back on Paige Fredrick, a refusal of further contact speaking volumes about how much he had been hurt by her lie.

If I had only said something sooner, would Everett have left? Would honesty starting at our first encounter have convinced him to stay?

Unable to stand in the wake of unanswered questions and bitter embarrassment, she scurried into the courthouse without casting a backward glance. How her body was able to carry her, she wasn't sure. Buckling legs nearly knocked her to her knees on the sidewalk. In addition to shakiness in her lower half, there was plenty in her upper half. Her head pounded, her heart thumped, and her chest contracted. Out of sight, she had escaped a final view of Everett, but she couldn't outrun pain.

A further sickening feeling was the realization she bore the brunt of responsibility in creating Everett's reaction. He left because of her.

Paige was out of his view, but she was no less a sight. She was a mess, through and through. Inside the cool interior of the courthouse, she tried to recalibrate herself with the air-conditioned temperature. Her interior stress had externalized in forms of heat, causing her to sweat and flush all over. If she could cool down, she could at least manage her emotions better.

She looked around at the surroundings, the space eerily familiar to where she stood to regain her composure on the afternoon after her finalized divorce proceedings. She expected fragility then; it was today's that came as a greater surprise.

Suck it up, buttercup. She repeated the mantra until her body reacted in kind to the cadence of the repetitive mental pep talk.

Her wallowing in self-pity complete, resuming her work duties gave her purpose. She needed to drop a file at the county clerk's and pick one up from an employee in commissioner's court. Back at the land and title office, there was a full slate of end-of-day activities. Her work helped her regain focus, enough to function like someone who didn't just have her heart broken.

Was that the true source of pain? Not her head, not her knees, but her heart? Just how deeply had Everett touched her?

Again, these weren't questions Paige could answer, at least not in the fog of the present. They would be ones to contemplate another time, when Everett's parting was not a raw wound but a distant echo.

Until that time, she had a job, which she returned to do that afternoon. She had motherhood, which she resumed when she picked up Nathan from day care. And she had a house that was experiencing a mini revival, DIY style. She resumed those projects that very night. Still, there was no amount of distraction that could take Paige's mind fully off Everett, even though touch ups and improvements to her domicile helped. They were a way to pass time, and they were a way to stay productive. She knew the routine of staying busy, for that was how she managed with the initial filing for divorce. If she could keep her days full, she could keep the worry and the sadness at bay.

HER HOME WAS still a sanctuary, and it was becoming an even better version of itself. As the week ended and the weekend arrived, it took on a renewed look. Drawers had never been more organized, closets had never been more streamlined, and cabinets had never been so ordered. There was a place for everything, and the emotional stress Paige experienced after her Tuesday courthouse meltdown was the test for whether those improvements could stay that way.

They could.

By the next week, Paige was living in her version of the Taj Mahal.

Paige cleaned—and cleaned and cleaned and cleaned. Carpets were vacuumed, floors were shined, baseboards were scrubbed. She managed to dust the top of the ceiling fans and give each of the two bathtubs in the house a good scrub. She even wiped down the microwave and the refrigerator shelves. Laundry was put away. Dishes were too.

It was a dream house.

Every evening after work, she tackled something new. And in the hour or two after Nathan went to sleep, she finished whatever she wanted to get done. She put things away. She didn't allow chores to pile up. She didn't spend any time at home through that week and the following weekend doing anything that wasn't productive.

And, by Sunday, she was utterly exhausted. And possibly coming down with a sinus infection.

She self-medicated with some Sudafed and a whole lot of orange juice. Seeing Nathan as chipper and bright-eyed as ever, she decided to take cues from him, at least for the day. She ate a balanced meal, but didn't overdo it. When he napped, she napped. When he played quietly, she put her feet up. When he went down for an eight o'clock bedtime on Sunday night, she followed.

And she didn't wake once through the night.

Monday morning announced itself through her alarm, a chance for her to try her success at a new week. It had been six days since she saw Everett, six days of staring at her phone, hoping some kind of text would ping its way through.

Nothing.

With still stuffy sinuses, Paige threw back the covers, swung her legs off the mattress, and stepped out of bed, resolving to make the most of the week ahead.

And coffee would help. Rich, strong, bold coffee.

Paige selected her darkest roast and popped the pod into her coffee maker. The aroma was an instantaneous pick-me-up, which she needed to help add some life into her Monday. She popped two more Sudafed before rummaging in the pantry for a can of chicken noodle soup to take with her for lunch.

Bingo! She tilted the soup can forward, choosing a sleeve of Saltines to add to her lunch bag as well. It wasn't exactly a meal of champions, more a lunch for the weak. But she hoped it would make her strong.

That—and facing her reality of work, responsibilities, and maybe even an outreach to Everett, if she could muster the strength. She had contemplated sending him something over the weekend, an olive branch correspondence to perhaps take the edge off the blunt end to their courthouse meet-up. But nothing seemed appropriate.

Nathan stirred from inside his bedroom just as the coffee finished brewing. *Child or coffee?* She weighed, debating which to grab first. With an internal grunt, she let the coffee cool as she trudged to get Nathan ready for his day. *A mother's work is never done.*

A quick diaper refresh and change of clothes later, Nathan was ready to go. One joy of having a boy was the ease of getting him dressed. He had no long hair to braid, no complicated outfits to coordinate, no accessories to add. She silently thanked his DNA sequence.

With Nathan dressed for the day, Paige was able to focus on her needs, at least in the short-term. She savored her coffee as Nathan ate his cereal for breakfast. She stretched her back and rolled her shoulders. She inhaled and exhaled deeply as much as she could to clear her nasal passages and throat. If she felt awake, she might look more awake.

She swapped her morning mug for a travel one beneath her coffee maker and added a second pod. It was already shaping up to be a two-cup morning. Stumbling back into her bedroom, it would be a no-frills Monday for her. She opted for an outfit that didn't need ironing, her chunky leather boots, and a no-nonsense hairdo of a simple, sleek ponytail. Lip gloss and a swipe of ivory eyeshadow woke up the parts of her face which needed it the most. She grabbed her purse, throwing in a tube of concealer and a powder compact for later. After she dropped off Nathan, she could touch up with them both in the car before she arrived at the office, if she needed it. Daylight would be her judge.

She reentered the kitchen, grabbed her mug, stowed her lunch bag beneath her arm, and extended her one free hand to Nathan "Ready?" As he gripped it, Paige realized his was the only human touch she had felt in days.

"PAIGE, JUST KEEP those folders from toppling over, okay?" Miguel warned of the growing stack of files on Paige's desk. Indeed, it was turning into a version of a leaning tower.

"Got it." Paige pushed the pile, righting it into balance. "Or you could stop bringing me new deed applications." She was only half joking.

"New files equal new customers. New customers," Miguel insisted, dollar signs all but absent in his gaze, "means more money. That's more money for me"—he pointed his thumb into his chest—"and more money for you." He extended an index finger toward Paige.

"Got it," she repeated again.

He held his gesture in place, clicking his fingers like a pistol at the start of a race. Yes, Paige was off.

And to think it was only Monday.

She swiveled in her chair with a sigh. Her two cups of coffee had made her more productive, but that was a short-term solution to her stuffiness. Her head still ached, and she mentally tallied how much longer she'd have to wait before she could pop two more Sudafed. If she could make it to lunch, the chicken soup might give her fresh pep and mental stamina. She was in need of both.

She grabbed a new file and thumbed through the documents inside for a preliminary administrative check. Property description, commitment for title insurance, and the survey were standard. Pages and the survey map appeared complete. A planned unit development rider was her signal this was not for an existing homestead but instead for a tract of land being subdivided, a piece of larger property being spliced into smaller lots for sale. That was happening all around Seguin. Real estate developers took gambles, but it seemed those were paying off, at least by the land and title office's approximation.

Would this one?

She flipped to the illustration of the property where she saw dotted lines that cut the page into twenty lots. There was an entrance from the existing infrastructure with a simple t-street design all ending in cul-de-sacs through the middle. This was a smaller project than some she had seen, but still one that could turn a large profit, especially depending on how richly it was developed. With buried utilities, strong signage, and proper curbing, those infrastructure improvements alone could net a turnaround profit on just the sale of a few of the lots.

But who was taking the gamble now? She thumbed to the signature page, and her morning coffee almost choked upward from the pit of her stomach.

Barry Van Soyt's name was a shock. Her ex—buying property? She gulped back the bitter taste of seeing his signature as *Undersigned*. She was trying to make Seguin her future, but now there was competition. Queasiness seized her as the realization hit that her ex-husband was making his indelible mark in the town, one that suddenly felt too small for the both of them to share.

But she kept reading.

There was more to the signature page.

A second name was listed below his, revealing a copartner in the development. Momentary shock gave way to full-blown panic, and she gripped the side of the desk to steady herself even while seated. If the name had been anyone else's, it wouldn't have rocked Paige in such a consequential way.

But it wasn't.

Unmistakably, she ran her fingers across the signature as if touching the ink would verify it before her eyes. Her sight did not deceive her.

Even through all the stress of divorce and the seemingly never-ending parade of paperwork, Paige had never been as mad then as she was in this moment to read a single document. Nausea overtook her, and it was more than the sinus headache. She swiveled in a flash, pulled out the garbage can beneath her desk, and heaved a sour cocktail of shock, disgust, and anger into the bin, the name Danica Lara on the paperwork inches away staring back at her.

Chapter Fifteen

A MANILA FILE folder had never felt so corrupt.

Paige slammed the cover of the file down. Pushing back her desk chair in a frenzy, she raced to the bathroom before any of her coworkers could ask her what was the matter.

And in case she needed to puke again.

Deeds of trust communicated intent to be part of location, not just on the surface but engrained in the very fiber of a place through acquisition. The documents served as a permanent and legal stamp of property ownership. Permanent enough, at least, until another owner came along. But twenty lots? Even in a best case scenario, preparing and moving those would take months, possibly a year or more. This wasn't going to be an overnight, fly-by sale, and this wasn't a project at the hands of some in-and-out contractor. This was a calculated development attempt by someone who knew the area and knew how to profit.

To some people, her job at the land and title office was just as a paper pusher. Those people didn't understand the role she played. Paige had been attracted to land work because she loved connecting people with the places they loved. Truly, she aimed to make a difference and help even in this behind-the-scenes way in making property dreams come true.

But there was a line.

And her ex just crossed it.

Her best friend—make that ex-best friend—had crossed it too.

Paige locked herself into a stall in the women's restroom, facing the toilet as if the two were in a duel. The walls protecting her were cold and sterile, the space private but unnerving. Pressure continued to build behind her forehead, her sinuses so heavy that her head drooped.

"You okay, Paige?" A female voice called through the entrance door. It sounded like the office's front assistant was checking on her.

"Fine," she lied. "Headache turned to puke." That was a bit more of the truth, even though it probably made little logical sense.

"Need some water?"

I need something stronger than that.

"Paige?"

Her name sounded foreign, even to her own ears. Paige closed her eyes, steadying herself against the frame of the stall. "Yes, on my desk." She wanted to be alone. "Can you just put a cup on my desk?"

"Oh, okay. Sure." The door squeaked close, giving Paige the privacy she craved. But having the space to herself wasn't a sanction on solitude. If anything, she felt more discombobulated and confused than ever. She was a recent divorcee whose best friend was in cahoots with her ex-husband. Her stomach wretched along with the thoughts in her mind. She was a woman both alone and lonely.

She dropped her head, giving way to the pressure behind her eyes that made tears pool at their corners. Paige didn't have the strength to combat them as they began quietly streaming down her face.

How could Danica not tell her she was planning to buy land with Barry? Developing a partnership that must have been in the works since—when? Before he was even officially divorced from Paige?

And was this only a business partnership—or more?

The tears streamed harder as the questions mounted. She couldn't wrap her head around the sickening possibilities of just how two-faced Danica had been. To think she knew all along that she was keeping a secret and she never once cracked in revealing her truth to her friend. What kind of person does that?

Me. The realization was a blunt and unexpected slap. She had done the very thing she was reacting to now. She had lied—and continued the charade through heavy omission. If she was going to judge Danica, Paige needed to take a hard look at herself. Squeezing her eyes tight at the parallel recognition, she admitted in her mind, *I'm that type of person. I did that. To Everett.*

She cried harder, tears for her friend and tears for herself. Paige stayed until no more tears came and, by then, she was weak with defeat. She unlocked the slider on the bathroom stall, stood at the sink, and ran cool water from the faucet. She splashed it through her hands and wrists before moistening a paper towel and blotting her face. Behind her ears, on the back of the neck, and across her chest she swiped in order to bring her temperature and her distress level down.

She wadded the paper, tossed it in the garbage, and cupped her hand beneath the faucet. She raised a handful of water to her mouth, sloshed it through her teeth, and spit it out. She repeated the process, trying to erase the traces of bitter taste from her earlier upheaval.

Satisfied that she was presentable again, Paige took a deep breath, squared her shoulders, and mouthed, "Suck it up, buttercup." It took every ounce of courage to march back into the office and not collapse into a puddle, disguising to her coworkers that her sudden sickness was nothing more than a bodily reaction to a bad headache.

Paige took slow, restrained steps to her cubicle, Miguel at her heels. "If you need to leave early," he urged, "go ahead. You don't look good."

Never tell that to a woman. Regardless of the circumstances—and especially when a person didn't feel well—it just wasn't a good idea to articulate it.

Paige shook her bangs away from her face, staging her bravest smile. "I'm fine now."

That was a lie.

A woman who says she's "fine" but looked like Paige did in that moment shouldn't be believed. What Paige wanted to say instead was—*I'm not fine. Miguel, you need to take this file. And burn it. The title can never be cleared, and we're not going to do a thing with this.* But she didn't. She couldn't.

Miguel conceded just the same. "If you say so." He

shrugged. Maybe he felt compelled simply to check. Maybe he was following office supervisor protocol. Or maybe he couldn't stand the stench coming from Paige's trash can, a potent and unpleasant odor lingering from her initial reaction to the documents.

That trash can needed to be dumped, just like Danica's dirty friendship.

PAIGE'S PAST COUPLE of years had been a series of starts and stops. Pregnancy, parenting, work, and marriage—challenges abounded. Her life was no different, perhaps, than some. Everyone weathered their own storms.

But weathering hers privately was taking a toll. Her sinuses didn't seem to get any better. Relief at the hands of pills and hot beverages was temporary. If she stopped crying, she could breathe easier.

It was just that she couldn't stop crying.

The smallest hiccup even after she left the office kept her on edge—a car tailgating too closely, a man walking whom she saw litter, the extra wait time at the day care picking up Nathan while his caregiver finished a phone call. Then there was Nathan himself. At home, he was cranky and irritable. He went from being hungry to not wanting to eat a thing to wanting to be held and then wanting to be let go. He cried for Paige and he cried at Paige.

"What happened to you?" she asked in frustration, as if

he could articulate a completely coherent response. He just sat cross-legged on the carpeted floor of his bedroom, uninterested in any toy she tried to produce to pacify him. At her wit's end, she planted one foot in front of the other and stood with a hand on her hip.

As if he were an adult able to determine as much, she fired a couple of further questions. "Did you discover a secret today? Did you find out your friend betrayed your trust?"

Nathan cried louder.

She wanted to take back her snappy comments as quickly as she had delivered them. She bent close to him and in a soothing voice, held his hand and admitted, "I'm sorry, little guy." She kissed him on his chubby arm. Maybe he was coming down with a sinus infection like she was. Or perhaps it was a summer cold, a bug of sorts he picked up from day care. She touched his forehead. It felt a little warm, but nothing quite feverish. It was probably just hot from his crying. Paige was told his nap was restless today, so that likely accounted for his crankiness more than anything.

"So, bad afternoon just like Mommy had, huh?" That was her verdict. She stood up. "Well, there's only one cure for that, Nate." When her feet got knocked out from under her, she could fall down—or she could find a way to get back up. She had done that today in the office, not succumbing to her emotions by taking off the afternoon and not even telling Miguel, "*You handle this because I can't.*" She found her own strength, and she made it through.

That was who she was, and that was what she did.

When she needed a little support underneath her, she

leaned on an old hobby.

"Want to go for a bike ride?"

Nathan immediately silenced, his attitude perking at the mere mention.

So that was easy.

She had little motivation herself to exert energy by cycling. Her greater motivation was for Nathan's well-being— to help calm him. Secondarily, her sinuses might benefit from fresh air.

Or maybe the heat and humidity would have the opposite effect and make her feel worse. She'd see.

Already changed from her work clothes into a comfortable set of shorts and a t-shirt, she just needed to lace up her sneakers. She gathered her hair into a quick and messy low ponytail before grabbing helmets from the garage. Nathan's went on first, then hers. She hoisted him into the ride-along, though he yelped with a sharp cry when she moved him.

"Sheesh." Paige reacted to his sensitivity. Everything was setting this little guy off. Maybe he needed a bike ride even more than she did.

It didn't take long for Nathan to quiet. His whimpers were soothed by the cruising lull of Paige's pedaling along the asphalt. She didn't need to go fast. The gentle breeze cut around them, cooling their skin even though daylight still hung in the air. Being on a bike was a simple pleasure, and she was thankful it had calmed Nathan's fussiness almost instantaneously.

They strolled through neighborhood streets, beneath live oaks, around bends, and past well-kept yards where blooms added to each home's curb appeal. Dainty petunias and zinnias announced themselves from pots and flower boxes. Color-bursting lantana dotted some front porches while evergreen bushes added a more stately look to lined walkways and driveways. Many homes favored an array of butterfly bushes, blooming to attract Texas' summer tourists of swallowtails and buckeyes. Street medians and subdivision entrances held beautiful knockout roses in characteristic rich blooms. The popular sun-hearty plants sprouted with countless buds that overpowered the leafy green stalks to create showy bushes in all types of lipstick-worthy shades from fuchsia to coral to deep salmon to hot pink.

Maybe I should do more with my front yard. Her mind flashed with images of grandeur if she could devote serious attention to expanding her flower beds or adding a few larger plants. Even small changes could have a big impact, as she was noticing when she passed certain homes. There was so much inspiration she could gleam from others. *But a project like that will have to wait for another day.*

Paige glanced back at Nathan, his eyes turning heavy as his chin nodded up and down to the rhythm of her cycling. The ride was tiring him out, and she took note of her own energy level, which was waning too. They should both sleep well tonight.

She circled through the end of a cul-de-sac before pointing her bike back in the direction of home. She cruised Nathan in comfort through the scenes they were passing for the second time but, since the sun was dipping, there was an entirely new view to be had.

"Fireflies." She breathed in delight at seeing the magical creatures, gushing over their presence with a coo.

The light of the night insects were one joy of this part of the region. Fireflies would descend in small groups at dusk, their little flickering lights brightening the horizon. The winged bugs were silent and, unlike mosquitos, did not wield an annoying bite. If she had to pick a favorite insect—and Paige wasn't much a fan of any—fireflies would most certainly be at the top of the list.

She wished Nathan were awake to see their magic, but there would be another evening. She made a mental note of the time to remind herself when a ride might yield another viewing like this.

It was a gorgeous end to an otherwise loathsome day. At least Seguin could offer her that.

THE LAST FEW evenings were rough at the Mullins farmhouse.

Ruby was restless, and Dale stayed worried. Everett had to be the voice of reason—medically and personally—to prevent both from imploding.

"And just why do those doctors think replacing my blood with someone else's is such a good idea?" Ruby's voice was laced with sass.

"It's not a replacement, Mom." Everett had already tried explaining the blood transfusion earlier in the day. "It's a procedure that a lot of chemotherapy patients have to—"

"I don't care about other chemotherapy patients."

"That's right," his dad chimed in. "All she needs to worry about is herself." On the one hand, it was admirable how his father spoke in defense of his mother. But on the other hand, it made it two against one.

Everett tried a more clinical approach. "You've got a low blood cell count. And your body needs energy to continue to fight this. It will help your bone marrow."

"My bone marrow isn't my blood." His mother was as combative as a child who refused to take a pill.

"That's right," Everett conceded, drawing on his best memory of what he heard the nurses explain. Pairing that with the rhetoric of the doctors, he continued, "But your bone marrow makes the blood cells. And the chemotherapy has damaged it so—"

"The chemotherapy was a bad idea." His father interrupted with an argument they were not going to have.

"Dad!" This was not the time to level criticism. They were all in with this. "The chemotherapy is working." There was evidence to support as much. "And this is simply a side effect. A manageable one," Everett stressed.

His dad turned his head and mumbled something Everett couldn't hear. His mother conceded to Everett, "You'll make me do it anyway."

When did this complete role reversal from child to parent happen?

Yes, he was going to make her do it. That was why he had taken all this time off work and had relocated temporarily back to Seguin—for her. Everett took a role in her recovery that was going to make her life better, nor harder.

"I love you." Those words always seemed to help. "And, Mom, the benefits will be immediate. Lots of people feel better right away after this."

His mother leaned back into the recliner, rocking it into gentle motion. "I'll feel better when this is all over."

Everett pounded on her minced words. "You will. That's the point."

"Fine," she concluded.

"Fine," his father echoed, though his agreement wasn't needed at this point. Still, Everett understood they were tackling this together, like the couple they had always been.

"It better be good blood," his mother snapped before tilting her head, settling further into the cushion of the recliner.

"I'm sure it will be," Everett soothed.

A transfusion was a new experience for all of them, but it certainly wasn't new to the doctors and nurses at the Guadalupe Regional Medical Center. Ruby could have the procedure locally instead of driving to San Antonio, which was a burden lifted. Placing trust in professionals was important, and they had all been assured this would be an easy morning visit that would last a few hours. Not that the actual transfusion took much time, but her body's reaction just needed to be monitored and healthy vitals confirmed before she was released. The majority, then, of the recovery would happen at home.

"There's going to be no Zika in it, right?" His father had

been hearing half of one too many news reports on the invasive mosquito-borne virus.

"No, Dad. The blood is screened. No Zika. No West Nile. No malaria or yellow fever either, I'm sure." Some days, he wondered how his parents functioned by themselves if there was no voice of reason to break into their worry.

"Good." He retrieved a copy of *The San Antonio Express-News* from the coffee table. "Because that virus is bad stuff."

Oh boy. Are we going to get into this? But Everett was saved by his father's distraction.

He folded the paper against the border of a large advertisement. "You know Tractor Supply Company is having a sale on pressure washers?"

"You've been talking about buying one." Ruby fielded a reply instead of Everett. "How much?"

And just like that, his parents were absorbed in an entirely new conversation. Maybe they didn't need Everett as much as he thought after all.

Chapter Sixteen

P AIGE AWOKE TO cries.

Nathan had a restless night, with a couple of fits that Paige had to soothe. She chalked it up to falling asleep early on their bike ride and not having a full nighttime routine. He didn't even get a bath because Paige didn't want to disturb him. She just settled him straight into bed. He needed his sleep.

But his routine had been thrown off-kilter, and Paige's week wasn't much better. She tried to put on her sweetest face as she entered his room. "Hey, buddy," she greeted.

He met her voice with a louder cry.

She kneeled next to his bed, wiping sleep from her own eyes. "What's wrong?" She brought her hand to judge the temperature on his forehead, and it was burning up. That spurred her into a more serious reaction than just a child having a rough night of sleep. "Are you sick?" He couldn't respond with much, though it still seemed natural to have a conversation, one-sided as it may be. "I'm going to get the thermometer."

She retrieved her trusty ear thermometer from the cabinet in his bathroom. It had been an incredible baby shower gift from her aunt, and Paige made a mental note to offer yet another verbal thanks to her the next time she spoke with her on the phone. She had received so many other fun items at her shower—charming outfits, adorable pairs of shoes, the softest blankets, the cuddliest stuffed animals—that unwrapping a medical gadget was a bit underwhelming. Blinded by the cute stuff, she didn't know then how very useful an ear thermometer would be, but it was a tool she used regularly both in Nathan's infancy and now in his toddlerhood.

Paige kneeled back beside him on the bed. "Stay still." She coaxed while the thermometer read his temperature. She angled the screen back to read it.

102.5.

Could that be right?

His gaze was glassy and his cries continued. "Come here." She set the thermometer on the carpet as she bent over him to scoop his body into her arms, but he wailed with a painful cry unlike one she'd ever heard from him. She kept him on the bed instead and poked gently against his side and across his ribs at the places that solicited the sound.

Nathan wailed again when she applied the slightest bit of pressure on his abdomen, kicking violently before crying even louder.

Something's not right.

Times like this, she wished her son could talk in full sentences to express what he was feeling. Without that, Paige had to interpret his feelings and be his voice.

But as a single mother, she was in tune with his needs. And he needed—something.

This isn't right.

She couldn't take any chances. Trusting her intuition, she would skip work and take Nathan straight into the pediatrician's office. No appointment didn't matter. Someone needed to determine what was wrong with Nathan.

"ALL READY?" A nurse addressed Ruby Mullins, who sat still on a reclining medical chair.

She pushed her palm against the stiff plastic cushion, little give in flexibility of the slick vinyl. "Not exactly like my recliner at home."

Everett stood at a distance, though if he had been closer he would have kicked his mother's foot to jostle her back into being polite.

The nurse, to her credit, didn't seem fazed by the jab, even agreeing with his mother. "It's no Lazy Boy."

"Maybe patients would be more comfortable if it were." She tightened her lips, as if her mere mention of this suggestion was going to change the future of patient care during blood transfusions.

"I'd vote for that." The nurse untangled a blood pressure cuff and released the Velcro with a quick rip. "But the hospital board probably wouldn't go for it."

Ruby Mullins wasn't ready to drop her argument just yet. She lifted her arm, allowing the nurse to slide the cuff around it. "Well, I can see how there would be too much chance for contamination on the fabric." The nurse secured the cuff in place, but even that didn't stop Ruby from continuing a mile a minute. "You know, at home, I've got this ottoman. It's supposed to have Scotch Guard on the fabric, but I swear whenever I go to vacuum that thing there's not a lick of protection on it. I think I got scammed at the furniture store, but—"

"Mrs. Mullins, I'm going to need you to take a break for a moment, please." The nurse secured the cuff and then poised her hand atop the rolling reader, ready to press the machine into action. "That way we can get an accurate reading of your blood pressure."

"Of course, sweetie." She smiled before sealing her lips by pressing them together tight.

The nurse punched the button to start the machine, a grinding sound filling the space of the private room as it compressed into action. Ruby closed her eyes, and Everett stayed still. He hoped his mother really was going to relax through all of this.

The machine beeped in completion, and the nurse read Ruby's vitals. "A little on the low side," she commented, bending to release the cuff. "But we'll get you fixed up and feeling fine with this transfusion."

Ruby stiffened her arm so the nurse could remove the band. "Will it be good blood?"

Here we go again. Everett was sure his eyes rolled.

"The best we have, Mrs. Mullins. I can guarantee you that." The nurse moved the reader back into its corner. "I've got to take this reading to the doctor, but I'll be back in a moment to start the prep work."

"Take your time, sweetie," Ruby joked. "I'm not going anywhere." She crossed her feet at the ankles as lazily as one might do lounging on a poolside chaise. Months of in and out medical care made her comfortable with nurses and doctors both. She knew when to be lighthearted and turn on the jokes.

She sometimes just didn't know when to stop.

But Everett couldn't fault her for that. Everyone their own way of dealing with cancer and, all things considered, his mom was dealing remarkably well.

"Can I get you anything?" Everett waited until the nurse exited to ask, even though he wasn't sure what she might be allowed before a transfusion.

"Just tell me when your father's going to get back." He had excused himself to get a cup of coffee—or so he said—but it certainly seemed like it was taking longer than it should.

"I don't know," Everett admitted. "Do you want me to track him down?"

"Don't bother." His mother waved a hand. "Just talk to me. Keep me company for a while."

Everett had been doing a lot of that. But, then again, it was part of the role. During treatments, there were long periods of waiting around. Here, too, it seemed there would be a fair share of that, even for a morning blood transfusion.

"What do you want me to talk about?" If Everett let her drive the conversation, the time might pass more quickly, at least for his mother.

"Oh . . ." She breezed. "Tell me anything."

There had been plenty on Everett's mind as of late, especially when it came to Paige, but there was also nothing much to say. He wasn't going to use this time to have his mother play arm chair psychiatrist for his psyche, though, admittedly, she was sitting in the perfect position. "Like what?"

His mother lifted and lowered her chest in a heavy intake before she turned her head to give him a better look. "You can tell me why you've been moping around for a week."

The accusation shook him with surprise. "What?"

"You heard me," she insisted. "I didn't stutter."

"Moping?" Everett repeated. "I haven't been moping."

She raised her volume and her tone into a high-pitched motherly outcry. "I beg your pardon?"

Everett tried to shush her. "Mom, please. We've got to be quiet in here."

"That wasn't a rule on any of the papers I signed." Now she was just being ornery. "Besides, it's true. You've been moping around ever since who knows what happened."

I know what happened. Everett still felt her in his heart. *Paige.*

"So if you want to get back to Amarillo that bad—"

"No." That wasn't it, and he certainly didn't want his mother to think so. He had a clear timeline in place for approved medical leave. He was here to care for his mother and would be leaving next week. That was already established, and he wasn't going to head north any earlier. "That's not why."

"Ah ha!" She pointed her finger as if she were a detective

who just found a primary clue. "So you admit. You have been acting mopey."

Can we please use a different word?

His mom furrowed her brow, detecting that his body language and words were serving as camouflage. "Something is bothering you, Everett."

Maybe he did wear his emotions on his sleeve. What were they revealing this week? Perhaps not the full extent of his empty heart, but perhaps enough of it. Still, what could be said about Paige? How could he explain her—and the untruth he learned about her—to his mother? And for what benefit?

He didn't want to try, and especially not here. A hospital was the furthest place from where Paige would be, so he didn't want to bring her into the setting, even just in name.

Yet he couldn't shake his thoughts and memories of Paige Fredrick, even when he had tried to do so for the past week. There was the Paige he had known in high school, and there was the Paige he had grown to know now. That's who filled him.

In his silence, his mother offered a more diplomatic request. Quiet and gentle, she prodded. "Want to talk about it?"

Even if he did want to talk about Paige, he couldn't do so without talking about Catherine. She was always there too.

And she always would be.

Everett scratched the side of his head. "I don't know if this is the time—"

"Mrs. Mullins"—the nurse poked her head back through the doorway of their room—"the doctor said you're all set. We'll prep for the transfusion."

Everett exhaled in relief. *Saved by the bell.* Or at least by that nurse.

His mother straightened in her seat, her arms by each side as she looked completely resigned to the impending procedure. She turned her head toward the ceiling, telling no one in particular, "Time to make this a memory."

Strange, Everett thought, seeing the ease with which his mother was approaching what was otherwise difficult. *If only I could do that in my life.*

THE RECEPTIONIST OFFERED a sympathetic smile to Paige in the waiting room at the pediatrician's office. There were no available morning appointments, but showing up with a wailing toddler pretty much guaranteed the doctor would see them at some point. And the receptionist worked her magic to force them in between other patients with minimal wait time. Paige was grateful, and so was everyone else in the room who cringed and shuffled in their seats at Nathan's desperate cries.

That poor receptionist. Paige walked as fast as she could through the door that led to the examination rooms. *She's got to deal with crying kids all day long.* Paige's nerves were fraying after less than one day of it, so she could only imagine a pediatrician office employee's level of stress. *Everything requires perspective.*

Resolving to stay as calm and level-headed as possible, Paige advanced under the guidance of a nurse who met her. "Right this way." She ushered Paige into the room, clearing the way with Nathan curled into Paige like a baby koala. The nurse wasted no time. "What seems to be the problem?"

Paige angled her chin at Nathan, though his presence was obvious. She gave a rundown of the symptoms. "Crying nonstop all morning. Fever at 102.5. Fussy and irritable through the night. Seems really sensitive around his stomach."

The nurse nodded. "Let's get him up here." She pointed to the examination table. "And I'll call in the doctor to have a look."

As Paige attempted to unhook Nathan's arms from around her neck and separate their bodies, she was met with resistance. Wails of discomfort echoed in the confined space, sounding even worse than before they left the house.

Though those cries at home had certainly been bad.

The nurse's eyebrows contracted in worry. "Did you say his stomach has been sensitive?"

"Yes," she managed through his noise, "to the touch."

The nurse fired a series of questions in rapid succession. At the conclusion, before the doctor even entered the room, she gave Paige new reason to worry. "Ms. Fredrick, the doctor can confirm my suspicion, but I think your son may have appendicitis."

The possible prognosis knocked the wind out of her.

That serious? What did that even mean for a two-year-old? How could this even happen?

The nurse disappeared, leaving Paige alone with her ailing son. Her disgust at her lack of foresight into considering appendicitis made her wretch. Her own stomach knotted in pain as if she had the ailment, though Nathan's experience was far worse.

She stepped close to him on the examination table, his hands grabbing for her waist from his horizontal position. *My baby.* Her heart puddled and poured in empathy, his pain her pain. *If only Mommy could take it away, sweet boy, Mommy would.* All she could do was soothe Nathan in her mind and try her best to gently calm through minimized but careful touch and comfort.

The blur of the doctor's arrival and confirmation heightened Paige's immediate need to get Nathan relief. After a quick examination and more peppering of questions, the doctor confirmed what the nurse suspected. "Nathan needs to be transported to Guadalupe Regional. We will need to perform a surgical removal of his appendix."

Paige had not been in the hospital since delivery of Nathan. She had two years with him free of medical emergencies, but now the possibilities in regard to this major one loomed at a level she didn't know how she could shoulder. The magnitude of what was impending weighed heavier than anything she could remember.

So much stress. So much worry. So much pain. She didn't want to take her eyes off Nathan, though she couldn't bear to look at him and see his level of agony. Her heart broke as if it were obsidian spliced into shards, the sharp points piercing her at the core. The pain stayed with her, a small comparison emotionally to the physical pain Nathan must be harboring.

Everyone worked fast, but not fast enough. There were calls and transfers, paperwork and permissions. Through the flurry of activity, there was little actual relief for Nathan. Paige, keenly aware of her helplessness, could only try to keep soothing in any small way until the surgery occurred.

CHILDBIRTH WAS AN event Paige could remember in crisp detail. Every moment of that special day was captured in her mind as if on a moving reel, image and emotion alike. It was a whirlwind, a day she could never forget.

Today was moving in a similar sequence, but the emotions held an undercurrent of fear, both for Nathan and for the unknown of what would happen in the hospital.

At Guadalupe Regional Medical Center, Paige had doctors, nurses, and staff aplenty to attend to Nathan's needs. There shouldn't have been reason to second-guess the level of care and attention he would be provided.

Yet . . . there was always fear.

The hospital staff took the lead in telling Paige exactly what to do, from where to go to where to stand and what to sign. Paige paced through the process.

A nurse touched Paige on her elbow, the small act verification that this was, indeed, real and not a horrid nightmare. "Do you want to take this time to call someone? Your son is in a stable position, so now would be a good time for a phone call."

Again, Paige took the professional's lead. "Sure," she agreed, though, truly, correspondence that took her attention away from Nathan was the last thing on her mind.

There were plenty of people in her address book. She didn't hurt for family or neighbors who would be concerned. Friends, too, would show support. Of course her coworkers would understand, and Miguel would be calling if he hadn't already since she didn't show up for work. So many people to call, yet she didn't have a strong pull to dial any particular number.

"Now's the best time," the nurse urged. "It will start getting hectic again in another few minutes."

Paige fished for her phone inside her purse and held it in her hand. Her parents and sister were in another state, and so many of her neighbors were at work. Her own office was busy with activity for sure. She tapped her thumb against the side of the phone, nervous and afraid. Taking a deep breath, she slid across the names to the one person who never skipped her call and who routinely helped at the drop of the word to do so.

"Danica." Even as she spoke her name, it tasted like disgust and betrayal. "I'm at the hospital with Nathan." She kept the details curt, wasting no time. She inhaled for strength before admitting, "I need your help."

Fathers needed to know about their children. Barry Van

Soyt needed to know about his son.

But typical of his absenteeism, Barry didn't always take Paige's calls and instead let most go to voice mail. Paige knew this, and she enlisted Danica for this reason. Since Danica was doing business with Barry, he would likely answer a call from her.

Chapter Seventeen

NOTHING CHALLENGED A parent's skill more than a crisis. Any emergency required an all-hands-on-deck approach, physically and mentally. Between the decisions and oversight as well as the quick reaction and response time needed, parents had to be sharp. There was a small window in which fast decisions needed to occur. Luckily, Paige had guidance from her pediatrician and from rural doctors and nurses who were already giving what seemed like their total attention to Nathan.

When it involved such a young child, there was also a dread and a complete giving over of emotion, the urge to help and ease and support.

And she was just one person.

Like childbirth, there were things she would remember about this day. There were memories forming from the surroundings—the antiseptic hospital air, the texture of the stiff hospital bedsheets, the rhythmic beep of the medical machines that punctuated the events. But there were images that were cementing themselves into her memory too. Nathan's wide eyes, his frightened look, his cries of desperate pain. These would be Paige's permanent mental marks whether she wanted them or not.

But everything about Paige—her needs, her thoughts, her worries—took a backseat to her child's.

As Nathan was prepped for surgery, every fiber in Paige wanted to take his place. If she could substitute herself for his being in that moment, she would. Bearing all she could, her love for him was that strong.

But the hospital needed to treat Nathan. And Paige would be there as his parent. She took all her cues from the nurses, for even childbirth didn't prepare her for the demands of a medical crisis. And she needed to follow someone's lead because she was alone. The staff was substituting for a significant other or another adult family member.

Or a trusted friend.

Preparations continued for the operating room. A nurse explained the procedure for a ruptured appendix. Three small incisions that would form a triangle around Nathan's belly button would allow laparoscopic insertion and then appendix removal.

"Will he have anesthesia?"

"Yes," the nurse confirmed. "The lowest dosage necessary will be administered by the anesthesiologist in order to prepare him for the surgery."

Paige just needed to make sure. "So he's not going to feel anything?"

"That's correct. No pain." Simply hearing the words erased some of Paige's anxiety. "But there will be pain to manage after the surgery, and he will have to stay a patient here until the doctor feels he is healing enough on his own to return home."

"Of course." Paige hadn't thought far in advance, but she certainly didn't foresee being able to drive home later in the day.

"Recovery for a little one can be tougher than the surgery." The nurse warned, her voice low but comforting. "So if you can make arrangements now for a recovery plan, that's what I would advise."

A recovery plan? Paige had so many questions yet no voice to ask them. Instead, her head swirled with scenarios and outcomes that she wasn't even sure belonged in her mind at the moment. As if sensing Paige's singlehood status, the nurse offered, "We'll be here to help you."

As heartfelt as the offer seemed, the nurse had a job. Bedside manners were kicking in, and she knew her role in calming a near-hysterical mother. But Paige was beginning to realize she needed more than a nurse to lean on.

"Paige!" An unmistakable male voice ripped through the room, the nurses parting to reveal the man she hadn't seen in weeks.

She choked a one-word acknowledgement. "Barry." She collapsed into his open arms in utter vulnerability. There was simply no one else to hold her, and she needed that.

He accepted her as she was, folding his arms around her to cover her in an embrace that kept her upright with legs that wanted to collapse. "Tell me what to do." His voice was level and low. "Tell me what Nathan needs."

Things were moving so fast, she didn't even know.

Then the offer heightened. "Tell me what you need."

So much.

Before she could answer, the nurse cut in to give a final overview and time estimate. "Parents can wait in a special area outside the OR. Would both of you like to do that?"

Barry slackened his hold on Paige as they each answered for themselves in the affirmative.

"Then let's go." The nurse led them into the hallway. Blinking hard to hold back tears, Paige focused her gaze on looking high ahead of her to regain composure. There was movement at the far end of the inpatient hallway. Adding to her shaky mental and emotional state, she could have sworn it looked like Everett walking toward the center reception area of the hospital. *That's it. I'm officially seeing things.*

Maybe the nurses could make room for Paige in a shared room with Nathan, for surely she was losing it and needed to be admitted to a medical professional's care.

EVERYTHING ABOUT BARRY'S presence was at once familiar and unfamiliar. Characteristics were the same, and even a slight bit of time spent close to him revealed that. But there was no pull toward him in any way other than yielding a shared supportive role. She and Barry were divorced, with love lost between them. Also, with time having passed, he was not a regular part of Nathan's life. That distance had made him a stranger in some ways. She might have collapsed into his available embrace, but Paige was not going to fall for anything.

Trust was shaken in regard to his motives with Danica. Why was Danica involved with him? And to what extent? So many questions eddied that she wanted to ask him, but only one rolled forth as they marched toward the OR. "Where's Danica?"

Barry didn't pretend. He knew. "She's here, in the hospital. Danica is waiting in the main room."

Paige couldn't have heard him correctly. Seeing the names of Barry and Danica together on a land deed were betrayal enough. Now, her former friend and ex-husband were under the same roof? Alarm rang through her, shock still pelting her from all directions.

Barry spoke in a calm tone. "She's here to see you—to talk—whenever you want."

"I don't want to talk to her." Paige picked up her pace through the hallway, the soles of her shoes hitting hard against the tile with each footfall. *I've got nothing to say.*

"That's fair." Barry eased off the accelerator of bringing them together, focusing on matching her speed instead.

But he didn't get too close, not like when she walked in Walnut Springs Park with Everett. Barry must have sensed he had gone too far, so he stayed a step behind. Timid, he revealed Danica had something for Paige.

Paige seethed. She had no desire to spend precious minutes in the hospital thinking about Danica instead of Nathan. "What does she have that I could possibly want?"

"It's a bag of overnight stuff. Things to save you a trip from going home. She wanted to make today easier on you."

Oh. Not what Paige expected.

Barry continued. "Plus I'll get whatever Nathan needs, if there's something the hospital won't provide." Paige doubted that would be the case. The hospital provided gowns, bedding, food, medicine. But Barry's thoughts were on comfort items. "Does he have a favorite stuffed animal or something I could bring?"

His baby blue snuggly giraffe. It was the one Nathan got as a gift from . . .

Danica.

Paige scrunched her face, holding back the urge to shout in complete frustration.

BARRY AND PAIGE were told to wait outside the OR entrance. A nurse assured them the staff was working to prep the area for surgery.

And waiting was the hardest task.

Paige used the downtime to cool her anger. Nathan needed her attention, and she owed it to him not to let her emotions get pulled away by a situation between Danica and Barry she didn't understand, and, frankly, didn't care to right now.

"Look, Paige." Barry's tone took his words into new territory, a tone of self-directed admission she hadn't heard before. "I know I haven't been the best father. And I could be a lousy husband."

"Go on." This was the first of any such acknowledgement by Barry, and she wasn't about to let him off easy.

It was just the two of them standing at the entrance to the operating area, waiting for confirmation to enter. Barry admitted, "You're so much better at parenting than I am—than I can ever hope to be."

"Don't play a martyr." She blew her bangs out of her eyes.

The sterility of the setting must have been Barry's motivation to continue. "I didn't embrace being a father, and I know that." He kept his voice low, speaking only to her. "But I want to be the father that Nathan needs now." Paige wasn't one to suffer fools, yet she was hearing Barry's words with a softness of heart. "I want to do my part so he'll be taken care of." Barry spoke the next phrase carefully, "and you'll be taken care of." He sounded so certain, a quality Paige didn't seem to have all morning. Or maybe she just wasn't giving herself enough credit. Either way, Barry was communicating a desire that had been nonexistent since Nathan's birth. He was offering help.

Paige's anger wasn't minimized, but she pushed it aside. She wasn't going to turn away words she had waited for since Nathan's birth.

"Thank you," she managed, finally answering with the strength of a parent who had resolved to manage a worst case scenario the best way possible.

She didn't look Barry in the eye, but she looked to him. And as she took in the sight of this man who had fathered her son, she saw for the first time not an ex-husband or an enemy who was fighting for territory in her town, but as someone more human. He wasn't perfect; he never would be. But Barry was no longer an absent parent. His very presence and his words communicated his desire to co-parent. Maybe it was the emergency situation or maybe it was the neutral setting of the hospital. This place was neither her turf nor his. Whatever the reason, this surprise stepping-up-to-the-plate approach as a parent was what Barry needed to do.

For Nathan's sake.

And for his own.

Paige couldn't control anyone else but herself. Nonetheless, she was optimistic this would be the start of a more unified front when it came to choices that mattered in the interest of their son.

Consciously, Paige made a decision in the hospital hallway not to be bitter. There was no energy for that. Better late than never, Barry's decision was representative not of the past but of the present. He had shown up when it mattered.

Paige came to another decision. Asking questions of Danica and her life choices could wait for another time, another place. As much as she would be cautious of Danica, she too had shown up when it mattered, and Paige could honor that. "Tell Danica thank you for coming when you talk to her." She wasn't ready to see her or confront her, and her priority was on the OR, wanting to be ready when the staff let them know Nathan's surgery was beginning.

"I will." They paused outside of the double doors of the OR, waiting for their next cue for the nurses. "She'll want to hear an update. And she'll want to help."

Paige wasn't sure about having that conversation. They fell silent, letting the topic go.

In the brief quiet of the space, Paige could hear herself think, and she started making a mental checklist of whom to call. She needed to reach-out to Nathan's day care. Then she needed to contact Miguel at the land and title office. She needed to get in touch with her parents, though maybe calling Mallory would result in a less hysterical response than speaking with her mother. *Who else?* She queried through other names.

A churning brain that could devise a list was a sign of clarity. Paige did need to give herself more credit.

"EASY DOES IT." Everett held his arm at a sharp right angle for his mother to leverage as he helped her to a standing position. "Take my hand." He extended his other to steady her.

"I'm a cancer patient, not a rising corpse." She pushed against Everett's forearm but didn't accept his hand.

"How does that new blood feel?" Everett's father waited for them both in the doorway of the hospital room.

Ruby's voice was full of pep. "Cool like a refrigerator coil."

"Don't those run hot?" Dale Mullins could be a critic.

"Would you like some assistance to your vehicle?" The

nurse reached to a hook on the wall and retrieved Ruby's purse. She held it out for Dale or Everett to grab.

"Honey," his mother responded, "if these two men can't get me to where I'm going, there's no hope for me."

"Fair enough." Everett took a step toward the middle-aged nurse, and she pulled her hand back slightly so Everett would have to get just a bit closer. She dropped her eyes and flashed a flirtatious smile.

No time for that. Everett wasn't in the mood to even entertain a female's attention.

He thanked the nurse instead and pivoted to join his mother, carrying her purse for her. The trio proceeded into the hallway, Ruby taking measured steps as her equilibrium adjusted to being upright after so long in a horizontal position.

When she made a joke about it, Everett's father responded, "And adjusting to that Zika inside of you."

"I swear, Dale . . ." If she had her purse in her hands, she likely would have swung it at him.

"I put your take-home papers in there." Everett's father pointed to the purse as he spoke to Ruby. "So you know what to do if that virus hits, just in case."

Let it go, Dad. Everett wasn't going to try to keep the peace between two adults acting like elementary school kids for the rest of the day.

They proceeded slowly through the hallway, across a center atrium, and around a receptionist area through the front. There was no need to exit any other way. "Do you want me to bring the car around? It's going to be hot when we step into that sunshine."

Everett offered to do it as well. Anything to minimize his mother's exertion would be helpful.

"I'll make it. That blood's perking me up already," she insisted, though Everett's couldn't see it. "Why don't you get me a bottle of water, though, for the ride home?" She wasn't thirsty initially after the procedure, but the nurse said she might be soon.

"All right." Everett passed his mother's purse to his father. Digging his hands into his front pocket, he found two folded dollar bills and held them up. "I'll see if the gift store has some."

The hospital gift shop and in-house florist held a surprising amount of items for a small hospital. Then again, big offerings in slim spaces were characteristic of much of rural Texas. Here, there was a quintessential array of cheerful presents for any hospitalization occasion. Cards, balloons, figurines, stuffed animals, books, and fresh floral arrangements stood at the ready. Medical center gift shops could be sources of bought cheer in the middle of tremendous agony and uncertainty, but there was still something a little awkward about being in one. They weren't a place people just stumbled into. Anyone who was inside of one was there with a purpose. There was no "just browsing" to be used as an excuse.

Everett had to wait behind a woman standing at the counter, signing a credit card receipt before he could pay for the water. He caught the clipped end of her conversation with the attendant.

"And these will be delivered to the recovery room, right?" The female's voice was laced with worry.

"Yes, we'll make sure they arrive." The attendant pointed to a tiny card on the counter. "Just seal that envelope and we can stick the message right in the center of the arrangement on a floral pick."

"Great." She picked up the card, sealed the edge with her tongue, and pressed the flap down. "Should I put the patient's name or his mother's?"

How sad. I wonder what's wrong? But as soon as he caught himself eavesdropping, he tried to snap himself out of the impolite practice.

Still, it wasn't like the space was big enough for him to avoid hearing the back and forth dialogue. The attendant continued. "That's up to you. The patient's name will be on the door, and we'll find the room number. But if the flowers are more for the mother, feel free to write her name on the card."

The woman buying the flowers scribbled a name on the front and slid the envelope and credit card receipt back across the counter. After a cordial exchange of gratitude, the woman exited, clearing the way for Everett. He was glad she didn't take long, for his mother must be close to the front entrance by now.

The attendant finished keying the transaction into the register and settled the receipt into the cash drawer before turning her attention to Everett. "May I help you?"

"Yes, just one water." He held up the bottle he had re-trieved from the grab-and-go cooler. The woman punched a series of keys until the total appeared on the digital screen facing Everett. He already had his two dollars ready, and he held out his hand to accept the change.

As his eyes cast downward, curiosity got the best of him. Everett read the name on the card, shuddering with recognition. Alarm rang in his head as dread replaced life inside his body. Suddenly cold, his hand seized in position, his limbs unable to move. His eyes were the only part of his body not paralyzed in total fear as he read the name "Paige Fredrick."

PAIGE PACED AND flicked her thumbnail with every step. A small distraction was the only way she could keep from having a complete meltdown.

"Do you want to sit?" Barry gestured to an open chair.

There were half a dozen in the private waiting area outside the operating room, and the two of them were the only ones occupying the space. Still, sitting next to Barry would be too coupled, too familiar. She had only collapsed into his arms earlier because she was distraught. She wasn't rushing back in complete abandon to his presence like some teenage girl. If she could rewind that moment, she might have rethought that move.

"No thanks. I'm happy here." But as soon as she heard her words, "happy" was overplaying it.

Paige was anything but happy. That word didn't exist for her, not today. Not for the past week. She froze in step to lift her hand as she pinched the bridge of her nose.

Barry continued his line of questioning. "Do you feel okay?"

Sure, never better. Sheesh. She wasn't going to dignify a stupid question by answering it.

Paige's silence had always grated on Barry, and she knew this. But rather than just let go, he filled the void with a baseless line about how Nathan would be just fine. Doctor's hands, or something like that.

She wasn't buying it.

At least not from Barry.

She wasn't in the mood to argue with him or critique the level of medical care. This was a procedure these professionals had probably performed dozens, maybe even hundreds, of times. Quality care was all that mattered.

And she had no complaints about the quality of what she saw.

The staff went out of their way to accommodate and to inform. Paige and Barry didn't have to be given access to this private OR waiting room, but they had been. The hospital didn't have to staff a nurse as a runner just to keep them informed, but they did. And Guadalupe Regional Medical Center Auxiliary volunteers didn't have to personally offer to place calls, contact clergy, or ask about public release of information to visitors, but they did.

All signs pointed toward positive, supportive care. And for that, she was grateful.

She was also glad to have another human nearby, as presence alone helped her manage her stress. Just being accountable in the company of Barry forced her not to lose it.

But even so, the close proximity brought to life Barry's idiosyncrasies, those that had surfaced during their marriage. They were deep reminders to Paige of how much he irked her, like his incessant need to fill silence with talking. Here, that didn't always work. He also had a managerial way of trying to stay one-up in everything. Whether he was even aware of this or not, Paige didn't know. She heard him pompously pontificate knowledge he learned in scrolling the internet on his phone about an appendix.

"Do you know the length of a typical human appendix?" he read, the phone screen illuminating his face.

"No," Paige stayed toneless. "And I don't care."

"You may care if you knew that . . ." And he proceeded to rattle off some fact he must have read on WebMD.

That doesn't make you an expert.

Another annoying characteristic of Barry in the waiting area was how he pretended to foresee the nurse's next comment before the door opened. "I bet she's going to tell us the fluid is clear."

Bet? This isn't Vegas.

But Paige bit her tongue. Barry was never going to change. Of that, she was certain.

Yet she could hope for change when it came to his role as a parent, and that tide was turning. He was co-parenting. All throughout today, he was doing exactly that. So if defining and operating in those roles could be their focus, they might just have a different future when it came to Nathan after all.

Paige's back was to the operating room door, so she heard the nurse before she saw her. "The surgery was a success!" The sweet words were what she had been waiting to hear. She clutched her chest in relief. "You're able to see Nathan now."

Paige wasted no time in turning and advancing toward the nurse. As she stepped through the doorway, she realized Barry was not at her back. She pivoted. Before she could even ask, he insisted, "You go on. Nathan will want to see his mother." And she didn't look at Barry long, but it sure looked like tears pooling in that father's eyes.

Nathan had a father. And he was present for his son when it mattered.

Maybe that counted for something.

Chapter Eighteen

B Y AFTERNOON, PAIGE was settled in a private recovery room with Nathan, still groggy from the anesthesia. There would be a lot of recovery, and no nurse would commit to an exact number of nights that would be required in the hospital.

"We'll base that on his recovery. Day-by-day," they all insisted.

She understood, though there was still fear when it came to anything unknown.

And, after major surgery, there were a lot of unknowns.

Paige did her best to question but not overdo it. She took notes. She tried to remember dosages and times. She called nurses by the names scripted on their nametags. She was exhausted, but she was going to be polite and responsible.

A steady stream of medical professionals paraded in and out of the room, Nathan at the center of their orbit. His vitals, the IV drip, his level of bodily elevation, the amount of liquid release pain medication. Everything was checked and checked.

Barry didn't stay in the room as Paige did, but he did stay in the hospital. She knew enough of his whereabouts, but she knew nothing of Danica's. She hadn't seen her, though she suspected Barry had talked with her. Besides, visitors were just now cleared for Nathan's room.

"Do you know where Danica is?" Paige asked Barry the loaded question the moment he returned to check on them midafternoon.

"In the waiting room. Where she's been." Barry delivered the answer as if the presence of her best-friend-turned-questionable-business-partner-with-her-ex-husband was perfectly normal.

Paige's jaw dropped. *How long has she been waiting? And what about her job?* Paige wasn't certain of the time, but it wasn't the end of the workday yet. *Did she even go in to the appraisal office today?*

"She has been here all day. She doesn't want to impose."

"Impose? That's ridiculous because she's my friend." The final word surprised her, escaping as naturally as it had for years, without the new label of "ex" she had assigned to Danica.

And the word must have surprised Barry. He pounced on an offer. "Do you want me to call her in here?"

Paige didn't know what she wanted, other than for Nathan to start showing real signs that his recovery was on track. She looked at the dry erase board mounted to the wall where the nurses wrote their names to help patients keep track of who was coming in and out, especially as shifts changed. Was that only to keep names organized, or was it a necessity when minds started to falter like hers was beginning to do? The stress, the fatigue, and the worry were all culminating. How much longer would Paige even be able to read

AUDREY WICK

that board with clarity?

"Paige?" Barry cut in. "Do you want me to tell her it's okay to come in for a visit?"

Paige looked across to Nathan, drowsy yet calm. The IV fluid dripped, and his limp body lay in recovery mode. He was still beautiful in her eyes, always her baby. "Sure."

Barry shuffled out of the room, and a few moments later a female voice replaced his voice. "Paige?" Danica's head poked sheepishly through the doorway, her feet still planted in the hallway.

Paige tore her eyes from Nathan long enough to see her, an odd mixture of betrayal and familiarity whirling inside her like a noisy blender she could only turn off if she made a decision on what she wanted her to do.

Taking the high road, she prompted, "You can come in now." She stood as Danica entered, dropped a duffel bag to the floor, and approached her.

Danica made the move first by extending her arms, and Paige was so in need of a friend that she followed her lead into an embrace.

"Oh, Paige." Danica repeated over and over, gripping Paige as if their separation had been for years. "I'm a terrible friend, and I owe you the biggest apology. And explanation. Oh, Paige." She repeated until Paige stilled her with a reply of her own.

"Not now," she leveled. *I don't want to get into this.*

Clandestine dealings with Barry were taking a backseat to Nathan's recovery. She still couldn't believe the former, but she needed to believe the latter. She held onto Danica, trying to extract strength and understanding from their peaceful embrace. Siphoning, too, any ounce of support she could in turn use to help her with Nathan, she only let go when she determined she had.

There were questions to ask of Danica—there were questions to ask of Barry—but now wasn't the time. Tough conversations would happen, but they could be saved for later. And they needed to be. Right now, the world revolved around Nathan's recovery. And to help Paige stay strong for that, she just needed a friend.

She needed Danica.

"I'm going to help," Danica swore. "Everything, anything." She held Paige at an arm's length, squeezing her shoulders and promising her with eye contact.

Danica stayed through another round of nurses' passes, moving the duffel bag she brought from the floor to a pull-out drawer.

"What's that?" Paige didn't recognize the bag.

"It's one of my extras." Danica pushed the drawer closed. "Just some stuff you might want for later. Little toiletries I had and a change of clothes." The day had unfolded hour by hour, and Paige wasn't thinking ahead to the evening. But knowing Danica had brought relief to Paige.

Danica settled in to a chair in the corner of the room while Paige stayed close to Nathan. They spoke in low tones to minimize the noise for Nathan, though there was plenty of shuffling, sorting, and beeping at the hands of the nurses and the equipment. As Danica sat, Paige was able to provide an overview of the surgery. When Paige finished talking,

Danica proceeded to tell her who was informed of the emergency and what she had taken care of throughout the day.

Paige's eyes popped at realizing the lengths to which Danica had been making calls, fielding others, driving to retrieve items, and generally running interception on all things Paige and Nathan related.

Paige was stunned. "How did you know to do all of this?"

Her one-word response was the man at the heart of prior pain for Paige and now at the heart of the week of tension with Danica. "Barry."

Barry had been in-and-out of the waiting area and the recovery room often. "So he was telling you?"

"Only so I could tell everyone else and not say anything that wasn't accurate." She popped the snap that held together the two sides of her purse and brought out a notebook. "I've been keeping track of who knows, how many calls have been made." She flipped to a page with a penciled chart of names, columns, and checkmarks. "Then I've written specific questions people have that can either be answered whenever you feel up to it or ignored completely. Tell me what you want when you're ready."

She pointed to some words Paige couldn't read. There were so many people to call, and she was sure they would have lots more questions. She still did herself. So having someone else be the one to handle those, at least on day one, was an incredible gift.

Danica flipped to another hand drawn chart in her notebook. "And I put together a list of your neighbors who have agreed to take care of things for the next few days. Watch the house, hold your mail, water the lawn if it needs it. That sort of thing." Danica was in complete crisis management mode. "Then here's a schedule of people who have agreed to deliver a home-cooked meal to you and Nathan every day for the next two weeks, once you guys are released."

"But that's not going to happen for days."

"I've covered that." She retrieved her phone and slid the screen to her digital calendar. "It doesn't matter what day, but the volunteer chefs will get started just as soon as you need them. The last thing you should be worried about is stocking the pantry and making meals. So that will be covered for you."

Paige could hardly believe the words Danica was saying. *You've done this? All of this?* Paige held out her fingers to touch the notebook for herself. Danica placed it in her hands, flipped to the page entitled "Meal Commitments."

It's real.

She glanced down at the names of people who were listed. Neighbors not just on either side of her house but from throughout the neighborhood, parents from Nathan's day care, women from her church, members of the yoga group Paige hadn't attended since before she gave birth. Danica's aunt was listed, and so were a couple of her friends who Paige knew of by name but didn't really know in person. Miguel was even written, with playful asterisks and an exclamation point after the words "Boss Man" next to his first name.

So many names. "We're going to have food for days." Paige couldn't even wrap her mind around such generosity.

"Eighteen families of volunteers, to be exact." Danica pointed to a series of tally marks at the bottom right of the page. "But more if you want it because some people already said they can bring a second meal. Two weeks' worth was on the shy side of my estimate."

Amazing. A small gesture to one meant so much to another.

"And if you're not home or don't eat it or whatever, we'll freeze it. I've already made myself a note to get some plastic containers and gallon zipper bags from the grocery store. And whatever else you need, tell me."

"Nothing," Paige whispered, still in utter disbelief at the efficiency and kindness of all Danica had spent the day doing. Lingering questions took a backseat to the here and now, and here—now—she had her friend. She reached across the space between them, clasped hands, and squeezed their friendship tight.

ALREADY PAIGE'S PERSONAL will and her skill as a parent were challenged. There was a lot of rest for Nathan, but little rest for Paige as she kept watch over his frail body as if she were holding a vigil.

"He's progressing well," one nurse said.

"Remarkable color to his skin for someone so fresh out of

surgery," another offered.

"Vitals are steady," several noted.

Compliments and optimistic remarks reigned. How much of that were nurses supposed to do, and how much of what they said was actually true? Paige couldn't sort the difference, so she just smiled and continued to thank them for their work.

Barry poked his head in around seven o'clock. "I know dinner was brought." He nodded to a courtesy tray with covered dishes Paige had barely touched. "But do you want me to pick up something?"

Paige should eat, but she wasn't hungry. "I'm fine." She would nibble on the mixed vegetables or the few packages of crackers that were part of the hospital meal later if she wanted something to settle her stomach.

Barry had asked about spending the night in the hospital, but Paige didn't want that. It was hard enough for one person to occupy the space beside Nathan with all of the activity from the nurses and with the size of the machinery. Aside from that, it would be too uncomfortable to have her ex sleeping—or watching them—in the same space.

Still, she was glad he offered.

"I'm going to be back first thing in the morning, six a.m."

That's awfully early.

"That way you can go home if you need, have a break, whatever." Again, Paige wasn't thinking past each hour, but those around her continued to prove that they were. "And I'm bringing you hot coffee. None of this hospital brew."

She smiled, a bit of unexpected warmth filling her heart at the thoughtful gesture.

"But I'll be back one more time before nighttime, okay?" He really wasn't asking permission, and that was fine. It was his parental right, and Paige was glad to have routine assistance. "In another hour or two, so see you then." Then he stepped close to Nathan's bed, leaned over the railing, and placed a careful kiss on his forehead. "Bye, Nate-Nate." But Nathan was in such a deep sleep, he didn't respond.

When Barry left, Paige leaned her head back in the chair that had become her permanent perch and closed her eyes. She couldn't sleep, but if nothing else, she wanted to still her body long enough to trick herself into thinking she had. Every bit of energy she could store would be useful in facing whatever the night brought. It was only a matter of time before Nathan's body started reacting in a greater way to the pain of recovery, and one of the nurses had already predicted by midnight the trials would hit. Even for a two-year-old, awareness of his discomfort was imminent, so Paige needed to be ready for that.

Paige was startled by a knocking on the doorway to the room. The door hadn't been closed because the staff was in and out, so the formality of the sound stirred her back into the present.

Expecting Barry, she invited, "It's fine."

But Barry wasn't there.

"Everett." She breathed, blinking back surprise.

How?

And why?

When?

Her tongue twisted in her mouth, trying to find its way into articulating something. "What?" She finally managed aloud.

Everett took a step and paused in the frame of the doorway. "Hi, Paige."

That really is you.

"May I come in?" Everett looked as casually handsome as ever in a chocolate brown tee and denim jeans.

"Sure, yeah." Paige straightened her posture, pushed her legs together at the knees, and tried to finger comb the back of her hair that was in chair-induced knots. She must have looked a fright.

"You're beautiful," Everett offered, as if sensing her self-consciousness.

The surprise of him and his words weighed heavily. "How did you know I was here?"

"Small town." He didn't add anything else aside from "News travels."

She tilted her head back into the chair cushion. "Great."

"Oh, no. Not like that." He countered, hastily backpedaling with his words. "I just mean, I heard. Or, I, um . . ." He looked to Nathan as he finished his thought. "I saw."

Paige was as confused as ever, but her curiosity took a temporary backseat to the focus on Nathan. She stared over him.

Everett spoke again. "This is your son?"

"Yes." She righted her gaze and patted the boy's exposed arm. "This is Nathan," she confirmed, motherly pride in her voice.

"I am so sorry," Everett began, "to hear about all of this. And to know you are, well . . ." He lowered his head and scratched the back of his neck before meeting her eyes again. Nervous words continued to congeal in various forms of outreach and apology at the current situation, sincerity shining with the attempt.

But whether his concern was for Nathan, for Paige, or for their stalled start as a couple, she wasn't sure. Either way, it was like inhaling a refreshingly cool breeze for Paige to be able to see Everett face-to-face.

He didn't get too close to either the hospital bed or Paige's chair, but, to her surprise, he did poise a gift bag on the lower edge of the mattress against the railing. "I thought your son might enjoy what's in there. Or maybe you could enjoy it with him."

"Thank you." She shifted in her seated position to the edge of the chair and looped the bag's handle beneath two fingers to bring it into her lap. "Shall I open it now? Or do you want him to see it later?"

"Now is fine." He gestured with a sweep of his hand. "Go ahead. It's not much, but it's something I thought would be appropriate."

Paige separated the handle and pushed aside dainty sheets of tissue paper to glimpse a glossy, navy cover of a hardback children's book. There was a classic look to the selection, though Paige couldn't put her finger on identification until she pulled the book from the bag and took in the full cover.

A cartoon drawing of the Eiffel Tower loomed over a nun leading yellow-attired children in two straight lines, walking through a tree-lined street. The scene was quintessentially Paris and quintessentially a children's classic. "*Madeline*," she read from the title, though she recognized the book from her own memory long ago.

Everett spoke with care. "The story is about a child who has appendicitis. She has the surgery and then is proud of her scar."

The memory of the actual storyline came rushing back to Paige. There was a hospital, and the cadence of the rhymed lines throughout the book rang through her childhood memories. But appendicitis? Really? Had she never recognized that before in the tale of *Madeline*?

"I read it to make sure," Everett admitted quietly. "It's a sweet story. Happy ending," he added quickly. "The girl gets well, and—well, now I'm just sort of spoiling it for you, aren't I?"

Paige clutched the book in one hand and held the flattened palm of the other across her chest. She countered in thanks. "You're not spoiling anything. You're really not."

For tonight, even through the uncertainty and pain of the day, mother and son were going to get to enjoy the bedtime story portion of their nighttime routine. A flood of gratitude rushed forth at Everett's small gesture, something so touching and grand even he couldn't have known the meaning it would hold to her. Or maybe he did. Regardless, Paige rose, stepped toward him, and swung her arms around him in one, great hug of overwhelming appreciation and utter exhaustion.

Everett could have frozen. He could have simply stood still. Or he could have turned and left. Instead, he did what Paige didn't expect but desperately needed from someone whom she cared about.

Everett met Paige where she was. He stood tall and strong, his broad shoulders cushioning her as she came close. She turned her head to the side to avoid his eyes as tears formed. But instead of pulling back, he pulled her in.

And hugged back.

Chapter Nineteen

S MALL TOWNS HAVE a way of surprising.

Rural towns like Seguin, even when their population swelled a bit, retained a congruence enviable to those in bigger cities. It was why so many from the nearby metropolitan areas of San Antonio and Austin frequently escaped to Seguin for weekends, holidays, and festivals. The town—and the people—held a certain charm.

Everett had left Seguin, but it never left him. There was always a piece of the town that he carried, even in his life in Amarillo. This was his old stomping ground—his school, the farm, the streets.

And then there were the people and the memories, old haunts from his past that surfaced again every time he visited. This extended trip was no exception.

His old haunt was Paige.

How he came to fold into her in their brief time together wasn't something he could explain. He didn't want to try. There was so much to like about her—grace, humor, intelligence, beauty, kindness. But more than anything, it was her personality, for he enjoyed feeling alive in her presence.

But his timeline for being in the area was expiring.

His mother's blood transfusion was complete, and he

had given her the one-on-one attention she needed from her only son. Additionally, he had helped at the farm by easing his father's responsibilities.

Then there was Paige.

This much he understood. There are important bonds between parent and child.

He saw it now, in the way Paige looked across the bed at Nathan. Her eyes never left him for long, and she doted without saying a word. There was no love lost even in a crisis.

Her love was beautiful to witness.

Everett couldn't fault her for having a son, for being divorced. Those weren't his to judge or dissect or try to understand. She, though, had kept those hidden. So what did that say about her? Maybe her heart just wasn't available.

Paige stowed the book on the bedside table next to the adjustable hospital bed. Folding the bag and tissue paper, she flattened them and slid them into the top drawer. Nathan stirred at her movement, releasing a moan. "Hey, sweetie." She bent nearer to him and stroked the top of his hair, combing it with her fingers across his forehead. "He feels a little cool." She looked at Everett.

I'm no nurse. Everett didn't know the first thing about toddler temperatures.

Paige proceeded to talk as if he did. "His body was so warm all afternoon. This is different." She spoke with the certainty of a mother in touch with her intuition. "Can you see if there's a blanket in one of those drawers behind you?"

Everett spun to face a built-in wardrobe, hospital style.

Smooth casters helped each drawer roll with ease. The first one he tried was empty, but the second one had a small knit blanket and an extra pillow. "Bingo." He held up both.

"I think just the blanket for him." Everett stretched to pass it to her. "But I'll take that pillow for myself tonight."

"Are you staying?" There wasn't even an extra bed in the room.

"This chair leans back. I'll be fine." She dismissed the accommodations as if they were no inconvenience at all. Everett, however, had spent enough time in and out of medical facilities over the past month with his mother to know that they were.

He watched as Paige carefully unfolded the blanket and lay it gently over the sheet that gingerly covered the small boy's body. A plush blue giraffe got a sweet and careful tucking-in as well. Nathan moaned another expression and then opened his eyes. He looked straight at Paige and whimpered in a way that probably only scratched the surface of the pain his body must be sustaining.

"Medicine is wearing off," Paige explained. "Staff said it would happen in waves." Then her words shifted back to Nathan where they belonged. She leaned close to resume stroking his hair and sung a soothing series of "there, there, there" assurances.

Learning about Paige's son by complete accident in the hospital gift shop, Everett wasn't even sure if he should act on the news. But he was glad he had. Seeing Paige with her son made him understand why she wouldn't share him with just anyone.

"Maybe I'll read the book to him now?"

Everett wasn't certain if she were asking permission or telling him of her intent. He nodded either way as she added, "Before the next round of nurses. It might help, you know?"

Everett hadn't a clue.

"Hearing my voice and just reading. We do that. Every night." She bit her bottom lip in a tight expression that showed both fragility and vulnerability—and beauty.

You're a beautiful mother. Everett recognized those qualities, but articulating them aloud wasn't appropriate. At least he didn't think so. Instead, he took her words as his cue to leave. Everett wished her well for the night, then told Nathan from afar to enjoy the book and get better soon. He excused himself out of the room and back into an evening spent in Seguin where he would again be alone.

No Catherine.

No Paige.

But thoughts of both.

FOUR DAYS IN the hospital was four days too many.

Nathan cried.

Moaned.

Ached.

And so did Paige.

She hadn't been this beat since he was a newborn. When Nathan was an infant, there were so many nights of little sleep followed by days where Paige would operate on fumes. Getting through each twenty-four hour period meant not collapsing before the end of it. These days in the hospital were like that.

Hours clicked by, but there was never notice for what they would bring. Nathan's toddler body was having to relearn how to operate with an internal organ missing.

There goes any progress on early potty training. Paige had resigned herself to one step forward and two steps back, given the surgery. That was just one of many challenges.

Barry peppered his presence in person at the hospital and on the phone, not only asking for updates but also asking what he could do. He was compassionate, and that was exactly what Paige needed him to be. Danica, to her credit and Paige's relief, was a stalwart friend though supportive calls and offers, then stepped aside only when Mallory arrived on the third day from Santa Fe.

"I'm here. You've got me for a week!" Her big sister always made an entrance. She loved Nathan, and she had been especially supportive with Paige through the divorce. Not always understanding or complimentary, but supportive.

She was, after all, a big sister, who still thought she knew best—about everything.

Mallory moved with a sound at every turn. She wore bangles and cuffs around her wrist in such volume they looked like parts of a superhero costume. Layered necklaces adorned her collar, and dangling earrings hung like tiny chandeliers from each lobe. To say she had a jewelry fetish was putting it mildly. Paige was convinced Mallory moved to

Santa Fe strictly for the sterling silver and turquoise.

Her older sister took it upon herself to organize the growing stack of cards, paperwork, and notes Paige had built into a squat tower on Nathan's bedside table. "Do you do this at work?" Mallory chastised.

"I'm not going to answer that." *But, yes, a leaning tower is one method I have of organizing. And it's so effective that I got a promotion, thank you very much.*

Mallory breezed on. She righted and shuffled until the arrangement was to her satisfaction. Then she blew her hurricane winds of organization to the wardrobe. "Nathan's going to need looser pajama bottoms than this." She held up a snuggly pair with footsies, a pair Danica had retrieved from the house. "That's a big wound, and elastic will do it no good when it's time to get out of that gown."

"I don't even know if that's going to happen tonight." Paige hadn't heard the nurses suggest anything of the sort. She was glad Danica had brought some things just in case. And how was she to know?

"Danica brought these?" Mallory was already wadding them and stuffing them back into the drawer.

"Yes. Clothes for us both, actually."

"I see." She wasted no time with a quick personal interrogation. "And Barry?"

Paige didn't know where this was going. "What about Barry?"

She cut right to what she wanted to know. "How has he helped?"

Paige didn't want to talk over Nathan as if he couldn't

hear, even when he was groggy and napping. And talking about his father—using his first name—wasn't normal either. To Nathan, his dad was Dad. Paige rolled her shoulders, answering her sister's prying question with a general, "He's helped."

"Humph." Her sister always huffed when she didn't approve of something in a conversation.

"Not now, Mallory." Paige wanted to have a deeper conversation with her, and she could even use a bit of her sisterly guidance in strategizing a next move with Everett. Every time Paige thought of him, a lump formed in her chest, as if it were moving in and paying rent until she could decide whether to swallow it or speak out about it. That was the problem with Everett—stay silent or speak?

"I can have a talk with Barry, you know." The defensive edge in Mallory's voice communicated her seriousness.

"Not necessary." Paige didn't need Mallory making their budding co-parenting relationship worse by any sort of intervention, no matter how well-intentioned it might be. "Just sit, okay?" Paige motioned to the extra chair a nurse had brought in earlier in the morning when Barry returned. Now, it was being used on a rotating basis for whoever else visited. That included Danica, Miguel, Nathan's main teacher at the day care, and one person she still held out hope would come again.

Everett.

But had he come for Paige? For Nathan? He had surely been in and out of facilities with his cancer-stricken mother so often that he must have known the joy a simple visit could bring. So was the late evening stop and the book for Nathan all just a sympathy visit and nothing on-track with what they had been sharing as a potential couple?

Paige didn't know.

She couldn't know.

Tired people didn't think straight. And tired people were prone to making mistakes, mistakes in action and mistakes in judgement. Maybe that was all Everett's visit was, a misunderstood gesture she had read far too much into to think he cared.

As Mallory sorted the room, Paige tried to sort her feelings. One of those tasks, however, was more hopeless than the other.

Nathan was released from Guadalupe Regional Medical Center on a Friday morning amid balloons and well wishes. A small fever setback delayed the release, but he was finally cleared on day five.

Paige drove him home, but Mallory sat in the backseat with him. The car seat was understandably uncomfortable for Nathan, the belts crisscrossing tender areas that were still swollen. The nurses were well aware and had bandaged his midsection enough for one car ride. Once he got home in his bed surrounded by his things, they insisted, he'd sleep better than he had been.

And Paige was looking forward to better sleep herself.

Mallory helped Paige and Nathan get situated in the house, Danica came by with the first delivery of promised food, and a neighbor brought her a stack of saved mail. It was an instantaneous flurry of activity, people, and questions. The difference here was that there was no medical staff to help her field them.

Nathan had a steady dose of pain medicine, and he was sound asleep less than half an hour after their arrival. That prompted the neighbor to leave, and the volunteer chef wasn't far behind. Finally on her personal turf with a little bit of home field advantage, Paige was strong enough to corner Danica with the question that had weighed heavily on her all week.

The need to know eclipsed holding back any longer. "So what's going on with you and Barry?"

Silence stole the space, the moment of truth demanding to be addressed now.

Danica counted with a cover. "It's not what you think."

Paige was over playing games, and she wasn't about to waste time on friendship psychoanalysis. "Just tell me."

"Financial, that's it." She held up her hands as if she were the target of a bank robbery. "Look, I didn't want to get into this at the hospital, and I didn't even want to tell you about the development partnership until everything was—"

"It doesn't matter. You didn't tell me at all," Paige reminded her.

"Fair enough," she conceded, balling her hands. "That was stupid of me, and I'm sorry about that." She rolled her fingers across her thumb as if the action could help her sharpen her words. "Barry approached me. At the appraisal district, he came in to get property tax information." A confession flooded forth with details about the land. "He wants to develop it as Cinnamon Ridge Estates. Homestead lots for young professionals. You know, the kind of thing that's trending in waves all around greater San Antonio."

Tart words sprang. "I know the market." Paige and Danica were, after all, both in the land business. They spoke the same language there. In fact, she had that with Barry, too, in his experience as a home inspector.

"Barry has wanted to get a foothold in something more than residential inspection."

Paige was ready to pounce all over that. "I know my ex-husband—"

"Which you know is something he's wanted to do for a long, long time."

The two weren't sharing anything that they didn't each know privately. Barry's desire for a second career—and his lack of financial means to get started with something on his own—was a source of contention for them in their marriage. But she hadn't ever shared specifics with Danica.

"You have every right to be upset."

Upset is one way to put it.

"We just got to talking, and between us both, it made more sense. I knew what land was a smart buy, and he needed a partner." Danica didn't stop there. "One development, one shot. That's it. We'll both see how it goes, but I'm not in this beyond the one project. Hopefully we'll turn a profit. Cash for me, seed money for him. Win, win."

Paige couldn't doubt the practicality of it. The location was perfect, the taxes were low, and Seguin's population was on the upswing. But what didn't make sense was keeping it a secret. "Why didn't you tell me?"

"I should have. And I was going to. But the timing didn't seem right with your divorce. I'm sorry about that. Truly, Paige, I am. It's just that this happened fast." She emphasized the speed by a snap of her fingers. "You know that about the real estate market."

I know a lot about the real estate market. Paige and Danica peppered real estate jabber into their conversations just like they did an occasional mention of an infinity scarf or a tulip skirt.

"So he needed to move quickly if he wanted this to work. I saw that. And I could help."

"Without jeopardizing your job?"

Danica raised an eyebrow. "I'm a partnership investor for real estate, not co-owner of a meth house."

"What's that about meth?" Mallory entered from the garage carrying two reusable grocery bags full to the brim that she dropped in the hallway before triangulating into their conversation.

"Nothing." Paige would take this up again at another time.

She wasn't ready to let it go fully, but she was ready to move on. Danica had shown through actions the past few days her friendship meant more than a business dealing. And they had been friends long enough to know theirs shouldn't be defined by one rough patch. After all, what relationships didn't have those? Paige looked to Mallory, with whom she had weathered many such mistakes and misunderstandings in the past, yet they had a strong relationship now. Paige wasn't ready to throw away all she and Danica had, and Danica clearly wasn't either.

Paige motioned both of them in close. "Group hug," she announced.

They obliged, though Mallory broke from the hug first. "No time to lose. Got to put this stuff away." She shuffled to the bags and bent over them. "So much stuff ended up at that hospital . . ."

Mallory busied herself with sorting the various items that made it home from the five-day stay. Danica reminded Paige of the hot meal waiting on her counter that was the first of her two weeks of promised delivery service to ease her responsibilities at home. But she knew Nathan's napping was temporary. "Go eat that while you can." She shooed Paige into the kitchen as she let herself out the front door with a standing "Call me" offer for whatever else Paige needed.

Peeling back the foil of the mystery dish, Paige's mouth watered with the combination of smells that she easily identified as king ranch casserole.

Once Mallory arrived back, she took the lead in spooning a hearty helping of the Texas chicken, tortilla chip, green chile, and cheddar cheese specialty onto a plate while Paige poured them two glasses of sweet iced tea. "I don't make this often enough." Mallory inhaled the savory aroma of the warm dish.

"I never do." Paige took her lead in serving a generous

portion for herself. They each carried their plate to the bar where the glasses of tea were set.

"Kind of hard to cook for one, you know?" Mallory had been single all of her adult life, but Paige's singlehood cooking was a new adjustment. Realizing, Mallory pushed the conversation back on herself to add no further discomfort to her sister. "I just mean by the time I roast a whole chicken and debone it for something like this . . . well, it's lots of work for me."

"It's fine, Mallory." Paige settled atop the bar stool. She was getting used to cutting comments that people didn't even realize might hurt. Sometimes people just spoke without thinking.

She had certainly been guilty of that enough times in her adult life. Like with Everett in the grocery store.

Sheesh, am I ever going to stop thinking about him? Previously, Everett's memory had silted like fine sand to the bottom of her Mason jar high school memory past. But seeing him back in Seguin as an adult brought that sand to the surface. So too did his arrival at the hospital. Now everything was muddied, and Paige couldn't see clearly enough to the other side of what any relationship with Everett might be.

What she could see to the other side of was next week. Mallory reminded her of her commitment to staying with her to help with Nathan, a sacrifice on his sister's part for which she was immensely grateful. "Through Wednesday," Mallory confirmed. "Got to head back to Santa Fe in the morning." She set her fork on the side of her plate, her bangle bracelets jingling as she righted the silver pendant that hung on a long leather chord.

"I know." Paige took a satisfying bite of casserole. Danica had dinner delivery covered, Miguel was lenient about her missing work, and Barry had offered to do whatever he could, short of invoking the divorce decree custody arrangement for taking Nathan to his house. Transporting Nathan there wouldn't have made sense anyway. She and Barry would deal with some shared visitation at a later date. He had already made a lot of progress in stepping up as the father Nathan needed, and Paige was glad for the budding relationship and their new co-parenting approach to his care. Hard as it was to admit, her life was in more order now than it had been for the past year.

Chapter Twenty

SUNDAY WOULD HAVE been like any other, had it not been for the call.

Nathan had recovered much of his personality over the weekend. He was engaging in play, laughing with Paige, and regaining his appetite for more than just popsicles and applesauce. His movements were still cautious, and the doctors had said they likely would be, even as his body recovered. Muscle memory was slow to return with children who had surgery, so he was favoring measured, safe movements. Paige was glad, as it helped her to keep a better eye on him.

Her parents called every day to check in, and several other friends and family did the same. Posting on social media seemed too much of a broadcast, and Paige had learned through her divorce not to overshare. Family matters were private, and if loved ones wanted to know, they could sacrifice time to make an individual call to ask.

In the hour before lunch, Paige saw a number flash on her cell phone screen and assumed it was another family member wanting an update, someone whose name wasn't programed into her phone. Calls around lunch were popular yesterday, and she suspected already that they would be today from family who didn't want to cut into Nathan's nap time.

Although he was sort of cat napping all the time.

She slid the phone and pressed it to her ear. "Hello?"

"This probably isn't the most convenient time," the caller started, by way of preemptive apology, "but can we talk, Paige?" Her name sounded smooth from the male caller's lips, though the rest of the words didn't.

She recognized the voice, having committed the contralto sound to memory over the past few weeks. It was the same voice from high school, but with a mature edge. The voice whether in sound or text was one she was beginning to relish, like a fine wine that she wanted to taste regularly. "Sure, Everett." She enjoyed saying his name when she could. Since this was their first ear to ear phone call, she wasn't even sure how his name would taste on the line.

Good.

Everett's call started like others she received. He asked for a requisite update about Nathan. Paige didn't imagine Everett knew much about parenting—or appendicitis—so she just gave a broad stroke answer. "Home since Friday. An adjustment, but the surgery was a success."

"That must be a relief."

You have no idea. A life turned upside down was righting itself, and having Nathan on a recovery path was a part of that. But even to someone like Everett with whom their lives had been absent from one another since high school, she didn't need to acknowledge the obvious.

Nathan's wellbeing cleared, his attention turned to Paige.

"And you? How are you?"

There were so many different ways she could respond to that, but she chose the first one which popped into her mind and mouth. "Tired."

She could hear Everett's understanding through the phone. "I can't imagine. Late nights and lots of keeping watch?"

"That's part of it." But would anyone really understand how lightly she was sleeping, on edge that Nathan would need her? Or when she did fall asleep, terrible nightmares came that shook her awake before she realized the images didn't apply to her reality? Surgery, parenthood, and too many days spent in a hospital caused some shaky reactions only time back home developing a routine could correct. That was her focus now. "I just want to get him back to normal and make sure I do what he needs. If he were older, he'd be able to tell me what he needs. But being so young, I still have to read and anticipate what he can't say."

Everett was quiet, and Paige didn't know if he were processing her answer or forming what he wanted to communicate next. Was finding out about Nathan why he called? If so, he wasn't making a motion to end the conversation. In a prompt to find out, she started again. "So is everything okay with you? How's your mother?"

"Oh, much better." He launched into an overview of her week, success of her blood transfusion, and the end to his semipermanent stay to take care of her through the past month.

"When you are going back to Amarillo?" Paige knew that

would happen. Temporary care of his mother was Everett's plan all along, though he hadn't been clear with Paige on which day would be his last at the farm.

"That's actually why I'm calling."

So that's the reason. Paige knew there was more.

Everett continued with unhurried words. "And I need to say this so that I can go back with peace. And give that to you too."

Paige could feel her face twist in confusion. "You have something to get off your chest?"

"A lot, actually." He breathed the words in relief, as if that small admission alone made him feel better.

"Okay." Paige wasn't one to delay. "So go for it."

If she could have seen Everett, perhaps it would have been easier to sense this wasn't an admission he was making lightly. And it wasn't one for which he was trying to bait her for sympathy or turn attention on him. Quite the opposite, his hesitation and quiet tone proved this was as hard for him to say as it was for Paige to hear.

Deafening silence stole the line before Everett summoned the courage to reveal, "Two years ago, my wife passed away."

CATHERINE HAD BEEN the love of Everett's life. A tragic vehicular accident claimed her just shy of their second anniversary. They were headed on their path toward happiness forever, but it was cut short through no fault of Everett's or Catherine's.

Tragedy struck. And it knew no bounds.

Having his wife ripped from him nearly sent Everett over the edge himself. There was no good way to deal, no pacing other than what he created for himself. It involved work—a lot of work—interspersed with a few trips to the Netherlands he jumped on because nothing else was keeping him stateside. Honing his expertise with water wells served as a healing distraction. He also made a few trips home to the family farm in Seguin to be with his parents. But holiday celebrations, weekend vacations, dinner invitations, or any activity that remotely resembled dating another woman was just too painful.

When Paige shocked Everett with her widowhood remark in the grocery store, there was no appropriate way to chorus with "me too." But he did understand pain. And he knew what not to say to someone in that position, so he kept his mouth shut. There was a sensitivity that surrounded tragedy and personal recovery, and he honored and respected that.

But learning Paige wasn't widowed had been a blow. Death wasn't something to joke about.

"I couldn't tell you I was a widower when you did." He needed to be straight. "I don't enjoy talking about the loss of my wife."

He could hear the wheels of recognition slowly turning through Paige's mind, her words whisper quiet. "So you're widowed?"

He cringed. Everett hated the word. Any form of it was

bad, but when it was used as a label, it carried the greatest weight. When it described him, the word morphed into identification, not just something outwardly applied but something inward. It was as if "widowed" had come to define who he was the past two years, and that had been long enough. He couldn't be that forever, and he didn't want to be. He just had no idea how to move forward.

And then came Paige.

The girl who was his simmering crush in high school had now become a woman who affected him just the same. Seeing her was a breath of fresh air. And talking to her made him breathe easy. They had a shared past, and they had shared pain.

Sort of.

Divorce must carry its own level of hurt. Not exactly widower pain, but emotion and adjustment of its own. However, as much as he enjoyed sharing with Paige and feeling normal again—for the first time since Catherine's death—he couldn't continue. What was the point? He was in Amarillo. She was in Seguin. And she had a son, a son who desperately needed her attention and focus, especially with his recovery. Everett didn't need to be stealing time away from either of them.

Perhaps under different circumstances, his unrequited crush could be given a fair shot. But they were too far apart in too many ways.

He said the words aloud even though they tasted sour. "Yes, I'm widowed." He had come to accept the hand he was dealt, and the word he hated was part of that. "We were married almost two years. Catherine." Even after so long, the admission still choked him.

"I am so sorry." That was the standard reaction he received. But Paige's next line wasn't. "That must be difficult, and you must be strong."

Most people expressed sorrow and that was it. They didn't extend a compliment.

Especially one of strength.

He never considered himself as such. *Weak is more like it.*

Catherine was part of who he was. He couldn't stop thinking about her, especially in quiet moments. And he feared when he did, he'd lose her all over again. He had been cautious with his heart, guarding it against further pain. He also didn't want to use its space for what was otherwise reserved for his wife. There was personal guilt in that.

But then came Paige.

Moments and conversations with her were a healing salve. He welcomed them. But he couldn't let them go too far. There was risk in that.

Everett got back to the business of why he called Paige in the first place. "I just wanted you to know I'm closing up my commitments here, and I'm heading back to Amarillo." The silence that followed underscored the finality of the words.

Paige cleared her throat with an answer. "Oh. Okay."

Is that all? He didn't know what he expected, but it was something more than that. *What's in your heart, Paige?*

Everett couldn't reach through the phone to see her, and he couldn't channel into her. As much as he might have wanted, he also knew he wasn't being fair because Paige couldn't see him. And while he had let his emotions be tapped by her, his conscious choice today was not to react to them. He was going to keep the flow of his emotions contained. Life was simply safer that way.

ONE SETBACK AFTER another.

Paige Fredrick could not catch a break.

All she wanted to do post-divorce was get her feet squarely under her, stand tall in her changing life. She wanted the compass of her life to point straight, not spin in confusion. Some strides at work, some improvements around the house, some simple joys—her life was pacing forward. She was headed in a positive direction.

Until speedbump Everett appeared in the aisle of the grocery store.

She never intended to lie to him. She never intended to have more than a passing conversation with him. She wasn't in the market for a boyfriend when they met, fresh from court. A relationship was the last thing on her mind.

But life had never asked what she wanted.

Everett wasn't asking either.

He was firm on the phone. He announced his decision to go back to Amarillo, which wasn't a surprise in the general sense because she knew it was coming. Instead, it was a surprise in the more specific sense.

She hadn't prepared herself to hear it today.

There would be no final lunch date. No stroll in the park. No face-to-face goodbye. She wasn't going to get to see him off in a way other than with the click of a phone call.

Perhaps that was why the anticlimactic end to whatever was starting between them—and Paige still wasn't sure—hurt like a scorpion sting. Everett Mullins wasn't a stranger, but he entered her adult life without warning. Now he was exiting without one either.

Or much of one. A phone call? Really?

I guess it's better than a text.

She wished him well, and he extended the same back to her. Simple goodbyes were their end punctuation.

As she ended the call, she held the phone as if it were a lifeline to him and their time together. In many ways, it was. Paige allowed herself a moment to capture a few images in her mind that formed a visual storybook of their reconnection. The first flash of recognition after the grocery store blackout, the smile and left dimple that broke his ruggedly handsome face, his humor across the table at lunch, the surprise flowers delivered to work, nearly sharing a kiss in the park, seeing him exit his truck looking breathtakingly gorgeous when they met at the courthouse, that hospital hug. These would be the images she chose to keep.

She could also scroll through their shared texts to bring a smile whenever the need arose. Those would help.

Paige had always made the best out of a bad situation. She was sentimental through and through. She had been in high school, and neither age nor parenthood changed that.

After sealing the memories, she wasn't going to dissect their last conversation or dwell in a fantasyland of improbable thoughts about a future with a man whose final call indicated nothing of the sort.

Amarillo was a world away for a single mother with roots in the heart of Texas. Distance alone was an incredible hurdle. She was opening herself fully to feelings and thinking Everett may be too. He was a widower—a real one—and had his own hurt.

At some point, Danica would try to set her up on a blind date. Mallory would insist on registering her for an online dating profile or having her fly to Santa Fe for a double female prowl on men there. At some point, those opportunities—comfortable or not—were coming. But it was too soon, and a steady relationship with a man—any man—wasn't in the cards for Paige.

Not now.

Everett couldn't be hers. She couldn't be his. That was that.

Suck it up, buttercup. One quick line of a pep talk helped her shift from thought to action. She put the phone down to resume the responsibilities of the day, which included life as a mother.

Not a widow.

Not someone's possible future girlfriend.

Not someone who was going to even attempt a long distance anything with a man who indicated nothing about continued texts, phone calls, or visits.

Everett hadn't made a move in that direction. Indirectly, he had given Paige an answer to a question about their future that she didn't even ask. What did he want from her?

The answer was absolutely nothing.

Chapter Twenty-One

NATHAN WAS SOOTHED by the *Madeline* book.

Just my luck. As precious as the book was, it made Paige think of Everett.

Again. And again. And again. Every time Nathan chose that book from his shelf, it was as if he was bringing a reminder of Everett to his mom courtesy of his tiny toddler fingers.

Thanks. Her bitter mental reaction, though, was kept sealed. It was going to take time to shake away from Everett, and she couldn't fault a two-year-old for unknowingly making the process just a tad more difficult.

"Yes, I'll read this one." She tapped her lap, and Nathan crawled in gingerly.

"Nest, nest." He used their code as he settled in for a story.

Since being back home, their nighttime reading routine resumed, as did morning reading. Noontime reading. Afternoon reading. Pre-nighttime nighttime reading. Since Nathan was still sore, stationary activities were good ones, and he couldn't seem to get enough of books of all kinds.

Luckily, Mallory was there to tag team with Paige. Otherwise, her voice would be sore from reading aloud so many

AUDREY WICK

tales. She might have even plucked her eyes out for sheer overkill of the same stories.

But fictional Madeline made Nathan smile, and he seemed to understand the connection to the protagonist's surgery and her scar to his. For that level of understanding Everett was able to provide, Paige was grateful.

"It is a cute book." Mallory agreed it was a fitting addition to Nathan's library and an appropriate way to help him recover. She didn't know about Everett. Explaining things to Danica had been challenging enough, and Paige didn't sense there was anything left to tell Mallory anyway. A man she once knew in high school popped into her life, stayed for a short time, and then popped back out.

Not exactly a storybook tale.

So she and Mallory talked about anything but men.

However, through Sunday lunch, afternoon, and the general business of the day, a feeling gnawed at her. It persisted through Monday morning, and Paige awoke with a strong need to do something about it.

Reflecting on the previous day's call, Everett was leaving for Amarillo this week, she just didn't know the day. Was it possible he'd leave on a Monday? Anything was possible at this point. It was even possible he was expecting an apology from her on yesterday's call for building their time together on the back of a lie, though that wasn't territory into which Paige ventured. In hindsight, maybe she should have done so. After all, she had privately faulted Everett for not sharing emotions. The reality was, though, that she never asked him to do so, nor did she share her own.

Am I condemning an action in another for which I'm to blame? Seesawing between directed blame and personal guilt, Paige realized the only way to balance her feelings was to address them with the other person in the equation who created them. But there was a right way to do that and a wrong way. Eliminating the wrong was easy.

No text.

No telephone call.

No waiting patiently for a chance meeting some ten years down the road.

She needed to see Everett, face-to-face. That was the only right way to have a proper conversation that would bring closure. Being honest with him wasn't a claim she could make. But if he heard from her how much she enjoyed their time, how it helped her move forward, how it made her alive again, perhaps they could both rest with the decisions that were made.

"Mallory," she called to her sister in the living room. "Can I ask you for a big favor?"

"Sure. What?"

Paige knew of the one place where she could find Everett, and catching him there would be uncomfortable but necessary. "I've got to run into, um . . ." Paige hated white lies, and she wasn't going to fall into one. "I need to tend to . . . to this thing." She stammered, trying to make her planned visit more laced with truth. "I've got something I need to take care of, and I'll only be gone an hour. Maybe less. Can you watch Nathan?"

To Mallory's credit, she didn't pry. "Not a problem. Go

do whatever you need, just tell me about it when you get back." She was a good sister, and Paige could fulfill that second part, especially if she were successful with the conversation. "Nathan and I will see how many books we can get through in that time."

"Great." She dashed to her bedroom to change into a slightly nicer blouse than the worn t-shirt she sported. A striped v-neck in coral with oatmeal-colored piping was simple and flattering. Paired with the distressed jeans she was already wearing, it was casual and chic without trying too hard. She slipped her feet into a pair of crisscrossed leather slides, her toes peeking through as they begged for new polish.

She silently cursed the chipped coloring. *Hopefully Everett won't be looking at my toes. He needs to look at me.*

Feeling suddenly vulnerable, she wondered if she was even making the right decision as she closed the door of her Mini Cooper, turned the key, and steered the car toward the direction of Everett's childhood homestead.

DRIVING TO THE Mullins' farm made about as much sense as wearing a wool bikini. And, in some ways, that choice might have been more comfortable than the one Paige was making.

But Paige hadn't lived her life without responding to a bit of fire that lit under her now and again. That was what she had come to realize Everett was. A fire. A flicker from her past, his presence now was heat she could fan or extinguish. And regardless of what he communicated on his phone call, she wasn't ready to extinguish him just yet. Not totally.

Dust fanned from her wheels as her car cut through the teeming dirt road to the homestead she remembered. In high school, friends and classmates made tracks all over Seguin and the surrounding area, for joyrides, drives, parties, and whatever they could conjure for fun. They had to make their own enjoyment, and memories of who lived where and whose parents were still in the area were a part of Paige's bank of small-town knowledge.

Finding the homestead was easy. It was steeling her courage to confront Everett that would be hard.

He had said on the phone he was going back to Amarillo this week, so she needed to act. Otherwise, if she waited, she would risk him already being gone.

White-hot, early morning sun highlighted fertile fields and gentle, rolling hills on the Mullins' property. Swaying grasses greeted her in waves as her car continued down the long driveway to their classic farmhouse, standing a little worn but still proud. Live oaks with heavy limbs held firm to the ground, rooting their presence to frame the house in shade. Across the fields that extended on each side, crisp colors poked in patches. Late-blooming wildflowers held over from spring quilted the landscape in a pattern that was uniquely Texas. Paige Fredrick loved land, and she loved Texas.

Paige checked her reflection in the mirror, swiping a bit

of lip gloss from the corner of her mouth that had spread too far. She readjusted her sunglasses on the bridge of her nose. She wasn't going to ask to be invited into the house. Hopefully a talk on the sprawling front porch would be enough. She rehearsed a few general phrases she wanted to say to Everett, but she'd also let his presence guide her exact words, giving way to a conversation she hoped wouldn't be one-sided.

Everett's black Tacoma truck wasn't visible as she pulled into the circle drive, but the Mullins' farm was large. He could be parked inside their garage or even in a barn. If he wasn't, maybe he was using the truck to make a quick check of something on the farm. If she had to wait for him to return from a pasture, she could do that.

She eased her compact vehicle to a stop, its body dwarfed by the shadow of the live oaks and two-story farmhouse. A little peeling paint, boards in need of replacement, and weeds invading the flowerbeds didn't destroy the majesty of the place. It was still quintessentially rural, with rustic charm and an inviting air.

Paige took a deep breath as she stepped from her driver's seat, dust settling around her car that was probably a clearer announcement of her arrival than any knock on the front door would be. Stepping away from her vehicle, the dust evaporated just as quickly as it stirred, clearing the sight of the farmhouse. It was hard to harbor any bit of worry or stress in a beautiful environment such as this. The setting alone made her melt into an ease of movement that helped her advance across the flagstone walkway, up the concrete steps, and onto the wooden beamed porch. The lack of a doorbell wasn't a surprise. She swung open the simple, hinged screen door that held a stately front entrance behind. Balling her fingers into a fist, she knocked with firm knuckles against the wood to signal her presence.

She pushed her sunglasses atop her head, strands of her bangs falling loose to frame her forehead. She wanted her full face on display, no hiding behind a mask of any means. Completely vulnerable, she propped the screen door into an open position with her foot, waiting for the start of a conversation with Everett she needed to have.

Dialogue she couldn't decipher echoed from within, but no voice seemed to belong to Everett. She planted her feet on the porch, rooting herself as if she were a sapling trying not to bow in the wind. Suddenly flush with anticipation, she steeled herself for whatever the situation would be when the door swung open.

When it did, there was no big reveal of Everett Mullins. Instead, a much older version of him stood before Paige, towering inches higher than her and with a broadness of build that suggested rural toughness. Age had added a few wrinkles, but the man was no less recognizable to her than from when she had last seen him years ago.

"Mr. Mullins?" She raised her chin to meet his eyes.

He squinted beneath a furrowed brow of suspicion. He studied her for a moment. Though his eyes had seen many decades pass, his recognition was sharp. "I know you."

The words were a breeze of relief, blowing across Paige like a wind against a dandelion globe. Uncertainty lifted, and she replied with confidence. "I know you too, Mr. Mullins."

He put out his hand. "Paige. Paige . . . Fredrick, is it?"

"Yes." It was a relief to be called by her reclaimed maiden name. As least that was one less bit of explaining she would have to do at the doorway. "I know it's been a while, but I'm here to see Everett. I understand he's been helping with . . ." She searched for a phrase so she wouldn't have to say the nasty c-word. "Cancer" was probably something they had all heard too much of in that house as it was. "Um, helping around the farm and spending time with you both."

"He's been mighty good about that," Dale Mullins admitted, overlooking her bit of sidestepping the obvious illness that had brought his son back home. "Everett's put his whole life on hold for his mother, and now he can finally get back to his."

"Dale!" A female voice rang from the interior. "Who is that?"

Paige stiffened as she prepared for how Everett's father would answer the query. But instead of the quick verbal one she expected, he opted for a gesture of invitation instead. He held the wooden door open, stepped to the side, and ushered Paige into the interior of their home. She followed his lead, letting the screen door swing closed behind her. In the wake of the spring closure that sealed against the frame with a snap, he lowered his voice. "Can you go up to her and introduce yourself? She'll never understand what I'm trying to say if we stay out of sight."

Paige nodded, mentally rehearsing her response as she stepped into the foyer. She followed Everett's father past the base of the staircase and into a living room replete with twelve-foot ceilings framed by wooden crown molding on top and stately wainscoting on the bottom. His wife sat in a recliner in the corner of the room.

She took one look at her and blew Paige's rehearsed lines away with her own. "Well you must be here to see Everett. Gorgeous girl, you are, like I expected. But you're a day too late."

Paige stopped short. "Pardon me?"

The lack of formal introduction came as a surprise, as much as did the accuracy of what she knew disguised as a question. "You're here to see Everett?"

"Yes." Paige shrunk in the presence of the space.

The diminutive woman continued to shock. "Honey, you should have driven faster." She shook her head, reached for a tissue, and blotted her face for no particular reason that Paige could tell. "That bird's flown north."

Still not entirely sure of this conversation, Paige stammered for clarity. "Is that, I mean . . . Everett's not . . ."

"Yes, yes," she insisted, as if Paige were the last to arrive at a party and out of sorts with the reason for it. "Everett left yesterday." She offered a few other quickened phrases that Paige couldn't process, for her mind was concentrating on only one that seemed to matter. The finality of the words pounded through her, an echoed despair ringing as soon as she heard them. "Honey, he's gone."

PAIGE WAS LIVING in a bad country song.

And the chorus was one word. *Gone.*

"Gone?" Paige repeated the last word she heard Ruby utter. The word was so finite, a conclusion not only to time with his parents but time with her.

"Sit down here, honey." Ruby waved her hand at the couch as if dusting it off. "You're looking sicker than a chemotherapy patient. And I should know."

Paige did need to sit. "Only for a moment," she insisted, her knees buckling as she lowered herself to cushion the shock.

Everett's mother called to her husband. "Dale, bring this gal some water." She edged forward in her seat. "We've got superb well water here. That's thanks to Everett. For decades we've lived with too much sulfur and he goes to college, gets his fancy job in Amarillo, travels halfway across the world, and learns all about fixing anything. Our good water is all thanks to Everett." She spoke with pride.

Water wasn't going to drown her hurt. But if that's all she was being offered, she'd down it just to try.

The sad tune continued. "Everett's been though a lot." His mother knitted her hands as she spoke. "Losing Catherine, which I'm sure you know."

Just barely. Paige couldn't find her voice.

"There's hurt in loss, no doubt about that." She didn't need to tell Paige about hurt. She knew her share.

"And loss unexpected is the hardest." The irony of the words spoken by someone battling cancer did not escape Paige.

She processed the words with an audible gulp. There was no way to mentally argue with what his mother expressed. Death from a vehicular accident came without warning, no time for preparation. Dealing with it required Spartan endurance, which alone spoke volumes about Everett's character.

Ruby tapped her foot against the wooden floorboard, a metronome of sound in an otherwise silent space. Paige still couldn't speak, and his mother seemed to want the words to settle into her.

"Here's some water." Everett's father returned with a tall glass and offered it to Paige, who grabbed it with more greed than she intended just to break the stillness.

"Thank you." She raised the glass to her lips and tilted it back, filling her mouth with the liquid instead of a response.

"Slow down there," Ruby warned. "You'll choke going that fast."

Paige lowered the glass and brushed the back of her hand across her mouth. She froze as she realized just have juvenile she must have appeared. Mute and thirsty could not have been a good look for her, especially as a guest in someone's home.

"I'm sorry." Paige's apology was meant to cover every embarrassment and misstep since she cut the engine of her car outside the Mullins' home, not the least of which was sitting in their home pining pathetically for their son.

As if reading that half of Paige's mind, his mother invited her to tell her a little bit about how she and Everett reconnected since he had been back. The opportunity to verbalize so much that she had kept internalized was an offer she couldn't refuse.

And it wasn't as if her legs were ready to operate again. Sitting and talking was the best thing for Paige.

She opened her mouth and surprised herself as her voice launched into a storied overview of the past several weeks. Without oversharing, she gave a rundown of short periods spent together and more tender ones like the flowers he sent for her promotion and the book he brought to Nathan. In the presence of Ruby, Paige didn't even cross the line of a white lie. She was completely up front with her about being divorced and having a son, and her blunt honesty came as a surprise.

As she shared more of the memories she stored, she found that she inadvertently commented on their joint emotional growth. Contrasting who she was now with who she was on the day of her finalized divorce, she realized, "I've opened around him." But more than that, there was a longer-lasting effect, perhaps the highest compliment she could pay him. "I'm a better me because of him."

Too bad he wasn't around to hear it.

But his mother was. And she found an even better verb, given her buttercup nickname. "You've blossomed around him."

Paige nodded. "I guess I have." She set the empty glass of water on the coffee table, finally able to still her hands as she rested in the recognition of just how deeply Everett had influenced her.

"Oh, honey, if you had been a day earlier."

Leaving on a Sunday made more sense than a weekday

for a man who had a job to resume. *Why hadn't I thought of that?* Paige kicked herself for not clarifying that on the phone. *But would it have mattered?*

Ruby entertained those questions and more. "I wish you would have told him these things." She leaned further forward so that she could place a hand on Paige's knee, delivering her words of wisdom with sass. "And I told that boy to tell you how he was feeling too."

How he was feeling? Paige wanted to make sure she heard the words correctly. "How *was* he feeling?"

Ruby removed her hand as if Paige's knee were suddenly engulfed in flame. Throwing both hands in the air, she couldn't be any plainer with Paige. "That boy is feeling better because of you too." She challenged Paige not to minimize the judgment of a woman who understood her grown son, who had seen him love and lose and close himself to loving again.

"But you opened him too. He didn't have to tell me anything like you just did," she insisted. "I saw it. In everything from his smile to his walk. I know he was stealing time to see you."

Like teenagers. Paige smiled.

"Plus he was hiding his phone all the time. I knew he was up to something with a woman, something special." Mothers had an instinct, no matter their age.

Ruby's words filled the void Everett had left. It was a boost of confidence to know Paige had an effect on him beyond what she alone saw. Then, because she didn't know who else to ask, she did so right then to the most available listener. "So what am I supposed to do now?"

Chapter Twenty-Two

PAIGE NEVER EXPECTED the pieces of her crumbling heart to be picked up by Everett's mother. But there was a comfort in their conversation, an easy way about Ruby that Paige observed in Everett as well. Now she knew where he got it.

Ruby Mullins didn't let Paige leave without a hug. She brought her in with the universal gesture from her recliner, and Paige bent to embrace her with appreciation for her listening ear and her kind, open heart. It didn't take long to see those qualities in an individual. She had them.

Everett did too.

His mother's final advice was to trust. Trust herself. Trust her emotions. Trust the process of healing that she needed. She urged Paige to place trust in her journey, whatever that might be. It wasn't earth-shattering advice, and it wasn't life-changing. But it was the sage, sound advice Paige needed to hear from someone outside of her bubble of existence that could help her move forward.

Opening the door to her Mini Cooper, she raised her arm high to give a grateful wave to Dale, who reciprocated from the porch to see her off. She lowered her sunglasses, climbed inside, and fastened her seatbelt for a journey away from the farmhouse. Her visit was more nourishing than a spa trip, more relaxing than a massage. For the price of free, she scored a private consultation with a woman who offered her wisdom about strength, both physical and emotional. Their impromptu heart-to-heart was nothing Paige could have expected, but everything she needed.

HIS PHONE RANG twice before he looked at the screen to see if he should answer it. He ignored some people, but seeing this caller's name, she wasn't one he ever did. Calls during the past few months had been ones for which he held his breath before answering, not sure what her health would dictate. And that was precisely why he had taken a leave of absence from work to help care for her.

Sliding his thumb to answer the call, he spoke loud and clear through the line. "Hi, Mom."

"Ev-er-ett!" His mother practically barked his name, in the annoying triple-syllable way she had of dragging out what was normally a two-syllable sound. "You've got some nerve."

Everett ducked his head and pressed the phone close to his ear. "What did you say?" He was already out in the field on a series of service calls with difficult water line and well repairs that had been waiting for his consultation expertise.

"You heard me." His mother's catch phrase was especially sassy today. "I didn't stutter."

"Well, actually . . ." Everett was ready to argue about that, but his mother had other plans.

She talked a mile a minute. "You were supposed to come to Seguin and not fuss. No stress, no problems. Head back to Amarillo better than when you came."

Where was this coming from? "Mom, I don't know what—"

"Don't play that with me."

"Play what?" Everett had taken time off for her, to help manage *her* health. Not for any personal reason related to himself.

"Everett, all mothers have intuition."

Here we go into a diatribe. Everett sealed his lips and was glad this was a phone call where he could keep his expressions under wraps.

"You might think you came to Seguin for me, but it was for you. You needed to get away to heal even more than I've been needing to heal." His mother paused for air. "Now before you go thinking that I'm wrong, listen to this. Two years. Two years is long enough. Catherine would have wanted you to remember her, but she wouldn't have wanted you to carry on like you've been doing."

A Monday morning conversation about his deceased wife was not what Everett expected. He certainly didn't need this on his first day back in the town he and Catherine shared together for their married life. Driving into Amarillo alone, as he had done ever since her death, was hard enough.

He nipped his mother right back. "And just what is that supposed to mean?"

"Alone." The word stole Everett's breath to respond.

I've heard that word enough. I've lived it.

His mother continued through his silence, perhaps mistaking his lack of a retort for acceptance. "You've been alone, Everett, and there's no need for that. You've grieved, but now you've got to grow."

His mother had made attempts at offering advice through the years, though he never solicited it. Why was she calling today? Why now? Maybe it was just easier over the phone to have a heart-to-heart, one-sided as it was becoming. If his mother had wanted to have this conversation with Everett face-to-face, he didn't give her much of a chance. After all, he left Seguin more abruptly than he originally intended. There was little time for proper goodbyes. And this conversation wasn't headed toward an end just yet either.

Ruby wasn't finished with what she needed to say. With the level tone of a psychiatrist, she continued with a one-word guide for Everett. "Trust."

Easier said than done. His heart was broken. Even two years couldn't erase his pain, though he had lived with it as best he knew how. But was his mother talking about him or about his ability to open to other people? "I do trust. When I'm ready."

His family hadn't pushed for him to get back into dating or start a relationship, but he did miss the joys of being in one. Before Paige, there wasn't anyone after Catherine.

His mother acknowledged, "On your own time. I know that." She spoke the next words with an evenness that forced Everett to hear them. "This is my wish for you. That you can learn to trust. Trust yourself. Trust your emotions. Trust the process of healing because it's already happened."

"Yes," he agreed. "I've done all that."

"Now it's time to place trust in your journey." She paused on the line before adding, "To her."

"To who?"

Of all the times for his mother to play coy, she chose now. "Everett, that's for you to know."

What wasn't his mother revealing? Did she know something he didn't? Or was she just planting a seed to see what grew?

Mothers. They think they know best.

PAIGE RETURNED HOME to Nathan, who had a surprise for his mom.

"Ta da!" Mallory announced from the kitchen, Nathan echoing the words in kind.

"What's this?" Paige stepped through the living room and around the bar to meet them there. She bent to his level, eye to eye as he placed a piece of paper in hands she outstretched.

Paige held the paper as if it were a sheet made of gold. Nathan pointed to a crayon blob of yellow coloring that he identified as "Mommy." Then he pointed to a blue blob next to it, a series of messy circles and spirals. "That's me!"

Mallory chimed in. "It's your first portrait together!"

Paige's eyes grew watery, and she frowned only because of the intensity of such raw emotion. She held the paper above Nathan's shoulder and she stole a hug, careful not to squeeze too tight since his torso was still sensitive. Sheer pride filled her.

"So you like it?" Mallory shouldn't have had to ask such a silly question, but it gave Paige the chance to put her emotions into words.

She pulled back from Nathan to address her thoughtful sister. "I absolutely love it."

Mallory beamed. "I suspected you might."

Paige couldn't help but return her wide smile. She really missed Mallory sometimes. Santa Fe was a lovely place for Mallory to land and create a life for herself, but times like this reminded Paige of the sweet, everyday joys they missed out on by being apart. She made a mental note to make more of an attempt to ensure she and Nathan could share other memories like this.

With a plate full of thanks for her sister, she looked again at the picture, an "N" in the lower righthand corner identifying the young artist-in-training. She stood and flipped it around for Mallory to admire. "What made you think to do this?"

Mallory shooed away a direct answer. "He was asking about you."

Paige read between the lines. When one of Nathan's day care teachers gave a response like that, it was a veil for some type of toddler crying tantrum. "So he threw a fit when I left?"

"I didn't say that." Mallory set a hand on her hip in defiance.

"You"—she leaned forward and playfully poked her older sister in the shoulder to try to knock her off balance—"didn't have to say that."

Mallory gave her best attempt at theatrical face shock. "You mean to tell me you don't think your two-year-old just casually colored a picture of you out of sheer love?"

Paige lifted an eyebrow. "Come on."

"Fine, fine." Mallory acquiesced, accepting the picture from Paige and turning to pin it to the refrigerator with a magnet. "But you have to admit it's pretty cute."

They both stood back and admired the drawing. "Yeah." Paige couldn't argue there. "Pretty cute."

But Mallory had one final question before the discussion of the drawing activity was put to rest. "And how did you know he was crying?"

Paige mused at the meaning of the colors and shapes, all crafted by her son's growing hands. Such self-satisfaction at his progress and development was one of the greatest joys of motherhood. "Guess it's just intuition. Something I sensed."

"Is all that really true about mothers?" Mallory wasn't one herself. "Or is that just part of the rhetoric you learn to say somewhere along the way?"

Paige could only speak from her experience. "It's true. Intuition. Gut feelings." And then words that had been spoken as wizened advice to her just a short time before sprang from her lips. "I guess I've just learned to trust."

Paige had learned that. And trusting was the most positive way to move forward.

Full of love and belongingness, Paige drew her sister in for an appreciative hug, sealing her thanks for all she was to her.

Maybe mothers did know best. But sisters weren't far behind.

"JUST ONE MORE errand. I promise." Tuesday morning started with a buzz, Mallory and Paige making a pajama-clad bee line for the single shot coffee maker after Nathan awoke them. No one was getting quality rest the past few nights.

Mallory rubbed the sleep from her eyes. "Fine. Go do what you need." Her hand hit the brew button first. "First cup is mine," she claimed with morning snark.

"I'll just have a cup when I get back." Paige stepped away from the machine. "If I get there first thing, I'll have Miguel's full attention and won't need to stay long." The land and title office was operating as usual in her absence, though she needed to sign some paperwork. She also wanted to make sure she shifted the right closing files to Miguel for coverage this week since she was taking off for Nathan's recovery.

"He's not interested in eating breakfast anyway." Her sister made an accurate observation about Nathan. His eating habits were still sporadic. "Which gives me more time for coffee." She hummed the tune to the Simon and Garfunkel classic "The Sound of Silence," with Paige singing behind her to their coffeemaker audience, "Hello, darkness . . ." Like sirens, the Fredrick sisters called forth the rich brew, dripping in time as the full-bodied aroma filled the air.

Paige moaned in longing for the caffeine. "Fine. Your cup. Then I'll have one when I get back." She pivoted to return to her bedroom to get dressed for a trip into the office.

Through the bedroom window, sunlight stretched to welcome her into the day. Paige decided she should take advantage of the crispness. Plus her body could use some exercise. She poked her head out of the bedroom and checked with Mallory. "Do you care if I ride my bike into the office?"

Her focus was squarely on the coffee, the machine and her mouth still humming away. She paused long enough to answer, "Do your thing, chicken wing."

Paige rolled her eyes. She loved her older sister.

And she found her incredibly weird sometimes.

Paige ducked into her closet, yanked a sun dress from a hanger, and changed from her pajamas into one of the most comfortable outfits she owned. Mallory had actually been the one to turn her on to the power of a flattering dress. As comfortable as her pajamas, a breezy non-wrinkle number certainly looked more presentable.

She twisted her hair into an upswept do and secured it with a jaw clip, letting loose strands fall where they wanted. She slipped into leather sandals that matched the dress but would allow her to still pedal. A quick swipe of mascara and lip gloss woke her face with pops of emphasis in precisely the right places. She was, after all, going into the office, and her coworkers would be pouncing on her for a Nathan update.

She also didn't know what clients she might see in passing, so she needed to look like someone who didn't just roll out of bed.

Even though she kind of had.

She grabbed her purse, slung it across her torso diagonally, grabbed her sunglasses, and snuck out through the garage with just a wave to Mallory. Nathan was in his room, and his uneven sleep schedule meant he might lull himself into another hour or two of dozing.

Positioning herself on the bike, she lowered her sunglasses before pedaling down the driveway and through the neighborhood she loved. Reflecting on the beauty around her and a peacefulness inside of her, she was filled with resolve in moving forward. She had everything she needed—family, friends, a supportive neighborhood, a warm and friendly community. Seguin was hers, and she was part of it too.

Cycling through the streets she knew well, she took note of all she loved about the area. Her thoughts overhauled her actions, and before she even broke a sweat, homes gave way to buildings that gave way to her arrival at the town center, the gem of a courthouse set in the middle. She took her time ambling around the square, her glasses shielding her view from the sun as she rode toward the land and title office.

The modest business sector around the square was just waking up, the retail section and eateries still quiet until their midmorning openings. Only a sprinkling of vehicles were parked around the courthouse, creating a smooth path for Paige to maneuver.

She rounded the corner by the landmark giant pecan,

and she lifted her glasses to make sure her eyes did not deceive her. A black Tacoma shone through streaks of sunlight, highlighting a single driver who was just now stepping out from the cab.

Wearing a smile as big as Texas, the male strode decidedly toward Paige. After saving the memories of him in her mind and looping them in a mental replay, she would know the sight of him anywhere.

That jawline.

His broad chest.

A sweet left dimple.

"Everett." She breathed, the first hint of perspiration breaking through as heat rose around her.

Her face flushed as she steered her bike to the curb, steadied the kickstand, and dismounted. Her dress fabric righted as she stood, smoothing against her skin through the morning's breeze.

Everett didn't say a word. He mirrored her advance, matched her steps, and met in the shadow of the place she knew well, the spot where they had formerly stood together. Leaning into her, he scooped his arm around her waist, pulling her in for a tender embrace. She accepted his advance, letting her arms fall around him as her head settled onto his shoulder.

"Is this really you?" Paige still couldn't believe he was here.

"I'm here," he confirmed. "For you. Because I made a mistake in leaving." He continued with short but heartfelt sentences, ones that were music to Paige's ears. "You opened me up. You made me come alive. And I want to stay that way."

"I want you to stay that way too." She hugged Everett tighter, feeling all that was in his heart.

As they stood with bodies pressed close, she let go of all inhabitations at who might see them, what gawkers might stumble past and point or how the rural gossip mill might churn later that day with whispered rumors. She heard none of that in her head. Instead, she heard only the calming sounds made by the word she was using as her mantra. *Trust.* This word offered by Everett's mother was one Paige now claimed. She wondered if it was a word of advice Everett had been told too.

He spoke up. "I drove all through the night from Amarillo to see you. Paige, I needed to see you." He inched back from her, adding physical space so he could look her in the eye.

There would be time to talk and ask questions. But now wasn't that time.

Everett looked at Paige in the way only a man filled with romantic intent could do. Talking no longer made sense. Only a kiss did.

They sealed their relationship with a first shared kiss in the center of the space where Paige was most comfortable. Surrounded by a town she adored and a solid frame of support she worked hard to build, her new normal was a life she loved. Her personal compass no longer in flux, she held Everett in her arms, happy she had found her true north.

The End

Don't miss the next book in The Texas Sisters Series!

Book 1: Finding True North

Book 2: Coming Soon!

If you enjoyed *Finding True North*, you'll love these other
great stories

Again, Alabama by Susan Sands

Until You by Jeannie Moon

The Real Thing by Tina Ann Forkner

Available now at your favorite online retailer!

About the Author

Audrey Wick is a full-time English professor at Blinn College in Texas. Her writing has appeared in college textbooks published by Cengage Learning and W. W. Norton as well as in *The Houston Chronicle, The Chicago Tribune, The Orlando Sentinel,* and various literary journals. Audrey believes the secret to happiness includes lifelong learning and good stories. But travel and coffee help. She has journeyed to over twenty countries—and sipped coffee at every one. Connect with her at audreywick.com and @WickWrites.

Thank you for reading

Finding True North

If you enjoyed this book, you can find more from all our great authors at TulePublishing.com, or from your favorite online retailer.

TULE
PUBLISHING

Made in the USA
Middletown, DE
21 April 2021

37903645R00177